T0034831

JINXED

"Regan Reilly is [an] amazing character. [Clark] has created another exciting mystery, which will keep her readers entranced and entertained."

—Nelson DeMille

"Plenty of fast-paced fun."

—*Publishers Weekly*

"Clark pours a Zinfandel that's light and fruity and perfect with cheese."

—New York *Daily News*

FLEECED

"A good old-fashioned mystery with the edginess and pulse of a modern Manhattan suspense thriller."

—Nelson DeMille

"Like an Agatha Christie incarnation, Clark knows how to pull out the whodunit stops of yore. . . . She cooks with the same three ingredients used by many great mystery writers of the past—elegance, wit, and a good plot."

—*The Ottawa Citizen*

"Good enough for holiday dessert."

—*The Calgary Herald*

. . . AND PRAISE FOR THE ENTIRE
REGAN REILLY MYSTERY SERIES

"Fast, glamorous, intricately plotted."
—Los Angeles Times

"Fun and funny."
—USA Today

"Upbeat, fast-paced."
—The New York Times

"No one can read just one page."
—The Washington Post

CAROL HIGGINS CLARK

BURNED

POCKET STAR BOOKS

New York London Toronto Sydney

A Pocket Star Book published by
POCKET BOOKS, a division of Simon & Schuster, Inc.
1230 Avenue of the Americas, New York, NY 10020

This book is a work of fiction. Names, characters, places and incidents are products of the author's imagination or are used fictitiously.
Any resemblance to actual events or locales or persons, living or dead,
is entirely coincidental.

ISBN 978-0-7434-7666-9

This Pocket Star Books paperback edition May 2006

20 19 18 17 16 15 14 13

POCKET STAR BOOKS and colophon are registered
trademarks of Simon & Schuster, Inc.

Cover design and illustration by Carlos Beltran

Manufactured in the United States of America

For information regarding special discounts for bulk purchases,
please contact Simon & Schuster Special Sales at 1-800-456-6798
or business@simonandschuster.com.

Acknowledgments

Writing is solitary work, but publishing a book is not. I would like to say a special "aloha" to the people who helped me bring another Regan Reilly adventure to my readers.

Special thanks to Roz Lippel, who is my editor. From the time we went to lunch together to discuss the idea for this book to the final edits, her guidance and contributions were invaluable. A frequent visitor to Hawaii, she shared with me her keen knowledge of those wonderful islands!

Many thanks to Michael Korda for his comments and advice. Roz's assistant, Laura Thielen, is always so helpful. Working with Associate Director of Copyediting Gypsy da Silva is a continuing pleasure. Gratitude to copy editor Rose Ann Ferrick and the proofreading team: Barbara Raynor, Steve Friedeman, and Joshua Cohen. Praise to Art Director John Fulbrook and photographer Herman Estevez, who did a wonderful job evoking the Hawaiian spirit on the cover and in the picture. Applause to my longtime publicist and dear friend Lisl Cade for promoting Regan Reilly.

Thanks to Hawaii residents Robbie Poznansky,

who was so hospitable as he familiarized me with the Big Island, and Jason Gaspero, who did the same in Oahu.

Finally, thanks to my mother, who understands what it is to write a book, my family, friends, and readers. Aloha one and all!

In Pectore

BURNED

Thursday, January 13

"This is going to be the snowstorm of the century," the action reporter, Brad Dayton, cried with a certain hysterical glee. Clad in bright yellow foul weather gear, he was standing on the side of the New Jersey Turnpike. Cars were inching by, sliding and spinning, as a gusty wind blew wet snow in every direction. The flakes seemed to target the reporter's face and the lens of the television camera. The sky was thick with gray clouds, and the whole Northeast was hunkering down for an unexpected blizzard.

"Don't go anywhere," he cried as he blinked to avoid the pelting precipitation. "Stay home. And forget the airports. They're closed, and it looks like they won't reopen for several days."

Regan Reilly stared at the television in her cozy

Los Angeles office in an ancient building on Hollywood Boulevard. "I can't believe it," she said aloud. "I should have flown out yesterday."

"Be careful out there, Brad," urged the cable news anchor in the climate-controlled studio. "Try to stay dry."

"I will," Brad shouted over the shrill wind. He started to say something else, but the sound was knocked out. The news director cut quickly to a weatherman standing in front of a map with lots of ominous arrows pointing in all directions.

"What have you got for us, Larry?" the smiling blond anchorwoman asked.

"Snow coming from all directions," Larry explained urgently as his hands made circles around the map. "Snow, snow, and more snow. I hope you all have lots of canned goods at home because this storm is going to stay with us for the next several days, and it is packing a *wallop!*"

Regan looked out the window. It was a typically sunny day in Los Angeles. Her suitcase was packed for New York. Recently engaged, Regan was a thirty-one-year-old private investigator based in Los Angeles. Her honey, Jack "no relation" Reilly, was the head of the major case squad in New York City. They were to wed in May, and she had been planning to fly out for the weekend to see Jack and her parents, Luke and Nora, who lived in Summit, New Jersey.

Regan and her mother were supposed to meet

with a wedding coordinator on Saturday to review all the plans for the big day—menu, flowers, limos, photographer, the list went on and on. On Saturday night she and her parents and Jack had arranged to hear a band they were considering for the reception. Regan had been looking forward to a fun night out. The snowstorm would have precluded those plans, but if Regan had gotten to New York yesterday, she could have had a cozy weekend with Jack. It was the second week in January, and she hadn't seen him for ten days. And what's more romantic than being together during a snowstorm?

She felt lonely and frustrated, and the sight of the shining sun she found irritating. I don't want to be here, she thought. I want to be in New York.

The phone rang.

"Regan Reilly," she answered without much enthusiasm.

"Aloha, Regan. It's your maid of honor calling from Hawaii."

Kit Callan was Regan's best friend. They'd met in college on a junior year abroad program in England. Kit lived in Hartford and sold insurance. Her other job was the hunt for Mr. Right. So far she was having better luck peddling her policies.

"Aloha, Kit." Regan smiled and immediately felt better just hearing her best friend's voice. She knew that Kit had gone to Hawaii for an insurance convention. "How's your trip going?"

"I'm stuck here."

"Not many people would complain that they were stuck in Hawaii."

"The convention ended Tuesday. I took an extra day to relax, and now I can't get home. My travel agent says you can't get anywhere near the East Coast."

"Tell me about it. I was supposed to go to New York today to see Jack. And my mother and I were going to meet with the wedding planner."

"Promise me you'll go easy on me with the bridesmaids' dresses."

"I was actually thinking of plaid pantsuits," Regan quipped.

"I've got an idea. Come out here, and we'll pick up some grass skirts."

Regan laughed. "Now there's an idea. People always want their weddings to be different."

"So you're coming then?"

"What are you talking about?"

"Get out here, Regan! How many chances will we have to be together like this again? Once you get hitched, that'll be it. You'll never want to leave him, and I don't blame you."

"I'm keeping my office in Los Angeles," Regan protested. "At least for a while."

"That's different. You know what I mean. This is a perfect opportunity for us to have a fun girls' weekend before your wedding. What else are you going to do for the next few days? Watch the weather reports? Come out here to Waikiki. I'll have a tropical drink waiting for you. I have a room on the second floor with two big beds and a balcony overlooking the ocean. You can almost dip your toes into the sand from here. As a matter of fact, I'm sitting on the balcony right now waiting for room service to deliver my breakfast."

"Be careful. With the sound of the waves crashing, you might not hear them knock," Regan muttered as she looked around the office that had been her home away from home for several years. The antique desk she'd found at a flea market, the black-and-white-tiled floor, the coffeepot in its place of honor atop a filing cabinet were all so familiar. But now they didn't feel welcoming. She had cleared the decks for a weekend away and felt the need to get out and go somewhere. It was true that she hadn't seen Kit much in the year since she'd met Jack.

"Where are you staying?" Regan asked.

"The Waikiki Waters Playground and Resort."

"That's a mouthful."

"You should see this place. It was just renovated, so everything is brand-new and beautiful. There are restaurants, shops, two spas, five pools, and several towers of rooms. We're in the best tower right on the water. And there's a gala charity ball this Saturday night. They're auctioning off a shell lei that belonged to a princess from the royal family. They're calling it the 'Be a Princess' Ball. So come on out. We'll both be princesses." Kit paused. "What's going on down there?" she said softly, more to herself than Regan.

"What are you talking about?" Regan asked.

Kit didn't seem to hear her. "I don't believe it," she said with alarm.

Regan's grip tightened on the phone. "Kit, what's going on?"

"People are suddenly running down to the water's edge. I think a body just washed ashore!"

"Are you kidding?"

"A woman just tore out of the water screaming her head off. It looks like she came across the body when she was out for a swim."

"Oh, my God."

"Regan, you're not going to let me stay by myself here this weekend, are you?" Kit inquired meekly. "This place could be dangerous."

"I'll call the airlines."

2

Nora Regan Reilly looked up at the snow falling on the skylight of her third-floor tower office at home in New Jersey. Normally a little snow would contribute to the cozy setting where she wrote her mystery novels. But the blizzard was causing havoc in her life and, it seemed, everyone else's in the tri-state area.

"Regan, I'm so sorry you won't be in New York this weekend."

"Me, too, Mom." Regan was in the bedroom of her Hollywood Hills apartment packing a suitcase with summer clothes.

"Hawaii doesn't sound so bad."

"It will be good to spend time with Kit. Things have been so busy, I know I'd never take a weekend like this otherwise."

"Your father has a big funeral scheduled for tomorrow. I don't know how it can possibly happen. They say the roads will be treacherous. Most of the relatives are from out of town. They're staying at a hotel nearby."

"Who died?" Regan's question was not an uncommon one at the Reillys' dinner table. Her father, Luke, was a funeral director. And with her mother, Nora, being a suspense writer, there was a lot of talk about crime and death around the house. The Waltons they were not. Regan was an only child, and as a result she had been privy to more adult conversations than most kids growing up. It seemed to be common with only children, Regan had long ago decided. Jack was one of six kids. She loved that. Soon they'd have the best of both worlds.

"Ernest Nelson. He just turned a hundred and had been a championship skier. He lived in an assisted-living facility in town, and his family is scattered all over. His wife just died last year."

"He was one hundred years old?"

"He celebrated his hundredth birthday in a very grand style two weeks ago. The family threw him a big party. Now they're all back to bury him. And there are a lot of them. He has eight children who all have numerous grandchildren. I think they're going to be here for a while."

"He sounds like the type who wanted to reach that milestone before he gave up. Somehow the weather seems fitting for his funeral."

"That's what they're all saying, Regan." Nora paused. "Have you told Jack your plans?"

"Of course. We're both disappointed that I'm not in New York for the storm, but I'll be there next weekend."

"How long will you stay in Hawaii?" Nora asked as she sipped steaming tea from the *Imus in the Morning* mug she was given the last time she was on his radio show.

"Just until Monday morning."

"Do you and Kit have any big plans out there?"

Regan dropped a red one-piece bathing suit into her suitcase. With her pale skin she wasn't a sun worshipper, but she did enjoy taking a dip and then sitting under an umbrella. She had inherited her black Irish looks from her father. Raven-haired, blue-eyed, and fair-skinned, she was five feet seven inches tall. Luke was six-foot-five and his hair was "long since silver," as he liked to call it. Her mother was a petite blond and had a more patrician look. "We'll sit on the beach, maybe do some sightseeing. I think Kit has her eye on a guy who lives in Waikiki."

"She does?"

"Well, she mentioned something about a few people she met who have retired young out there or gone to start second careers. One of them sounds interesting."

"Kit's probably happy she can't get home then."

"I think you're right, Mom. She only admitted it

to me when I called her back with my flight information. But as she said, a long-distance relationship takes on new meaning when you're talking about Connecticut to Hawaii."

Nora laughed. "I'm sure you two will have fun. Be careful in the water. Those currents out there can get pretty strong."

She has that Irish intuition, Regan marveled. Or was it her motherly radar? Regan was not going to mention that a body had washed ashore in front of Kit's hotel room, but her mother probably had a sense of something. When Regan had called Kit back, Kit was down on the beach. The body had been identified as Dorinda Dawes, a woman in her forties who was an employee of the Waikiki Waters. She had started there three months ago and was the hotel's roving photographer and reporter, in charge of their newsletter. Kit had met her at one of the bars at the hotel where Dorinda was taking pictures of the guests.

When she washed ashore, Dorinda wasn't wearing a bathing suit. She was wearing a tropical print dress and had a shell lei around her neck. Which meant she wasn't out for a casual swim.

No, Regan had decided. No sense mentioning it to her mother. Let Nora think she was going to have a relaxing weekend at a peaceful Hawaiian resort. Who knows? Maybe things would turn out that way after all.

But knowing her pal Kit, she somehow doubted it. Kit could find trouble at a church picnic. And once again it looked as if she had. Sometimes Regan thought that's why they were such good friends. In their own ways, they both had an affinity for the hazardous side of life.

"We'll be careful," Regan assured her mother.

"Stick together. Especially when you're swimming."

"We will." Regan hung up, zipped up her suitcase, and glanced at the picture of her and Jack on the dresser. It had been taken moments after they got engaged in a hot air balloon. Regan couldn't believe how lucky she was to have found her soul mate. They'd met when her father had been kidnapped and Jack was on the case. Now Luke always joked that he never knew he had such good matchmaking skills—after all, Regan and Jack got to know each other while he was tied up on a boat with his chauffeur. But they were terrific together and had so much in common, especially their senses of humor. What they both did for a living also made them kindred spirits, and they often discussed their cases with each other. She had dubbed him "Mr. Feedback." At the end of every conversation he always told her he loved her and to *be careful!*

"I will, Jack," she said now to the picture. "I want to live to wear my wedding dress." But somehow as Regan spoke the words aloud, they seemed to get caught in her throat. Brushing off the odd feeling of uneasiness that came over her, Regan pulled the suitcase off the bed and headed out the door. Here I go on my bachelorette weekend, she thought. How bad can it be?

3

As Regan's plane made its descent into Honolulu, she peered out the window and smiled at the sight of the red neon letters on top of the airport tower—A-L-O-H-A.

"Aloha," she murmured.

When she got off the plane, a rush of warm fragrant air hit her. She immediately pulled out her cell phone and called Jack. It was late in the evening in New York.

"Aloha, baby," Jack answered.

Regan smiled again. "Aloha. I just arrived. The sky is bright blue. I can spot a row of palm trees swaying in the breeze, a pagoda in a garden below, and I really wish you were with me."

"Me, too."

"What's happening in New York?"

"The snow is coming down fast and furious. I had a couple of drinks with the guys after work. People are out on the streets having a great time, throwing snowballs and pulling kids on sleds. Someone already built a snowman that is standing guard outside my building. But he doesn't have much to do. Crime goes down during snowstorms."

Regan felt a pang in her heart. "I can't believe I'm missing all that," she said wistfully.

"I can't believe you are, either."

Regan pictured Jack's spacious homey apartment that was so Jack with its handsome leather couches and beautiful Persian rugs. He had told Regan he wanted to make his place more than just a bachelor pad because he never knew when he'd meet the right girl. "I was afraid it might never happen," he admitted. "But with you this is finally the way it's supposed to be."

"Maybe there will be another snowstorm next weekend," Regan joked. "I'll just be sure to arrive ahead of it."

"Regan, have a good time with Kit. There will be other snowstorms, I promise. And believe me, a lot of people in this city would give anything to trade places with you right now. Not everyone thinks this is fun."

By now Regan was at the baggage claim. People were in shorts and sleeveless shirts. It was late afternoon, and there was a laid-back, peaceful feeling in the air.

"I'll be fine," Regan said. "Kit met some people out here who we'll hook up with. There's even a guy she likes."

"Uh-oh."

"Uh-oh is right. But this one sounds promising. He worked on Wall Street and retired to Hawaii at age thirty-five."

"Maybe I should run a check on him," Jack suggested. He laughed, but there was a note of seriousness in his voice. "He sounds too good to be true." Jack was fond of Kit and felt protective of her. A couple of the guys Kit had gotten involved with since Jack had been on the scene had been real lulus. He wanted to make sure whoever she dated was on the level.

"It won't be long before I learn his name and hear every detail of his life that Kit knows already. I'll fill you in. If you find something out about him that's not so great, she'll want to be told. She learned her lesson from that last loser she went out with."

"She sure did," Jack agreed.

They were referring to a guy Kit had several dates with who failed to mention that he was getting married and moving to Hong Kong.

"Hey, Regan," Jack continued. "I have a buddy out there in the Honolulu police force. I'll give him a call and let him know you're there. Maybe he'll have some suggestions about what to do or where to go."

"That's great. What's his name?" Regan asked as she pulled her suitcase off the carousel. She was always amazed at how connected Jack was. He knew people everywhere. And everyone respected him.

"Mike Darnell. I got to know him when some of the guys and I used to go there on vacation."

"I'm about to grab a cab to the hotel," Regan said as she wheeled her luggage outside.

"Don't have too good of a time."

"How could I? You're not here."

"I love you, Regan."

"I love you, too, Jack."

"Be careful, Regan."

"I will."

The cabdriver tossed Regan's suitcase into the trunk. Regan got in the back, and they sped off for the Waikiki Waters. So much for being careful, Regan thought as the taxi driver dodged in and out of traffic on the congested highway. Regan found it odd that the road was called Interstate H1. Where were the other states?

Six thousand miles away Jack hung up and looked around his apartment. "This place is so lonesome without her," he said aloud. But he cheered himself with the thought that she'd be there with him in one week. So what was that nagging feeling that came over him? He tried to shrug it off. He was a worrier when it came to Regan. And now he had a particularly good reason. Whenever she was with Kit, something odd always happened.

Jack stood and walked over to the window. The snow was piling up quickly. He walked across the room to his desk, got out his address book, and dialed his friend in the Honolulu Police Department. But the conversation only made him feel worse. Regan hadn't told him anything about the drowning of a hotel employee at the Waikiki Waters. There was no way Kit wouldn't have mentioned it to her. Regan knows me too well, he thought.

"Mike, would you do me a favor and give Regan a call?"

"Of course, Jack. I've got to run into a meeting. I'll talk to you later."

Standing by his window, Jack watched the snow coming down on the darkened street. I'll feel so much better when she's *Mrs.* Reilly, he thought. He turned, went into his room, and lay on the bed.

Back in Waikiki, people couldn't stop talking about the death of Dorinda Dawes.

4

Kit stepped out of the shower and wrapped a towel around her medium-sized frame. It was five-thirty, and she'd just come up from a late afternoon swim in one of the many pools at the Waikiki Waters Playground and Resort. After the morning's excitement a lot of guests at the hotel, including Kit, had the jitters about taking a dip in the ocean. The pool had been overflowing with swimmers.

Regan should be here soon, Kit thought happily. It was a miracle that she'd been able to get a reservation. She'd gotten one of the last seats on an afternoon flight from Los Angeles. Hundreds of Californians had decided to head for Hawaii when they couldn't travel east.

There had been a lot of buzz at the Waikiki

Waters about Dorinda Dawes. It seemed she had caused quite a stir in the three months that she'd worked at the hotel. The Christmas newsletter was more gossipy than most people liked, and she had run around taking pictures of tourists who didn't necessarily want to be in the paper. "You loved her or hated her," Kit heard more than once in the last few hours.

Kit bent over and towel-dried her shoulder-length blond hair. Straightening up, she ran a comb through it and then flicked on the little television set next to the sink. I'd love to have a TV in my bathroom at home, she thought as she applied a dab of styling cream to her golden locks.

The local news came on, and a female reporter was standing on the beach outside Kit's hotel room.

"The body of forty-eight-year-old Dorinda Dawes, a recently hired employee here at the Waikiki Waters, washed ashore this morning. The police believe it was an accidental drowning. She was seen leaving a party here at the hotel last night at about eleven o'clock. Dawes was alone, and employees say she liked to take the beach path back to her apartment building, which was almost a mile away, but she often stopped to spend some quiet time out on the jetty. Police suspect that she slipped and fell into the water. The currents here can be very strong, and there was a strong undertow last night.

"What is puzzling detectives is that she was wearing a lei around her neck made of old shells that are more valuable than pearls. Sources say it is a historic lei that was stolen from the Seashell Museum more than thirty years ago and is a match to the lei that belonged to Princess Kaiulani, a member of the Hawaiian royal family who died tragically in 1899 when she was only twenty-three. She was caught in a rainstorm while horseback riding on the Big Island and contracted a cold which lingered until her death. Princess Kaiulani's lei will be auctioned off at the 'Be a Princess' Ball here at the hotel on Saturday night. The lei around Dorinda's neck belonged to Princess Kaiulani's aunt, Queen Liliuokalani, who was queen for only two years when she was forced to abdicate and the monarchy was dissolved. No one at the hotel recalls ever seeing Dorinda wear this royal lei, and everyone we've spoken with says she was not wearing it at the hotel last night. Descendants of the royal family donated both leis to the Seashell Museum when it opened. Both leis were stolen in the robbery, but the princess's lei was quickly recovered. So the question is, how did Dorinda Dawes, who has lived in Hawaii only since October, get hold of the queen's lei that has been missing all these years?"

Regan will be all over this, Kit thought.

The phone on the wall rang. That's another thing I'd like to have at home, Kit thought. A phone in the bathroom. She sighed and answered.

"Kit?"

"Yes." Kit's heart quickened at the sound of the masculine voice. Was it who she thought it was?

"It's Steve."

Kit's eyes brightened. How could they not? Steve Yardley was about as eligible as a guy could get. A handsome thirty-five-year-old retiree from Wall Street who moved to Hawaii when he got sick of the urban rat race. He wasn't looking for a second career like so many others who made the move. He thought he might eventually do some consulting, but he had plenty of money and was enjoying this chilling-out period in his life. He'd only been in Hawaii six months. Long enough, though, to buy a house in an exclusive development in the hills east of Waikiki with a stunning view of the ocean. Kit smiled as she chirped, "Hi, Steve. What's going on?"

"I'm sitting here enjoying my view of Diamond Head from my lanai, and I thought you would make it even better."

I could faint, Kit thought as she looked at herself in the mirror. She was glad to see that the little bit of color she'd allowed herself to acquire looked good. She also silently thanked God for the snowstorm that was crippling the eastern United States. "You do, do you?" she said and immediately wished she'd thought of a wittier response.

"Yes, I do. I'm so glad you had to stay this weekend. Why were you headed back so soon anyway?"

"It's my grandmother's eighty-fifth birthday. We were going to have a big party on Saturday," Kit answered, thinking that he had already asked her this question last night when they'd met at one of the hotel bars. A lot of people who couldn't fly out had crowded in, and there was a real party atmosphere, with drinks flowing freely.

"My grandmother is eighty-five, too," Steve said incredulously. "It sounds as if we have a lot in common."

Is this guy for real? Kit wondered.

"And she's dying for me to settle down," he added with a laugh.

"That we definitely have in common," Kit added with a wry note in her voice. "And now my best friend is getting married, which is really getting Granny worked up. As a matter of fact, Regan will be arriving soon."

"Really?"

"No, Reilly."

"What?"

Kit laughed. "Her name is Regan Reilly. She's a private investigator in Los Angeles. She's certainly going to be interested in what's going on here at the Waikiki Waters. Did you hear that the woman who was taking pictures in the bar last night drowned in front of the hotel and was wearing a stolen lei? Regan will be all over that. She can't help herself when it comes to investigations."

"I just saw it on the news." Steve coughed. "Excuse me."

"Are you all right?"

"Yes, yes. Anyway, would you and your friend Regan Reilly like to come over for a sunset drink? I'll come and fetch the fetching lasses, and later I'll take you both to dinner."

Kit paused. For the briefest of moments. She and Regan were planning to catch up tonight, but they'd have plenty of time for that. Regan would understand. Heck, she was already engaged. To turn down a chance to get to know Steve, who was handsome, eligible, and rich, was not making the best use of her time. She thought of her granny's face and practically blurted, "Why don't you come get us in an hour?"

"I'll be there," he answered and hung up the phone.

5

Will Brown, the manager of the Waikiki Waters, was in a sweat. His job was to keep the resort running smoothly, keep the guests happy, and now, since the renovation, add new and exciting features to life at the upscale vacation spot. It had been his idea to hire someone like Dorinda Dawes to liven things up. Well, she certainly managed to do that, he thought as he sat in his office just steps away from the sprawling front desk. He could have had a big office in a suite overlooking the water, but that was not for him. Will liked to keep his finger on the pulse of the whole operation, which for him was where guests checked in and out. Most people were happy, but he didn't need to put his ear to the wall to hear the complaints—some valid, some bogus.

"I found mold growing under the bed. It looked like my kid's science experiment," one woman had charged. "I think I should get a discount."

What was she doing under the bed? Will wondered.

"I ordered a soft-boiled egg two days in a row. Both times my egg came out hard-boiled," another had cried. "I go on vacation to enjoy myself. I hate the smell of hard-boiled eggs! I just can't win."

Will was thirty-five and had been raised in a small town in the Midwest. When he was in kindergarten, his parents took a trip to Hawaii. For all the talk and planning, it seemed as if they were going to Oz. They brought him back a Hawaiian print bathing suit that he treasured and brought in to show-and-tell at school. He wore it for a couple of seasons until the seams burst at a pool party. Will's dream had been to visit Hawaii, and after torturing his parents for years, they finally took him and his sister to paradise when he graduated from grade school. With the warm ocean breezes, the fragrant flowers, the swaying palm trees, and the beautiful sandy beaches, he was hooked. He returned after college graduation, took a job as a bellboy at the Waikiki Waters, and worked his way up to manager of the hotel.

He never, ever wanted to leave.

But now his job could be in jeopardy. He had pushed for the renovation, which was expensive and could take years to recoup. He had brought in

Dorinda Dawes, and she turned out to be a troublemaker. And then she drowned at the hotel. Not very good for PR. He had to make things better. But how?

One thing that had to go well was the "Be a Princess" Ball on Saturday night. The gala event would bring a lot of attention to the hotel, and it had to be the right kind. It was the hotel's first big black-tie affair since the renovation. Five hundred people were expected, and they'd gone all out with the food, flowers, and decorations. Convincing the Seashell Museum to auction the royal lei was a real coup. If the event bombed, the buck stopped on Will's desk.

He shifted uncomfortably in his seat. A decent-looking guy, he had reddish hair that had been thinning of late, and pale blue eyes. He always had a ready smile, but sometimes it appeared a little too forced. That was probably a result of spending so many years in the service industry. You had to smile no matter how much people complained.

The coffee cup on his desk was half full. He took a sip and swallowed hard. It was cold. He'd been drinking it all day. With all the guests calling and the news reporters and the police, he hadn't eaten a thing. Everyone was asking about the stolen royal lei around Dorinda's neck that had once belonged to the last queen of Hawaii. Nervously he kept drinking the now bitter brew—which only made things worse.

Will was relieved that the police ruled the

drowning an accident, but he didn't believe it. Dorinda Dawes had gotten under too many people's skin. But what could he do? Was it better to leave well enough alone and hope the whole incident blew over quickly?

He couldn't do that. Something was going on at the hotel. There had been too many problems lately. Misplaced luggage. Purses gone missing. Toilets overflowing, not due to the call of nature. Guests getting sick after eating but not enough of them to cause too much of a stir. And now this: the death of Dorinda. Will felt a knot in his stomach.

He wanted to get to the bottom of things, but he didn't quite know how. The hotel hired consultants to call in and make reservations and then rate the clerks on their efficiency and friendliness. The consulting company also sent people in to act as guests and rate the overall service. The resort had a security staff, but Will felt he needed to find a professional investigator who could snoop around without everyone knowing and find out the dirt. Find out the dirt on everyone except him. Will grabbed the coffee cup and drained it.

He stood and stretched his arms up in the air. He needed to move. He went over to the sliding glass door that looked out on a little secluded grassy area outside his office. Feeling restless, he turned and walked out of his office, past his secretary's desk, and out to the reception area where he spotted the pretty blond girl he had helped yesterday. Her name was Kit. She was supposed to check out, but her flight was canceled because of the storm in the East. All of the rooms were booked, but he had managed to move things around so she could keep hers. She was nice and sweet and seemed to be the type of client they liked to have at the Waikiki Waters. A front desk clerk was handing her a room key.

"Will," Kit called to him.

He put on his best smile and walked over. The open-air lobby was bustling. People were checking in and out, taxi doors were slamming, bellboys were loading up their carts. The air was filled with excitement and possibility.

Kit was standing with an attractive dark-haired woman who had a suitcase at her side.

"Regan," Kit said. "This is Will, and he's the manager of the hotel. He was so nice to me yesterday. He let me keep my room when they were all booked up. Wait till you see it. It's great."

Will extended his hand. "Will Brown. Pleased to meet you."

"Regan Reilly. Thanks for taking care of my friend," she said and smiled.

"We do our best." Almost by rote he added, "And where are you from, Regan?"

"She's a private investigator in Los Angeles," Kit announced proudly.

"Kit!" Regan protested.

"I just know that she's going to be interested in

the story of that lei Dorinda Dawes was wearing when she died."

Will felt the blood rise in his face. "May I buy you two ladies a drink?" he offered.

"Thanks, but a friend is picking us up in a few minutes. Can we get a rain check on that?" Kit asked.

"Of course," he answered. "Perhaps tomorrow."

"We'll be here." Kit smiled. "Now we're just going to drop Regan's suitcase in the room."

As they walked off, he could hear Regan Reilly ask, "What's the story with the lei?"

Will hurried back to his office, his heart racing. A computer whiz, thanks to all the organizing he had to do at the hotel, he quickly looked up Regan Reilly on the Internet. She was a well respected detective who was the daughter of the mystery novelist Nora Regan Reilly. Will had seen guests reading Nora's books by the pool. Maybe Regan could do some work for him. Thank God he'd been nice to Kit and extended her room. Goes to show. Be nice and it'll often pay off. One hand washes the other and all that.

Will thought about going home but decided to hang around. What would he do if he went back to his empty house anyway? Watch the TV reports about Dorinda Dawes? No way. I'll stay here until they get back. Hopefully it won't be too late. Then I'll buy them a drink and see if I can get Regan Reilly on the case.

6

"I can't believe she was wearing an antique royal lei that belonged to the queen and was stolen thirty years ago!" Regan said to Kit as she wheeled her suitcase into the room that had two double beds covered with pale green and white floral quilts. Sand-colored carpeting and dressers and a sliding glass door that opened onto the balcony with the water view gave an immediate feeling that one had stepped into a zone of calm and relaxation. Just like the travel brochures promised.

Instinctively Regan walked over to the door and slid it open. She stepped out, leaned against the rail, and stared at the vast turquoise ocean. A warm tropical breeze fluttered around her, the sun was gently sinking into the west, and the sky had a beautiful pink cast. It all seemed so peaceful.

People were meandering along the beach, palm fronds swayed gently below the balcony, and the reporters covering the Dorinda Dawes drowning were gone.

Kit came up behind her. "It's a perfect time for a piña colada."

Regan smiled. "I suppose it is."

"Steve will be here in a few minutes. I hope you don't mind."

"Not at all. I'm a little tired from the flight, so it's good to keep moving. I want to meet this guy."

"He thinks we have a lot in common."

"Like what?"

"We both have grandmothers who are eighty-five."

"It's a start."

"You've got to start somewhere," Kit laughed.

"True enough." Regan turned and looked back at the beach. "It's hard to believe that Dorinda Dawes was probably walking this beach last night. When did you meet her?"

"Monday night at the bar. A bunch of us from my company were there after our last seminar. She was taking pictures. She sat down with us for a few minutes, asked a lot of questions, then moved on to the next table. You could tell she was the type who tried to get people to say things they'd regret."

"Really?"

"Nobody in our group took the bait. She was a lot nicer to the men than she was to the women."

"One of those, huh?"

Kit smiled. "One of those."

"Was she taking notes?"

"No. She was just acting like the life of the party. And she asked everyone to speak their names into the camera after she took their picture."

"Was she wearing a lei?"

"No. But she had a big orchid in her hair."

"So where did she get the lei she was wearing when she died? And who stole it thirty years ago?"

Kit shook her head and looked at her best friend. "I knew it would get to you, Reilly."

"You're right. It does. You know, drowning is the most difficult form of death to diagnose. It could be murder, suicide, or an accident."

"The police believe it was an accident. She used to walk home on the beach every night. Well, Steve will be here soon," Kit noted, hinting that Regan should get moving.

"I'll be ready in fifteen minutes," Regan promised. She could tell that Kit was excited about this guy and didn't want to keep him waiting. When you find out your grandmothers are the same age, the sky's the limit, Regan thought with a smile.

Twenty minutes later they were standing in the reception area when Steve pulled up in his big, expensive Land Cruiser. Kit waved enthusiastically and hurried to open the front door. Regan hopped in the back and breathed in the new-car smell. Steve turned around and extended his hand to Regan.

"Hello there, Regan Reilly."

"Hello, Steve," Regan said, having no idea of his last name. He certainly is cute, she thought. He looks like that clean-cut Wall Street I-deserve-to-be-rich kind of guy. He had on a baseball cap, khaki shorts, and a short-sleeved shirt. He was tanned, with brown hair and brown eyes. On the seat next to him Kit was glowing. They should be in an ad for something that makes you happy, Regan thought.

"Welcome to Hawaii," he said as he turned to face front. With style he pulled out of the driveway and onto the road filled with hotels, shops, and tourists that led through the heart of Waikiki. He turned up the volume of the CD player, a little too loud for Regan's taste. It precluded much chance for getting-to-know-you conversation. People were out in force, many wearing shorts and flip-flops and floral leis around their necks. It was a beautiful night. Soon they passed a large park where locals were barbecuing and playing guitars and ukeleles. The ocean glistened just beyond the picnic tables. They passed more hotels and then Diamond Head—the famous volcanic crater where Santana once gave a concert.

Steve's cell phone rang—a loud, jarring noise obviously designed to be heard over the stereo. He looked at the caller ID. "I'll let it go to Voice Mail," he said.

Interesting, Regan thought.

When they got to Steve's house, which was in an exclusive neighborhood up in the hills not too far from Diamond Head, several people were already there. "A few of my friends dropped by," he told them when they walked into the house where loud music was also playing. "I thought we'd make it a party."

7

The Mixed Bag Tour group came from a little town in the Pacific Northwest where it had rained 89 percent of the time over the last one hundred years. Hudville, nicknamed by the residents Mudville, could get a little depressing. So a club was formed twenty years ago called Praise the Rain. Twice a month members got together and sang and danced and bobbed for apples in buckets of rainwater. They played songs about rain and raindrops and rainbows, and did rain dances just for fun. It was a pleasant release from the leaky basements, waterlogged lawns, and soggy shoes that they dealt with on a daily basis.

"Into every life a little rain must fall," was their motto. "Or maybe a lot."

"But we have the best complexions in the world," the women cried.

In other words, they did their best to cope. But when an elderly member, Sal Hawkins, got up at a meeting three years ago and announced that he knew his days were numbered and that he was leaving a pot of gold at the end of the rainbow to the group, there was reason for cheer. Sal planned to leave the group money to go on trips to Hawaii. "Those who go to Hawaii must bring back sunshine in their hearts for the rest of you," he said. "I want my money to make the people of Hudville smile after I die."

Five people would be chosen by lottery every three months, and they would be led by Gert and Ev Thompson, sixty-something identical twins who owned the general store in town where they sold lots of umbrellas. Lucky for Gert and Ev they lived next door to Sal and always gave him rides to the Praise the Rain meetings. They also baked him casseroles and cakes just to be nice. He appointed the twins as leaders of the tour group, and as soon as Sal kicked the rain bucket, they arranged for the first trip to Hawaii. He was barely in his grave when their bags were packed and they were on their way. On that first trip Gert and Ev dubbed the group the Lucky Seven.

They'd had eight trips now. Membership in the Praise the Rain Club had increased tenfold since the lottery for the trips started. But everyone was

glad because it made the meetings more interesting, and it brought the town together. On the lottery nights every member was in attendance. With
all the excitement over whose name got picked,
you'd think they were giving away tickets to
heaven.

Gert and Ev loved being in charge of the Lucky
Seven trips. They were now the most relaxed
people in Hudville. But some of the townsfolk
quietly griped, "Who wouldn't be relaxed if you
went on a free vacation to paradise four times a
year?"

The Waikiki Waters Playground and Resort was
their choice of hotel. Every three months the twins
booked four rooms and stayed for a week. Sometimes the group did things together; sometimes
members broke off and went on their own. Every
morning those who had risen early took a walk on
the beach. They had been taking that group walk
when Dorinda Dawes's body had washed up. It had
been upsetting. Gert and Ev quickly herded everyone off to the breakfast buffet so they'd feel better.
"Don't forget," Gert advised, "we must keep a positive attitude about everything. We must bring
sunshine back to Hudville."

Now the Lucky Seven were sitting around one of
the pools under the hau trees as they did most
nights. Cocktails in hand, they talked about their
day as the sun slowly sank over the horizon and the
sky filled with streaks of red and blue and gold.

There was one couple and three singles who ranged in age from their twenties to their sixties. To have called the group eclectic would have been an understatement.

Gert, clad in her favorite flowered muumuu, held up her mai tai punch, which naturally had a floating umbrella bobbing happily among the ice cubes. "First we must have our nightly toast to our deceased benefactor, Mr. Sal Hawkins."

"Here's to Sal," they all agreed, and clinked glasses.

Ned, the hotel's tour guide/physical trainer, had joined them for cocktails. He had worked at the hotel for three months and spent his days swimming, surfing, jogging, and doing push-ups in the gym with any hotel guests who cared to join him. His boss, Will Brown, had hired him to be a roving Jack La Lanne who lived at the hotel, moving in and out of whatever room was available. Will had told him to pay special attention to the Praise the Rain group. They were steady customers, and the hotel liked to keep them happy. So happy that they saved the group the cost of a room by having Ned bunk in with the only single man on the trip.

"How can I help but pay attention to them?" Ned had joked to Will. "This guy is sleeping three feet from me!"

In his forties, Ned was physically fit and attractive, with a bald head and dark brown eyes. He always had a five o'clock shadow by lunchtime. His thick dark hair had had a tendency to frizz. When he had separated from his wife the previous year, he'd decided to shave it off and start over with a new look. He hadn't yet found a woman to his liking but was always on the prowl. I don't have anyone to calm me down, he often thought. I need that. But she has to be athletic. He sipped his scotch, then turned to Gert. "Why don't we go up to the surfing beach tomorrow? I'll get one of the hotel vans. We can rent surfboards."

The beaches up north on the island of Oahu were some of the best surfing beaches in the world. The waves were twenty-five feet high in the winter months, and the scenery was gorgeous. The mountains in the background were an inspiring sight for the surfers hanging ten as they steered their boards toward the beach.

Ev snorted, "Are you out of your mind?" She and Gert were both hefty-sized women who only shed their muumuus for a quick dunk in the pool. They loved their dunks and found them most refreshing. Very occasionally in the evenings they went to the water's edge and flung off their muumuus for a dip in the ocean. They were modest and didn't like walking around on the beach in their bathing suits in the light of day.

Ev had opted for blond hair at this stage of life, and Gert decided on red. Otherwise their round, pleasant faces framed by oversized glasses looked strikingly similar.

"We can bring a picnic lunch. I'm sure some of the others would like to try surfing, wouldn't they?" Ned looked around the group hopefully.

Artie, the thirty-nine-year-old masseur who believed his hands were healers and was Ned's unlikely roommate, replied, "I was thinking that I'd like to swim with the dolphins. I hear there's a great place on the Big Island where they really communicate with humans." Artie was fair and blond and usually quiet. He'd moved to Hudville from sunny Arizona because he figured with all the rain there must be a lot of aching bodies in town that could use a massage. He claimed that he could reduce the size of swollen feet by placing his hands over them and drawing out the negative energy. So far most Hudville residents had continued to ease their swollen feet by putting them up on a hassock while watching television. It was a lot cheaper.

"I would absolutely adore the idea of surfing, I would just adore it!" Frances cried. Francie was an exuberant fiftyish woman who never divulged her age and believed she was the most talented, gorgeous, insightful woman on the planet. Self-confidence was not something she lacked. She had curly black hair, a pretty enough face, and after a mostly unsuccessful acting career, she'd moved to Hudville to teach drama at the high school. Francie always wore heels, even on the beach, and plenty of jewelry. Every day she went out and bought herself a new lei.

"Francie, I can't picture you on a surfboard," Gert said practically as she fished out the sliced orange in her drink and bit into it.

Francie placed her hand on her chest and smiled. "I'll have you know that when I was sixteen I surfed in my hometown of San Diego. I got on the board and was exhilarated!" She now threw her arms up in the air. Her bracelets jangled and slid till they were halted by her elbows.

"Well, that's one taker," Ned said. He looked over at the Wiltons, a couple in their late fifties who were writing a chapter in a book on the joys of an exciting relationship. Only problem was they were dull as dishwater. How could they not have writer's block? Ned wondered. "Bob and Betsy, what do you say? Want to go up to the surfing beach?"

They stared back at him. The Wiltons were both thin and expressionless. Everything about them was nondescript. If you walked away from them, you couldn't remember what they looked like. They just kind of blended in.

"I'm sorry, Ned, but we're working on our chapter, and we need to be alone," Bob informed him.

Gert and Ev both rolled their eyes. The Wiltons were clearly not the best people to bring sunshine back to Hudville. They were downright drippy.

The last group member, Joy, was twenty-one and had no interest in hanging out as part of the Lucky Seven. Winning the trip had thrilled her, but she really wanted to go off and find people her own age. She'd rather go surfing with the lifeguards she'd met. Sharing a room with Francie was driving her crazy. "I have, like, plans for tomorrow," she said meekly as she licked the salt on her margarita glass.

Ned looked disgusted. Because he was a most athletic tour guide, he liked people to do things as a team. "What about the good of the group?" he asked.

Gert put her foot down. "Ned, we appreciate your spending time with us, but the Praise the Rain group is free to do what they want. We come together in the mornings and the evenings and share occasional activities. That's it. We don't want to get on one another's nerves."

"Ned, I'm going with you!" Francie exulted.

"Doesn't anyone want to go to the Big Island to swim with the dolphins?" Artie asked mournfully.

"Our budget doesn't cover trips to the Big Island," Ev noted somewhat sternly. "And Gert and I can't go on a surfing expedition tomorrow."

"Why not?" Betsy asked, her expression belying no curiosity whatsoever.

"We are conducting a private survey of the hotels and services in the area. See what we can do better for the next trip. See how we can save money."

"You're just doing that to drive Will crazy," Ned half-joked. "You know you're not going to get a better deal than what he gives you here."

Ev shrugged and smiled a Mona Lisa smile at him, then pulled the straw of her drink close to her lips.

"Come on, Artie, why don't you join us?" Ned asked. "We can swim with the dolphins here in Oahu on Saturday."

Artie slowly rubbed his hand back and forth. "All right, Ned. But we'd better get life preservers. I hear that surf is treacherous. I can't bear the sight of another dead body in the water."

Francie was the only one who laughed.

❀

8

Standing out on the deck of Steve's house, Regan was awestruck by the panoramic view. Oahu's most famous landmark, the magnificent Diamond Head crater, could be seen in the distance. On the plane Regan had read that the volcano had risen from the sea half a million years ago and earned its name when British seamen mistook its calcite crystals for diamonds. Those poor guys, Regan thought. Talk about getting bummed out after months at sea! But diamonds or not, the volcanic crater was a sight to behold. It stood proud and majestic as it watched over Waikiki and an endless stretch of sea. Glints of light from the setting sun were bouncing off the water below.

It looks like a postcard, Regan thought, taking a

seat in one of Steve's comfortably padded outdoor
chairs. The music was blaring, but there weren't as
many people as Regan might have guessed when
she first walked into the brand-new house with its
gleaming blond wood floors and floor-to-ceiling
windows. The walls were white, and the furniture
was pale wood, simple but expensive. The state-of-
the-art kitchen opened onto the living room/dining
room area, and the deck ran the length of the
whole room.

Five of Steve's friends were seated on the deck.
A painter and his wife, who crafted Hawaiian dolls,
two guys who were Steve's fraternity brothers from
college and had just looked him up, and a woman
who minded a house on the Big Island for a businessman from Chicago who was almost never
there.

To Regan she immediately seemed like a phony.

"I just love to party," she exclaimed, tossing
back her mane of long dirty blond hair. "But it's so
cool having this house in the wilderness to yourself. I love to sit up there and reread the classics."

"I'm sorry," Regan said. "I didn't catch your
name."

"Jasmine."

Of course, Regan thought. She didn't expect it
to be a run-of-the-mill kind of name. Inwardly,
Regan smiled, remembering her Catholic gram-
mar school where most students had been named
after saints. Regan hadn't even met people with

unusual names until she got to college. "How did you get the job?" Regan asked Jasmine.

"I was a corporate lawyer in New York City and couldn't stand all the pressure. So I came to Hawaii for a vacation and met my boss. When I complained about my work, he offered me the job. At first I was like, I can't do that, then I said, Oh, yes, I can. I've met so many wonderful and interesting people. It can be a little bit lonelier over on the Big Island. It's so vast, and there aren't as many people. But I come over to Oahu all the time. Steve is such a doll. He lets me stay in his guest room whenever I want."

Regan could see Kit's face out of the corner of her eye. Her look was less than thrilled.

"I met Jazzy when I first got here," Steve chimed in quickly. "She's great for introducing people around. She's been a real friend."

One of those, Regan thought. Nothing more annoying for a woman interested in a guy than the girl who is his really good pal.

"Jazzy" threw her head back and laughed appreciatively as she curled her tanned legs under her. "Before you know it, Steve, you'll know everyone in this town . . ."

Regan didn't dare look at Kit.

". . . because the thing is it becomes a small town very fast. Almost everyone in Hawaii lives on Oahu. They call it 'the gathering place,' and let me tell you, it certainly is. It's getting more and more exciting all the time. And after you're here for a while, you hear all the gossip. You just can't help it." She laughed again and winked at Steve. "My boss actually wants to buy a house in this area. I tell you, I would love that!"

What about rereading the classics? Regan wondered. "Jasmine," she began. She just couldn't bring herself to call her Jazzy. "Did you know the woman who drowned today at the Waikiki Waters Resort, Dorinda Dawes? She was writing a newsletter for the hotel."

The former corporate lawyer wrinkled her button nose at Regan. Jazzy was petite, tanned, attractive, wore little makeup, and looked as if she could pick up a tennis racket or swim twenty laps at any moment. The type who was born for country club living. "Who didn't know Dorinda Dawes? She butted into everyone's business and got on a lot of people's nerves."

And may she rest in peace, Regan thought. "Really? How so?"

"The newsletter wasn't so bad because the hotel had to approve it. But in the last issue that covered all the Christmas parties, she printed the worst possible pictures of the women. And she was planning to produce her own gossip sheet called 'Oh! Oh! Oahu!' Everyone was bracing for that. Word got out that Will, the hotel manager, rejected the first newsletter she wrote. And he edited all the others. She was saving those 'edits' for her gossip sheet. People were afraid that she'd make them look like jerks. But she managed to get into parties all over town. She wanted to become the queen of gossip in Hawaii. Now she's the subject of gossip herself. What was she doing with Liliuokalani's royal lei? Did you hear it matches the one that's being auctioned off at the 'Be a Princess' Ball? The one that belonged to poor Princess Kaiulani?"

"Yes. Kit told me," Regan answered.

"I'm putting together the gift bags for the ball. No one on the committee can believe that she was here three months and managed to get her hands on that stolen lei. Only Dorinda. I tell you, she worked fast. She was out to make a name for herself one way or another. I think she was getting desperate. She'd been trying for years."

"How do you know?"

"I met her several times in New York City."

"You did?"

"Yes. Dorinda was on the scene there for a long time. She had a lot of different jobs and then started a gossipy newsletter on the Internet. But it didn't fly. Then she got a job as a columnist at an Upper East Side newspaper that folded. Last summer she read an ad placed by a woman in Hawaii who needed an apartment in New York for six months. So they traded places. Dorinda wanted to settle here. The few times I talked to her, I got the feeling she thought it was her last shot at making a name for herself. Not that she came out and said that. But I've got to give her credit. She managed to get a job at the Waikiki Waters quickly. It didn't pay much, but it didn't take up too much of her time and it gave her access to a lot of people and parties."

Kit put her glass down. "Dorinda was having a swell time the other night when we saw her at the Towers bar. I think what she loved having access to was the men. And I think she'd had a few drinks."

"She enjoyed her wine," Jazzy sniffed, "which could be why she drowned."

"Can I refresh anyone's drink?" Steve asked, clearly wanting to change the subject.

"Mine!" Jazzy said. "Add lots of club soda! Hurry! You don't want to miss the sunset!"

Regan took a sip of her drink. It seemed that wherever one went, it turned into Peyton Place pretty quickly. Gossip mills are everywhere. So are people like Jazzy. There's no escaping them.

Steve's two male friends, Paul and Mark, walked back inside to grab a couple more beers. They seemed like nice guys, Regan thought. So did Steve. Whether he was a good prospect for Kit was another story, and she didn't have much time to find out.

Together they watched the sunset, oohing and aahing as the colors changed in the sky. Everyone was telling Steve how lucky he was to live in such a glorious spot. When the last bit of the blazing red and orange constellation slipped under the hori-

zon, the painter and his dollmaker wife stood.
"Thanks, Steve," he said. "We're on our way.
Tomorrow we're getting up early and flying to
Maui for a crafts fair. Hopefully we'll have a good
day peddling our wares." She was a native Hawaii-
ian, and he called himself an aging hippie who
came to Hawaii twenty-five years ago to find himself. He wore his blond hair pulled back in a pony-
tail while her black shiny hair cascaded down her
back.

The remaining six piled into Steve's car and
headed into town to Duke's Restaurant and Bare-
foot Bar, the restaurant named in honor of Duke
Kahanamoku, Hawaii's most famous citizen and
the "father of international surfing." Duke won
worldwide fame as a swimmer, appeared in over
twenty-eight Hollywood movies, and in later life
became Hawaii's ambassador of goodwill and
aloha. Decades after his death he was still considered the greatest athlete in the history of the
Hawaiian Islands. He had never seen snow and
was quoted as saying, "I am only happy when I am
swimming like a fish." A large statue of Duke, his
arms outstretched as if he were saying, "Aloha,"
stands on Waikiki Beach. Every day dozens of leis
are placed around his neck by adoring tourists.
Steve had pointed out the flower-covered statue as
they drove to his house.

The bar was packed, but they managed to get a
table in the open air. Jasmine seemed to know

more than her fair share of people, which didn't
surprise Regan in the least. A woman at the bar
stopped Steve, put her hand on his arm, and
started talking to him. To Regan he looked annoyed and seemed impatient with her. He quickly
broke free and sat down with the group, and they
ordered drinks and burgers. Regan was feeling
pretty tired. It was Thursday night, a little after
nine, which meant it was eleven in Los Angeles
and two in the morning in New York. A television
over the bar showed a clip of the snowstorm in the
East. I'll be there with Jack next week, Regan
thought longingly. She was glad that Kit looked
happy but wasn't really thrilled at the prospect of
spending all weekend with this group. And somehow she figured it was going to turn out that way.
There was talk of a dinner party tomorrow night at
Steve's house. I'm sure "dinner party" is a pretty
loose term with him, she thought.

Regan glanced over at Paul and Mark who were
blatantly checking out the babes at the bar. I guess I
shouldn't feel insulted, she mused. This ring on my
finger doesn't exactly go unnoticed. Jasmine was
leaning over and talking to people at the next table,
and Steve was whispering something in Kit's ear.

With all the noise it took a few minutes for
Regan to realize that her cell phone was ringing.
Regan fumbled in her purse for it. Who would be
calling me at this hour? she thought nervously.
Everyone at home should be asleep.

"Hello," she answered when she finally retrieved it.

"Regan?"

"Yes."

"This is Jack's friend Mike Darnell. I'm a detective with the Honolulu Police Department. He asked me to give you a call."

"Oh, hi, Mike," Regan said with a smile. "That's nice of you."

"I've been working late, but I was thinking of heading over to a place called Duke's. I thought you and your friend might like to meet me there."

"I'm at Duke's now."

"You're kidding."

"Would I kid you?"

"I don't know. If you're engaged to Jack Reilly, you're capable of anything."

Regan laughed. "We're with a group of people. Come join us. We're to the left of the bar on the outside. There are six of us, but there could be more by the time you get here."

"I'll see you in a few minutes."

Regan hung up the phone as Jasmine inquired, "Who was that?"

"A friend of my fiancé's who's a detective in the Honolulu Police Department. He's coming by for a drink."

"Oh," she said dismissively.

Am I imagining things, Regan wondered, or does Jazzy look nervous?

9

Nora Regan Reilly woke with a start. The wind was howling outside, and she heard a thump against the side of the house. The clock on the nightstand glowed 2:15. Beside her, Luke was sleeping peacefully. He can sleep through anything, Nora thought with a slight smile.

Thump. Thump.

Nora got up and reached for the bathrobe she kept on the satin-covered bench at the foot of the bed. She and Luke liked to keep their bedroom cold, and on this night that was no challenge. She wrapped the robe around her, walked to the big picture window, and pulled aside the curtain. She was just in time to see a huge branch from one of the trees in their backyard snap off and go crashing to the ground. Chunks of icy snow broke apart as they scattered on the sea of white below. That was Regan's favorite tree when she was a little girl, Nora remembered.

She could hear Luke's gentle breathing across the room. No sense waking him, she thought as she peered out at the yard. There was nothing he could do about it now. And tomorrow will be a tough day. There's no way they can have a funeral in this weather—the roads are impassable. All those relatives of the elderly skier will be stuck at the hotel, and they'll be looking to Luke for answers about the storm. As if he can change the weather.

Nora crept back into bed as the wind whistled outside. I hope things in Hawaii are calmer than they are here, she thought. She lay huddled under the blankets, her thoughts jumping from one topic to the next. She wished Regan was in New York this weekend. It would have been so much fun to go and hear the wedding band with her and Jack and find out for themselves if they were as good as everyone swore they were. Hopefully we'll do it next weekend, she mused. She tossed and turned a bit and finally fell back asleep.

Then she started to dream. She dreamed they were at Regan and Jack's wedding and a band was playing, but they were very loud and out of tune. The music sounded screechy and discordant. Nora kept telling them to stop, but they wouldn't listen. She was so thankful when she woke and realized it was just a bad dream. The hissing of the wind had incorporated itself into her unconscious as she slept.

What's wrong with me? she wondered. Well, for one thing, Regan hadn't called her when she arrived in Hawaii. She's a grown-up, Nora reminded herself, and doesn't have to call home all the time. But she usually checked in when she was traveling. Nora felt jittery, and the fact that the branch snapped off Regan's favorite tree made her a little sad. Once again Nora slipped out of bed, grabbed her robe, and stuffed her feet into a pair of slippers. Quietly she opened the bedroom door and padded down the hallway.

Downstairs she turned on the kettle and picked up the phone. It's not that late in Hawaii, she thought. I'll give Regan a quick call on her cell phone.

It was still six of them crowded around the table at Duke's. When Mike Darnell arrived, Jasmine floated off to talk to a group at the bar. Mike had just ordered a beer when Regan's cell phone rang again.

"Mom," she said with alarm when she heard her mother's voice. "What are you doing up at this hour? Is everything all right?" Regan covered her free ear with her hand so she could hear over the noise of the crowd.

"I couldn't sleep," Nora replied. "And I just wanted to make sure you got there okay. With the weather we're having, it's hard to imagine that it's nice anywhere in the world."

"We're sitting outside a restaurant looking out at the ocean and the palm trees. It's a beautiful night," Regan assured her. "A friend of Jack's just joined us. He's a detective in the Honolulu Police Department."

Somehow that made Nora feel better. Why do I worry so much? she wondered. The kettle started to whistle, a loud shriek that Luke said was designed to wake the dead.

"Are you making tea?" Regan asked.

"Decaf."

"I can't believe that kettle can be heard so clearly six thousand miles away."

"Dad would say you don't even need a phone for that."

Regan laughed. "Well, we're fine. Why don't you try to get some sleep? You'll be exhausted tomorrow."

"It won't matter. I'm certainly not going anywhere."

"Don't let Dad shovel the driveway."

"I won't. Greg Driscoll was here today three times with his plow, and he'll be back in the morning. He probably shouldn't bother. The snow's just going to keep piling up." Nora poured the tea, turned away from the stove, and gasped. "Luke!"

"Dad's up?"

"When I left the bed, he was dead to the world."

"You know he can always tell when you're gone from the bed for more than five minutes."

"What are you doing up?" Luke whispered to Nora as he rubbed his eyes.

"A loud noise woke me up, and then a branch snapped off the big tree in the back," Nora explained as Regan listened at the other end.

"The big tree?" Luke and Regan asked at the same time.

"The big tree," Nora confirmed.

"My favorite tree!" Regan noted. "Mom, remember you wrote the story about the tree that hit a house and then the family ran into a string of bad luck?"

"I forgot about that story. It was so long ago. Thanks a lot for reminding me."

"Well, don't worry. The tree didn't hit the house. I've got to go. This place is so noisy, it's hard to hear."

"Give a call over the weekend."

"Okay."

Regan hung up and reached for her wineglass. "Sorry, Mike," she apologized to the tall and attractive man with brown hair and dark skin who was sitting next to her.

"That was your mom?" Mike asked.

"Yes, they're having quite a storm back east."

"That's what Jack told me. By the way, he invited me to your wedding. You'd better be careful. I just might show up."

Regan smiled. "We'd love it."

"I should tell you that when Jack called me, I happened to mention there was a drowning at your hotel today."

Regan grimaced. "Oh, you did?"

"Yes. He sounded surprised."

"I purposely didn't tell him," Regan admitted. "What's the story on that?"

"We believe it was an accident."

"Really? Why?"

Mike shrugged. "There are no signs of a struggle on her body. She doesn't have any known enemies, from what we can gather. Her credit history is good. She didn't have a lot of money, but she paid her bills. We were told she walked home along the beach and liked to stop and sit on the jetty. They're doing toxicology tests, but people have said she'd had a couple of drinks. She probably just slipped and fell into the water. Those jetties can get incredibly slippery, and there's a strong undertow out there."

"What about her family?" Regan asked.

"The only immediate family is a cousin. The hotel had his number, and we were able to reach him. He was naturally upset but said they weren't close. I guess you heard about the stolen lei around her neck. Our big question is where she got it."

"I heard all about it. How was it so quickly identified?"

"It has a very unusual arrangement of shells and different shades of coral stones that is really distinct. One of the guys who brought the body in today had been to the Seashell Museum last weekend with friends who were visiting from the mainland. He had seen the other royal lei on display and knew that its mate had been stolen. He put two and two together."

"What are you going to do with the lei?"

"We gave it back to the owner of the museum. He's so happy, he's out of his mind. They're auctioning off the matching lei this weekend at the ball at the Waikiki Waters to raise money for the museum."

"I heard. I wonder if he'll have them auction off this one as well."

"I don't know."

"So the pair of leis are back together again after having been separated for thirty years."

"That's right. They'd been together in the museum for over fifty years, separated for thirty, and now they're reunited. It's quite a story."

"But Dorinda Dawes arrived in Hawaii only three months ago. Does anyone have any idea where she might have gotten that lei?"

"She probably didn't even know what she had. And she probably didn't steal it. Apparently she claimed that she had never been to Hawaii before three months ago, and she was a teenager when it was stolen."

"That girl over there"—Regan pointed to Jasmine who was posing at the bar—"knew Dorinda Dawes in New York."

"I've noticed her in here before," Mike said. "Something tells me she's a real player."

10

Back at the Waikiki Waters, Will Brown kept himself busy with paperwork all night. He called Kit and Regan's room a number of times to see if they were back yet. No luck. He wandered out to the reception area for about the twelfth time when he saw them get out of a Land Cruiser.

"Hello," he said as he ran to greet them.

"Hi, Will," Kit called out. "You're burning the midnight oil."

"No rest for the weary," he joked. "As you know, it's been quite a day around here. I'd love to buy you two a drink."

"Actually," Regan began, "I'm a little tired."

Will lowered his voice. "I need to speak to you about a professional matter."

Noticing how anxious Will looked, Regan acquiesced. "Maybe a quick one," she said and looked at Kit who nodded in agreement.

"Thatta girls!" Will boomed too forcefully.

This guy is definitely on edge, Regan decided.

Will led them to an airy and spacious outdoor bar that was situated between two of the largest towers. Lilting Hawaiian music was being piped in through speakers hidden in the palm trees and hibiscus plants surrounding the tables and chairs. Everyone must be resting up for another day of sitting on the beach, Regan thought as she glanced around the nearly empty lounge.

"Here we go." Will indicated a table that was off to the side, under a large palm tree lit with small white lights. A waiter, upon seeing the big boss, hurried over.

Regan and Kit ordered glasses of wine while Will decided on a vodka and tonic.

"Coming right up," the waiter announced cheerily and hurried off.

"Thank you, girls, for joining me." Will looked around cautiously to make sure no one was within earshot.

Kit looked at Regan and raised her eyebrows as if to say, "What gives?"

Regan shrugged.

After making sure the place was secure from eavesdroppers, Will cleared his throat and ran his fingers through his hair, which only made his anxiety worse. It somehow felt thinner than it did an hour ago. Maybe I am tearing my hair out, he thought. "Regan, Kit . . .," he began. "The Waikiki Waters Playground and Resort is a very reputable hotel. We just did a big and expensive renovation. We have many repeat customers every year. We pride ourselves on our service and our accommodations—"

"What's wrong?" Regan asked quickly. May as well make him get to the point, she thought.

"Right." Will nodded as beads of perspiration rolled down his forehead. He cleared his throat. "I feel there are people out there who are intent on ruining the good name of this hotel. There have been lots of little things going wrong. Maybe it's some of the employees. And the drowning today of Dorinda Dawes . . . I just don't think it was an accident."

Regan leaned forward. "What makes you say that?"

"I saw her before she left, and she said she was going straight home."

"Did you tell the police that?"

"Yes. But they knew she often walked along the beach to get home. They said she could have decided to stick her toes in the water. It was pretty warm last night."

"But you don't believe it?"

"No."

"Regan," he continued, "I know you have a great reputation as an investigator."

"You do?"

"I looked you up on the Internet."

"Oh."

"I was wondering if I could hire you to spend the next couple of days talking to people around here. See if you pick up on anything unusual. Lately we've had more than our share of petty thefts. We've had tubes of suntan lotion dropped into the public toilets, which caused several floods. Several people got sick at the salad bar, which is unusual because we're very careful about our restaurants. We pride ourselves on the quality of our food. Now Dorinda's drowning. It'll be all over the local papers tomorrow. I've already had calls from stringers for national papers—all because of that royal lei around her neck and the coincidence that it matches the lei that will be auctioned off at our ball Saturday night. That ball has to be a success!" Will paused and looked off into the distance.

Regan waited. She knew he had a lot more to say.

"I hired Dorinda to work here. I know she got on people's nerves, and now I feel somehow responsible for her death. If she hadn't been working here, she would have been someplace else last night. And if there is a murderer at the Waikiki Waters, who's to say he or she won't strike again? There's something going on around here, and I would be grateful if you could help me out. Maybe her killer

is in one of those rooms right now." Will gestured
to the towers in the distance.

Wow, Regan thought. He might be overreact-
ing, but who knows? "I understand your concern,"
she assured him quietly as the waiter approached
and served them their drinks.

"Can I get you anything else, Mr. Brown?"

"Thank you, but no."

The waiter tapped his tray with his fingers and
retreated to the bar.

Regan took a sip of her wine. "If there is someone who is responsible for Dorinda Dawes's death,
that person might have had nothing to do with her
personally. Her death may have been a random act
of violence. It may be related to the stolen lei. I'd
love to help you out, Will, but I'm only going to be
here until Monday."

"That's okay. I'd just like to get your read on
things. And you'll be here for the ball. Who knows
what someone might pull that night? We have a
security staff, but I'd like to have someone around
who isn't obviously checking things out for the
hotel. I don't know what else to do. You can probably get people to talk. Just play the nosey
tourist—or whatever it is you do. Maybe Dorinda
did accidentally drown. I don't know. But did you
ever get the feeling that there's something that's
not quite right but you can't quite put your finger
on it?"

"Sure," Regan replied.

"Sometimes when you're the boss, people don't want to tell you things. You, I bet, will get people to talk. I just don't know who to trust anymore." Will took another swig of his drink. "I'll be frank with you, Regan. I'm also afraid I'll lose my job. This all happened on my watch, and the big boys are not happy at all. Dorinda Dawes made herself known around town, not always in the best way, and they feel her life and death reflect badly on the hotel. And on me in particular because I hired her."

Kit looked at Regan with a raised eyebrow.

He knows more than he's telling me, Regan thought. "Do you live at the hotel?" she asked him.

"No. My wife, Kim, and I have a little house up the coast. It's about forty-five minutes away."

"Your wife?" Regan tried to keep the surprise out of her voice. He wasn't wearing a wedding band, nor did he have the aura of a married person. Whatever that aura was.

"Yes. We've been married for two years. We visited her mother in northern California for Christmas. She stayed on for a few extra weeks with our son. They'll be back tomorrow night."

This is getting more interesting, Regan thought. Did he have a personal interest in Dorinda Dawes? Maybe he's afraid his name will come up in an investigation, and he wants me to help prove he's not involved.

Kit had listened throughout. Regan had noticed that Kit also seemed surprised when Will said he was married. But Will did seem genuinely anguished. He has a wife and child to support, and he has a good job. If he loses it, he could be out of luck. Regan knew it wasn't easy to find another job like his in Hawaii. There were too many people who wanted to fill those "executive" spots and live in paradise.

Regan was interested in pursuing the case, but she had come out here to be with Kit. As if Kit could read her mind, she said, "Regan, I know you want to do this. I don't mind. As long as we can spend some time together."

"Ain't love grand?" Regan asked.

Kit laughed. "Yes, it does help that Steve suggested he come over and join us at the beach tomorrow."

"Lucky for both of us." Regan turned to Will. "All right. I'll help you out. But right now I need to get some sleep. I'm still on Los Angeles time. Should I meet you in your office tomorrow morning?"

Will looked as if some of the weight had been lifted from his shoulders. "Thank you, Regan. I'll pay you whatever your rate is. And your next trip here is on me."

"Fine," Regan agreed quickly. "Nine o'clock okay?"

"Perfect. Just tell them at the front desk that

you have an appointment with me. They won't question it."

"Good enough. I'll be there at nine."

Will pulled his handkerchief out of his pocket and mopped his brow as Don Ho's famous song "Tiny Bubbles" floated through the air.

11

"You take me to the safest places," Regan teased Kit as they headed back to their room.

"Leave it to me," Kit muttered. "But it is a little scary to think that there could be someone at the hotel who murdered Dorinda Dawes."

"Let's take a quick walk on the beach," Regan suggested.

"I thought you were tired."

"I am. But now my mind is focusing on this case. I want to see what it's like out here at night."

They walked past the Grand Pool where a hula show was performed every few nights and stepped out onto the sand. The Pacific Ocean lay before them. The waves lapped gently at the shore. Palm trees swayed softly in the breeze. The moonlight reflected on the water, and the lights from the

Waikiki Waters and hotels down the strip made for a beach that was not too dark at all.

Kit followed Regan out to the water's edge. Regan kicked off her sandals and walked into the water until it covered her ankles. She then turned left and started walking, staying close to the shore. Kit did the same. The beach curved around, and they hit a dark cove that couldn't be seen from the hotel. Just beyond it was the jetty that Regan figured must have been where Dorinda would stop and sit on her way home.

A couple was sitting there on the rocks in the cove, kissing. They pulled away from each other when they felt the presence of Regan and Kit.

Kit watched in amazement as Regan said, "Excuse me. Could I have a word with you?"

"I just proposed to my girlfriend on a moonlit beach, and you gotta interrupt?" the guy asked Regan incredulously.

"I guess you weren't here last night then?" Regan prodded.

"It was too cloudy last night. I always wanted it to be a moonlit night, so I waited. Tonight there's moonlight, so I proposed."

"I assume she said yes," Regan quipped.

"I did," the girl cried happily. She held out her hand to Regan and displayed a diamond ring.

Regan stepped toward them and leaned down. "It's beautiful," Regan said sincerely. "I just got engaged, too."

"Let me see your ring," the girl enthused.

Regan held out her left hand.

"Wow! Yours is gorgeous, too!"

"Thanks."

"Where did your boyfriend propose?" the guy asked. He seemed to be thawing.

"In a hot air balloon."

"That must have been real special," the girl cried. "A hot air balloon!"

The guy frowned. "I should have thought of that."

"No, sweetie. A moonlit beach is perfect." She leaned in for a little kiss. He gave her two.

"Were you by chance out here at all last night?" Regan asked.

"No. I walked out to see if the setting was right to get engaged, but it was too cloudy. So we went dancing."

"What time was that?"

"Just after ten."

"Did you notice if there were many people on the beach?"

"I didn't see too many people. People wander out from the pool area sometimes, but the pool closes at ten. The outdoor bar is open late. We had drinks there the other night and saw a few people stroll out to the beach and take a quick look at the ocean before they went to bed. But most of them are on the beach all day, so they've seen enough. You know what I mean?"

"You didn't see anyone swimming?"

He shook his head. "No. You'd be crazy to swim at night. There are riptides and strong currents around here. You get sucked under, and nobody's around to help. We stuck our feet in here and felt the swirling."

"We did, too," Regan told him.

"You trying to figure out how that lady drowned?"

Before Regan could answer, he continued, "I find that a lot of people take a walk on the beach at night when they're very upset."

"Jason!" the girl protested.

"It's true, Carla." He turned to Regan. "I woke up at three in the morning last night, and she's gone. I was a wreck. Where is she? I got dressed, and she walks in the door. She told me she couldn't sleep and went for a walk on the beach. At three in the morning! I said it would have been nice to leave me a note. Now she tells me she was upset because she was sure I was going to propose last night and didn't. It was our anniversary yesterday. Ya know, the day we met. Ten years ago."

Ten years, Regan thought. I'm glad Jack didn't take that long.

"She transferred to my school in the middle of the seventh grade."

"My father's job required a lot of moves," Carla explained. "But I didn't walk far on the beach. It felt a little scary. I figured if he was never going to propose, then so be it. There are other fish in the sea."

"Thanks a lot, honey."

She hit his arm playfully. "You know what I mean."

"Did you see anyone out here at that hour?" Regan asked.

"Not a soul! That's why it was scary. I ended up running back. And to think that body washed up just a few hours later. Oh, my God!"

Her fiancé pulled her close. "Don't leave me like that again."

"I won't." They started to kiss again.

"We'll leave you two alone," Regan said quickly. "But if you recall seeing anything even a little bit odd last night, could you let me know? Anything at all, even if it seems insignificant, might be important. The hotel just wants to ensure the safety of the guests. You can never be too careful." She gave them her name, room number, and cell phone number.

"Sure," the girl said. "I can't think of anything now. I'm kind of too excited. But if I think of something, I'll give you a call. My name is Carla. We're in the Coconut Tower."

"Thanks, Carla."

Regan and Kit walked back to their room. Kit flopped on her bed. "You're amazing. Only you could interrupt a couple in a clinch who just got engaged and end up being their pal."

"I don't know whether I'm their pal or not," Regan replied, "but if they call me with anything that might help explain what happened to Dorinda Dawes, then they'll be my pals. And something tells me that when the excitement of their engagement dies down just a little, she'll want to talk. Believe me, I'll be hearing from her."

12

Ned and Artie were in their room. It was decent-sized but small for two adults, particularly two adults who didn't want to spend much time together during the day, never mind those vulnerable hours at night. Artie liked to play tapes of his mystical healing as he drifted off to sleep, which drove Ned crazy. Ned always had the television turned to the sports channel, which drove Artie nuts.

Roommates.com would never have paired them up, but the twins had snapped up the opportunity to save money, so Artie was stuck. He couldn't complain too much since the trip was free, and as Gert and Ev pointed out, everyone shared a room and you should only be in the room to sleep when you're in a beautiful place like Hawaii.

Ned loved his job at the Waikiki Waters. Because they'd given him a room, he was on call almost all the time, but he didn't mind. His personality was such that he needed to be on the go continually. His colleagues thought he was intense. Some called him crazed.

It was now midnight, and Ned was doing a set of one hundred sit-ups. Artie was in bed, with his earphones plugged into his CD player. The light was on. Artie had his eyes shut tight, with the sheet over his head. Finally he pulled the earphones out of his ears.

"Ned, could we please turn out the light? I need my rest."

"I've got to finish my sit-ups," Ned said, breathing heavily.

"I thought it wasn't good to exercise right before you went to bed," Artie whined.

"It relaxes me."

"Last night you took a swim in the pool. Why don't you do that again?"

"Why don't you take a walk on the beach, Artie? You've been doing that every night. But you didn't tonight. Something tells me you need it."

"I like to think things through at the end of the day when I walk on the beach, but tonight I'm tired."

"What do you think about?" Ned asked as he kept count of his sit-ups.

"Like whether I should move on from Hudville."

"Move out of Hudville?"

"Yeah. Too much rain and not enough people willing to pony up the money for a massage. I'm thinking of moving to Sweden. I hear people like massages there."

Ned rolled his eyes. "They must have plenty of masseurs. Maybe you should move to Hawaii. That's what I did. I moved here when I separated from my wife last year, and I feel much better."

"I don't know," Artie said as he clenched and unclenched his hands. "I feel restless. I feel as if there are new things out there that I should be doing."

"Those relaxation tapes aren't helping you much," Ned noted.

"Don't make fun of my tapes."

"I'm not. Why don't we go for a run?"

"Now?"

"Why not? You have too much tension built up inside. Run it off, and you'll sleep like a baby."

"I'll sleep like a baby right now if we just turned out the light."

"Ninety-eight, ninety-nine, one hundred. Done!" Ned jumped up from the floor. "I'll take a quick shower, then lights out."

I can't take it, Artie thought. I just can't take it.

Down the hall, the Wiltons were lying in bed. They were discussing their chapter of the book on how to keep a relationship exciting.

Bob thought Betsy got a little too jealous at times. He liked to kid around with the ladies. No harm intended. But Betsy didn't like it one bit. That brought excitement to their relationship, but it wasn't the right kind. Some couples liked to fight so they could have fun making up. Not Betsy Wilton.

"Now, for instance," Bob said as he folded his hands across his chest, "when that lady who drowned was taking pictures of us last night and I told her how good she smelled, you gave me the evil eye. Then you left in a huff and went back to the room."

"The reason you knew how good she smelled was because you put your arm around her and gave her a big hug. Just because she took our picture. That wasn't necessary."

Bob considered this. "Well, it doesn't matter now."

"I guess it doesn't."

"She's dead."

"That she is."

"I came back to the room, and you were fast asleep."

"I took a little piece of a sleeping pill."

"No wonder you were out like a light." Bob smiled mischievously. "You know, Dorinda Dawes was wearing a shell lei when she died. I think they're sexy. I'll see if I can buy you one tomorrow. Good night, dear."

"Good night," Betsy said as she stared up at the ceiling. *Writing about bringing out the excitement in a relationship is bringing out the worst in him,* she thought. *It's getting downright scary.*

Two single women sharing a room when they were thirty years apart in age presented challenges all its own. But thankfully Francie and Joy were both slobs. On that score they were a match made in heaven. The bathroom counter was littered with makeup, creams, suntan lotions, and hair care products of every variety. Towels and clothes were piled in heaps everywhere.

They probably could have been good friends if Joy were a little older. But Joy was still sowing her wild oats and had no interest in anyone who was north of twenty-five. It was nearly three in the morning when she tiptoed into the room. She had managed to hook up with a group of young people who worked at the hotel. They had gone to Duke's and then partied on a stretch of beach in front of the restaurant. Zeke, the lifeguard she had a crush on, was there, and he'd spent the night talking to her. He didn't walk her back to her room because the staff wasn't supposed to socialize with the hotel guests, but he'd told her to meet him the next night at the bar at the Sheraton Moana. Joy was thrilled. It would make her day with the Mixed Bag Tour group bearable.

Joy tried to be quiet as she slipped into the bathroom and undressed. She picked the T-shirt she slept in off the floor and pulled it over her head. Too tired to take off her makeup, she did manage to give her teeth the once-over with a tattered toothbrush.

Holding her breath, she turned out the bathroom light and slowly opened the door. Five seconds later she was under the covers. That's a relief, she thought as she felt herself relax. Across the table, Francie's voice rang out: "How was your night? You must tell me all about it!"

Oh, my God, Joy thought. I can't cope!

Gert and Ev had a suite with a sitting room and a bedroom that was larger than all the others in the group. That's because they were in charge. They tried to book the same rooms for every trip, but of course it wasn't always possible. But they always managed to get rooms next to one another with adjoining terraces overlooking the water. Sometimes the Lucky Seven stood out on their terraces and chatted back and forth. There was no escaping each other.

Having lived together all their lives, Gert and Ev were as in synch as two people could be. They possessed a sixth sense often shared by twins. They still wore the same clothes, used the same products, and now shared many of the same aches and pains. Ev had more of an edge than Gert. She didn't always take to the people they had to drag on the trips.

"Those Wiltons are so annoying," she called to Gert from the bathroom as she was flossing her teeth.

"No sunshine from them," Gert agreed.

"I'm glad we have the day off tomorrow. We'll have our own fun."

"I can't wait."

Ev threw the floss in the trash, washed her hands again, rinsed her mouth, and went in and flopped on her bed. "Do you think we'll find us some good deals tomorrow?"

Gert smiled at her twin. "You betcha. We'll make ourselves some real good deals."

The twins high-fived each other, said a prayer for their deceased parents, an extra-special prayer for Sal Hawkins, and went to sleep.

Friday, January 14

13

Still on Los Angeles time Regan had awakened early, dressed, and left a note for Kit who was sleeping soundly when she left the room. By 7 A.M. Regan had already gone for a walk on the beach. Not wanting to deal with the big buffet in the main dining room, she went into one of the smaller cafés for breakfast.

It felt good being up so early. The air was fresh, and the beach was quiet and calm. Whenever Regan dragged herself out of bed at the crack of dawn, she told herself she had to do it more often. But her resolve never lasted. Rising with the roosters only worked when she went to sleep early or when her body was on a different time zone from where she happened to be.

In the Pineapple Café, Regan took a seat at the

counter. The Waikiki Waters wanted to cater to all types of people, so they had all kinds of restaurants. This particular café felt like a coffee shop in New York except that it had wallpaper depicting pineapple fields. Regan reached for the stack of local newspapers on the counter that were shared by the customers. She pulled over the newspaper on the top of the heap as the waitress approached her.

"Coffee?" she asked and started to pour before Regan responded. I guess she doesn't get too many negative responses to that question, Regan thought.

"Yes, thanks," Regan answered unnecessarily as she stared at the front page. There was a picture of a smiling, attractive woman with a big orchid in her hair, identified as Dorinda Dawes, the tragic victim of a drowning accident at the Waikiki Waters.

"Shame, isn't it?" the waitress remarked.

Regan looked at the woman who appeared to be in her late sixties—quite a bit older than the typical employee at the Waikiki Waters. She had a tight pageboy hairdo, a dark tan, and a wry smile. A pineapple-shaped name tag that said Winnie and about a dozen buttons that dispensed advice on life were pinned to her pink jacket. One of them read "Live every day as if it's your last. Someday you'll be right." How appropriate, Regan thought, then asked, "Did you know Dorinda Dawes?"

"I saw her around a little bit. But you know I only work when the young folks call in sick. Whenever the surf's up, you can be sure that they all suddenly come down with bad colds. Then they run off to the ocean with their surfboards. That's why they're in Hawaii. So the management has us older, more reliable types on call." She raised her eyebrows. "It gets me out of the house. I must say I like it because I can say no if I feel like it. And sometimes that's just what I do. I tell them, 'No way, José.' "

"It's good to be in that position," Regan noted as she glanced back at the newspaper. "I hear the real mystery is where she got that historic lei."

"I know it!" The waitress's eyes snapped. She dropped her voice. "The word is that she was running around the other night taking lots of pictures and asking too many questions. People were getting annoyed. Then she talked about having to go home and get her newsletter done. Next thing you know, her body washes ashore and she's wearing a lei no one had seen her with."

"Had she been drinking?" Regan asked.

"How do I know? I wasn't here. But I've seen her in action with a wineglass in one hand and the camera in the other. My friend Tess works here, too, and we were talking about this on the phone last night. Dorinda was always in the middle of every cocktail party they held here. Taking pictures, asking questions. Enough already!" Winnie lowered her voice. "If you want to know the truth, we think she was on the hunt for a guy. Well, why not? She was a nice-looking gal. And some of the men who come to the conferences are mighty handsome. Problem is, most of them are married. But let me tell you, she was some flirt!" Winnie nodded her head for emphasis. "You know what she seemed like to me and Tess? One of those women who love, love, love the men but have no use for women. Did you ever meet one of those?"

Oh, yes, Regan thought. She's still alive, and her name is Jazzy.

14

At 9:01 A.M. Regan was seated in the chair in front of Will's desk. He looked a little weary, she thought. This guy has a lot on his mind. His bright blue and white Hawaiian shirt did not off-set the gray pallor of his face.

"Sleep well?" he asked her.

"For several hours. But then I woke early. How about you?"

"Okay. But I'm used to having my wife and son around. I'll be glad when they get back tonight. I'll also be glad when this Princess ball is over and done with."

Regan nodded and pulled the newspaper out of her bag. "Did you see this?" She indicated the front-page article on Dorinda Dawes.

"I read it at six-thirty this morning."

"I was interested to read that Dorinda Dawes was writing a series of articles about life in Hawaii for a new travel magazine. She was profiling people who had come to Hawaii to start a second career."

"In the few months she was here she managed to get into a lot of things. She was like dandruff. All over the place. At first I didn't mind. What we paid her to do the newsletter wasn't enough to live on. But she also had plans to start her own gossip sheet about goings-on in Waikiki and Honolulu. She told me she really wanted to uncover big stories. That made me nervous. I insisted that she keep the newsletter friendly. It wasn't easy. Let's just say it wasn't in her nature to be nice. But who wants to come to a hotel where they might write snippy things about you? The first newsletter she wrote was all about the celebrities who stay here, but I wouldn't print it."

"I heard about that."

"You did?"

"Yes. From a girl named Jazzy."

Will rolled his eyes. "More dandruff. She's trying to get into everything. She's organizing the gift bags for the ball."

"She told me that, too. You don't like her?"

"Jazzy is out for Jazzy. She's also out for her boss. He's actually helping to underwrite the ball because he's trying to kick off a line of Hawaiian-style clothing. He's donating his Hawaiian shirts and muumuus for the gift bag."

"She didn't mention that. Have you seen the clothes?"

"No. But I understand there are sketches of shell leis on them. It goes along with the princess theme."

"I take it this is an important ball for the hotel."

Will nodded. "It's our first big event since the renovation. And it's a very important ball for the organizations that will benefit from this fund-raiser."

"What organizations?" Regan asked.

"The Seashell Museum and a group called Aloha Artists. Basically it's a bunch of people who got together and built a studio for young artists and sculptors and craftsmen who produce native Hawaiian art. They can go to the studio to work and just be with one another. They sometimes have guest artists, and they're trying to organize more formal classes. That's why the auction of the royal lei is such a big thing. It shows how important native art is and how good art can be passed down for generations. Now that Liliuokalani's lei has been found, the board of Aloha Artists is in a frenzy. They want to auction off both leis, although they're trying to be tasteful about it. After all, one of them was found on a dead woman. And of course they have to convince the owner of the Seashell Museum to hand the lei over for the auction."

Regan raised her eyebrows. "I thought I'd go over to the Seashell Museum this morning and see if I can talk to someone about when the lei was stolen. Maybe it'll lead to something. I can't help but think that lei has something to do with Dorinda's death. If I can find out where she got the lei, it may provide some clues as to how and why she died."

"Sounds like a good idea," Will agreed, his voice barely audible.

"In the meantime could you gather together all the newsletters that Dorinda Dawes wrote? I'd love to take a look at them." Regan looked down at the newspaper. "I'd also like copies of the travel magazine. It says here it's called *Spirits in Paradise.*" Regan looked back up at Will. "Do you know whom she interviewed for the pieces she did?"

Will shrugged. "It's a monthly magazine. She had only one article published so far, in this month's issue. She was working on another. I think she mentioned something about maybe going over to the Big Island for an interview. I must admit I never read the magazine. Dorinda talked so much, it went in one ear and out the other. But I'll get the article for you. We have the magazine for our guests in the spas and beauty salons."

"Thanks. I was wondering, did Dorinda have a locker here?"

"No. Only the employees who wear uniforms have lockers."

"What time did you last see Dorinda on Wednesday night?"

"It was about eleven-thirty. We both worked late. She had been taking pictures at a couple of events at the hotel and as usual went into the bars and restaurants to see who might want their picture taken. She poked her head in my office door and said good-bye. Her camera was still in her hand, and I think she had a bag over her shoulder."

"And she wasn't wearing the lei."

"No, she wasn't."

"And her purse hasn't been recovered."

"No."

Regan pushed her chair back and stood. "I'll take a cab to the museum. I assume you'll be here when I get back."

Will looked at her with wide, concerned eyes. "I'm not going anywhere."

15

The Seashell Museum was about a twenty-minute ride from the Waikiki Waters Hotel. Regan looked out the window as the cab drove down the main street of Waikiki, headed in the direction of Diamond Head. It was a beautiful Friday morning. Shoppers were going in and out of the stores, and swimmers were crossing the street, headed for the beach, surfboards and boogie boards in tow. The water looked blue and inviting, the temperature was about eighty degrees, and the sun was shining brightly. Perfect Hawaiian weather.

Regan thought about Dorinda Dawes. People seemed to have definite opinions about her. She certainly must have come on strong. There were a lot of people Regan wanted to talk to about

Dorinda, but first she wanted to read the news-letters and take a look at *Spirits in Paradise*.

At the museum, which was on a hill overlooking the beach, Regan paid the cabdriver and got out. It was a beautiful, somewhat secluded spot. A handful of cars was parked in the lot in front of the museum. The entrance was around back. Regan followed the walkway to the front door, went inside, and was told by a young girl behind the cash register that they didn't open until ten o'clock. The girl had long shiny black hair adorned with an orchid.

"What I really wanted," Regan explained as she handed the girl her card, "was to talk to someone about the shell lei that was found on the body of the woman who drowned. I understand it was returned to the museum."

The girl squinted her eyes at Regan. "You need to talk to Jimmy. He's a conchologist, and he owns the museum."

"Conchologist?"

"He's a person who can tell you everything you ever wanted to know about shells and some stuff you could care less about. He's down the hill, sitting on the beach. Go talk to him."

"Maybe I should wait . . ."

The girl waved her hand at Regan. "Nah. Go ahead."

"Okay, thanks. What does he look like?"

"He's big, pretty old, mostly bald, and he'll be sitting cross-legged."

Regan smiled. "How do you know he'll be sitting like that?"

"Because he's always looking at his feet. He walks so much on the beach that he occasionally gets cut by the shells. He's fascinated by the marks they leave on his skin."

"How interesting," Regan murmured, more to herself, as she went back outside and paused briefly. The view of the Pacific was awesome. She inhaled a breath of fresh fragrant air and headed down the stone steps on the side of the museum to the beach.

There was no missing Jimmy.

He was a big man indeed and was sitting cross-legged on the sand. His eyes were closed, and he was wearing what looked like a toga. The toga reminded Regan of fraternity parties she'd been to in college where people acted rowdy. But Jimmy was the only one at this party, and it certainly wasn't lively. There was no one else around. He looked like some sort of spiritual guru. His brown skin was deeply tanned, and a slight breeze blew back and forth the little bits of sparse hair that remained on his head. His eyes were closed.

Assuming he was meditating, Regan stopped a few feet behind the lone figure. She was deciding what to do when he opened his eyes and turned to her.

"Howzit. You looking for Jimmy?"

"Yes, I am."

"Jimmy's here."

"Hi, Jimmy," Regan responded, wondering why people would refer to themselves in the third person. She wanted to add: "Regan Reilly here, too."

"You like the beach?" Jimmy asked almost accusingly.

"Oh, yes." Regan gestured toward the ocean with her hands. "Of course with my light skin I can't take too much sun."

Jimmy looked at her sternly.

He thinks I'm an idiot, Regan decided. Oh, well. "I'm staying at the Waikiki Waters, and I'll rent an umbrella so I can enjoy the surf and the sand."

Jimmy's eyes finally showed some interest. "Waikiki Waters. A lady drowned there yesterday. She was wearing a very special lei that was stolen from the museum here." He gestured with his fist toward the building behind them. "What was she doing with my lei?"

"I couldn't tell you, Jimmy," Regan answered. "But I understand you're the one to talk to about the history of the lei." She took out her ID. "The hotel hired me to look into her death. The police think it was an accidental drowning. The hotel manager isn't so sure. And the lei complicates matters."

"You like pineapple juice?"

"I have to say that I don't drink it very often, but I do enjoy a glass now and then."

"Good. Let's go up to my museum. I will show

you the lei, and we can talk. I started working here fifty years ago. Now it's mine. It's not as big as the Bishop Museum, but we have valuable shells." He pushed down on the sand with his hands and managed to hoist himself to his feet. He was over six feet tall with a big belly, but his arms looked thick and strong.

Regan followed the large man back up the stone steps and into the museum. It was an old building that smelled of the sand and the sea. Seashells of all shapes and sizes hung on the walls. In front of the register was a cabinet of shell jewelry for sale. Earrings, necklaces, bracelets, and rings were all on display. The girl at the desk nodded when he walked past her. Regan followed him down the hall. He pointed to his office. "Sit down in there," he instructed Regan. "Jimmy be right back."

Regan did as she was told. So much for coming to Hawaii for a load of laughs and fun, she thought. But it was all right. New cases always excited her, and this one was no different. She'd rather be talking to a conchologist than sitting on the beach all day. I guess that's why God made my skin burn so easily, she reasoned as she took a seat in Jimmy's little office. A large poster of a shell adorned the wall behind his desk. It reminded Regan of the magnified picture of a dust mite hung in all its glory behind her allergist's desk. Different strokes for different folks.

Jimmy returned with two glasses of pineapple

juice and a shell lei around his neck. Could it be the one that was around Dorinda Dawes's neck yesterday morning? Regan accepted the drink, and Jimmy clinked her glass. "Aloha," he toasted.

The fresh juice was tangy and delicious. Regan could almost feel the sugar race through her system. She watched as Jimmy walked around the desk and lowered himself onto the chair.

"Jimmy loves shells," he began. "I grew up in Hawaii and spent many hours walking on the beach collecting them. I had a problem with my back when I was a child, so I couldn't surf. But I liked to be on the beach. It made me feel good. If shells cut my feet, I didn't care. Jellyfish bother me. They sting. Shells don't hurt anyone. Now I own the Seashell Museum. Jimmy very proud." Reverently he removed the lei from around his neck. "Thirty years ago this was stolen. I never dreamed I'd get it back. Here, take a look," he offered Regan. "The police brought it back to me yesterday. I've missed it."

Regan put down her empty glass and took the lei in her hands. It was truly beautiful. The shells were intricate and gorgeous, and the colors running through them ranged from coral to white to beige. Some of them were slightly chipped, but the lei was even more beautiful than many expensive necklaces she had seen.

"Jimmy knows what you're thinking," he said. "It's like fine jewelry. The royal ladies liked them better than pearls."

"I heard the story that this one was made for Queen Liliuokalani and the other for her niece Princess Kaiulani."

"They loved these leis!" Jimmy answered vehemently. "They wore them in public all the time. The leis were donated to the Seashell Museum when it was founded in the 1920s. They hung side by side in a glass case until the burglary."

Regan caressed the shells. "It's hard to believe this was worn so long ago."

"Then on a dead body."

Regan sighed. "On someone who had never been to Hawaii until three months ago. I can't imagine where she found this lei. Can you tell me what happened when the lei was stolen?"

Jimmy leaned back on his desk chair and looked up in the air. Regan noticed that the pencils in a mug on his desk had shell-shaped erasers. "We didn't have an alarm system yet. But now we do!" he said with sudden force, then calmed down again. "Someone broke in and smashed the glass cases holding the precious shell leis. The thief also gathered up a lot of our famous seashells and threw them in a bag. A cop on patrol noticed a light coming from the museum and checked it out. The thief jumped in a stolen car and raced into town, the police in hot pursuit. The cops cornered him in an alley downtown, but he managed to escape. He dropped the bag when he climbed over the fence. If you can believe it, they never found him. Everything was recovered except this one lei, the lei that was worn by our last queen."

"You're absolutely sure that this is it."

Once again he looked at Regan sternly. "Jimmy be right back."

Sometimes he starts a sentence with "I" and sometimes with "Jimmy," Regan observed. I wonder how he decides when to refer to himself in the third person. Regan stared at the priceless lei in her hands. Where had Dorinda Dawes been when she placed it around her neck? Leis were given in a spirit of hospitality, love, and peace. Regan had read that the memory of having a lei placed on your shoulders should last forever. Forever didn't turn out to be too long for Dorinda. She must have put the lei around her neck shortly before she died. No one had seen her with it that night. Was it possible that whoever stole the lei years ago knew Dorinda Dawes and had been the one to give it to her?

Jimmy reentered the office. He handed Regan another shell lei. It was uncanny. Shell for shell, they were a perfect match, except for the fact that Liliuokalani's lei had one small black lava bead.

"Now you believe Jimmy?" he asked.

Regan nodded. "I certainly do."

He took both leis from Regan and hung them over his beefy index finger. A dark expression came over his face. "If you find the guy who stole this lei, kept it from us for so many years, I will

———❦———

take care of him." He banged the desk with his free hand. "Makes me so mad."

"That won't be necessary," Regan assured him.

He turned and stared down at Regan. She felt the bottom of his toga brush against her foot. "That lady who died," he said, disapprovingly, "something tells me she stuck her nose too much in other people's business."

"You could be right about that," Regan noted as she shifted in her seat. "One final thing. I know that Princess Kaiulani's lei is going to be auctioned off at the Princess Ball tomorrow night."

"Yes. Half the money goes to Aloha Artists, half goes to Jimmy's Seashell Museum."

"That's wonderful. I understand they're asking you to auction off this other lei as well."

"Jimmy hasn't decided yet. Those special shells have been away a long time. Maybe I should keep them here for a while. I've missed the lei so much, my heart broke every day for thirty years." He paused. "But we could use the money."

"There's always that. Will you be at the ball?"

"Of course. Jimmy will sit at a special table. I will wear both leis around my neck. People will see how beautiful they are before the auction starts."

They could probably use a better-looking model, Regan reflected as she reached for her purse and made motions to leave. "Thank you, Jimmy, I'm sure I'll see you at the ball."

"I think I will decide whether to let them auction Queen Liliuokalani's lei after I see how much Princess Kaiulani's lei fetches."

"Makes sense," Regan muttered.

"Call Jimmy if you need me. I will be of help to you."

I wouldn't be surprised, Regan mused. I wouldn't be surprised at all.

16

The Mixed Bag Tour group was finishing up their breakfast in the largest restaurant of the Waikiki Waters hotel. It was a busy place, filled with rattan furniture and tropical plants. A large waterfall cascaded down one wall. Tourists were lining up for the buffet of pancakes, eggs, and fresh Hawaiian fruit that tasted much better than the fruit back home. Gert and Ev always managed to secure a large table in the section closest to the open doors that looked out on the ocean. Ned had already gotten up and down a number of times to refill his plate.

"I've got to have the energy to surf," he explained, more to himself than anyone at the table. "Man, am I pumped." He picked up his spoon and dug into a bowl of oatmeal.

"I hope you all have a lovely day," Ev said. "We'll meet back here for sunset cocktails and share our experiences."

Betsy pursed her lips. "Bob and I won't discuss our writing, and that's what we'll be doing today. What we write is much too personal."

What are you going to do if that book ever sees the light of day? Ev wondered. Won't it still be just as personal? I'd love to silence her. She belongs in the rain in Hudville. But Ev just smiled. "That's all right. We'll just enjoy being together. I want the three of you who are surfing today to please be careful and return to the safety and comfort of the Waikiki Waters."

"This place isn't so safe," Joy declared as she picked at the dollop of cottage cheese on her plate. She wanted to look good in her bathing suit for Zeke. She had a nice figure but wished she'd gone to the gym more before this trip. She hadn't had the motivation. Now she did. Too late. Washboard abs were thousands and thousands of crunches down the road. Her curly blond hair was pulled on top of her head, and she was wearing shorts and a little pink top that she'd bought at the one semi-hip store in Hudville. Maybe I'll go shopping today, she thought. Pick out a new outfit to wear tonight. After I catch a few rays.

"What do you mean it isn't so safe here?" Gert asked. She and Ev had a practiced schoolmarm tone they used when they wanted to express disap-

proval to one of their group members. Ev was better at it than Gert.

Joy looked up from her plate and stared at Gert.
Sometimes she got the twins mixed up. She
thought their matching outfits were a bit much for
women their age. Today they didn't have on their
usual muumuus. That was a surprise. They were
wearing stretch pants and long-sleeved shirts,
which seemed a bit odd. It was eighty degrees, for
God's sake. "Aren't you hot?" Joy replied.

"Hot?"

"Why don't you have your muumuus on?"

"When we go in and out of hotels, inspecting
them for the good of the future residents of
Hudville who make this trip, we don't want to
catch a cold," Gert explained.

"Air conditioning can be so drafty," Ev agreed.
"And the last thing I need is to get on the plane
home with a cold. Makes you feel like your head is
going to explode."

"You're darn right," her sister nodded as she bit
into a large pastry. Her mouth half full, she realized she hadn't yet gotten an answer from Joy.
"What do you mean this place isn't so safe?" she
asked, holding a napkin in front of her mouth as
she spoke with her mouth full. The pastry wasn't
chewed enough to swallow, but Gert couldn't wait
to ask the question.

"I heard things last night."

"Like what?" the twins asked in unison.

"Like the woman who drowned might have been murdered."

Gert and Ev both inhaled sharply. "Who says that?" they both asked at once.

The group all had fixed their gazes on Joy. Ned looked up from his oatmeal. Artie, who had been staring out at the water, finally started paying attention. Francie, who had been applying makeup, put her lipstick down on the table with a dramatic flourish. As usual, Bob and Betsy's expressions didn't change. Well, maybe Bob's did a little. Sometimes Joy wondered if they were alive. Now, as the whole group stared at her, she realized she liked the attention. They don't think I'm such a baby anymore, she told herself proudly. "I'm not at liberty to tell you."

"Why do they think she might have been murdered?" Ev asked, her expression steely.

"Because the hotel has had some weird stuff going on. Things going wrong. They think there's a phantom who is pulling pranks, and just maybe this phantom is getting a little more dangerous. There have been a couple of incidents—problems with food, and people who had a few drinks and ended up much more hungover than they should have been. Now maybe the phantom is stepping things up!"

Gert and Ev looked at each other in horror.

"They made me promise not to say anything," Joy added.

Artie rolled his eyes. Joy annoyed him because she clearly considered him an old person. "Then why did you? That's bad karma."

"It's ridiculous," Ned protested. "This is a good hotel, and the manager does a great job. Dorinda Dawes drowned. It's that simple."

Gert cleared her throat. "It seems to me that rumors and troublemakers abound. They are everywhere. This is a lovely hotel, and we shouldn't let other people's idle gossip destroy it. Perhaps people were hungover because they had way too much of a good thing. Ever think of that?"

Joy shook her head. "I heard one lady had a Shirley Temple and threw up all over the place."

Ned looked at his watch. " 'Surf's up!' as they say. I'm disappointed to see that only two of the Lucky Seven are coming with me. Next time I hope to do better. Gert and Ev, you shouldn't be worrying about other hotels. As you say, this is a good place. The renovation made it even better." He laughed. "After all, I was hired. Will would be disappointed if he thought you were checking out other places and thinking of going elsewhere. You should come up north with us today. It's a beautiful drive."

Gert shook her head. "We're always looking out for the good of the future trip-takers from Hudville. It's up to us to make sure there are many. The funds are not limitless, you know. Ev and I are worried that many people will be disappointed because they won't get to come to Hawaii."

"That'll be hard for you two," Francie said as she inspected herself in her compact mirror. "After going on these trips for years, how will you cope when the money is gone?"

"We have inner strength," Gert replied.

"Inner strength coupled with the fact that some of the other elderly church members are thinking of leaving some of their money to the Mixed Bag Tour group," Ev added.

"I didn't know that," Francie exclaimed. "Who plans to be so generous? Because let me tell you, if they're in the Praise the Rain group, I haven't met them."

"I can't divulge that information," Ev replied quietly. "The potential benefactors wish to remain anonymous."

"That I'll never understand," Francie announced as she picked a piece of mascara from under her eyelid. "I just have two questions about them: Are any of them single? And how close to the end are they?"

Ned laughed. "Francie, find someone your own age to pick on."

Francie snapped her compact shut. "There are no good ones left my age."

Get me out of here, Joy thought. This is depressing. I'm only twenty-one.

"You know," Francie continued, "now that I've been on this trip and am out of the running to be in the lottery, I'd like to see what the other hotels have to offer because I would like to come back. Maybe I should go with you today," she suggested to the twins.

"Francie!" Ned protested. "It's you, me, and Artie together today."

But he didn't have to worry about losing one of his charges. Both twins looked as if they'd been hit in the head. Ev reached over and put her hand on Gert's. "You see, Francie," she began patiently, "today is what we call our 'twin time.' Just the two of us together."

"It's almost as if we speak our own language," Gert added. "No one else understands it."

"I guess the answer is no," Francie said.

"That's right."

"But don't you two live together at home?" Francie asked rhetorically. "If that were me and my sister, we'd be on each other's nerves. Working together at the store, living together, traveling together. Sheesh!"

"We've been blessed with a special bond," Gert said, trying to make it clear. "We're not just sisters. We're best buds."

I'm going to be sick, Joy thought.

"Francie, you'll have a great time with us," Ned said. He looked insulted.

Francie, who recovered in no time, smiled flirtatiously. "I know I will."

They all got up from the table. Bob and Betsy headed back to their room without saying good-bye. Joy headed for the beach as fast as she could. Ned, Artie, and Francie went out front to look for the van that was picking them up. Gert and Ev proclaimed they were going back to their room to brush and floss before heading out, and waved good-bye.

At the elevator bank Gert looked at Ev and winked. When they got up to the door of their room, Ev pulled out her key. "I thought we'd never get out of there," she said.

"Oh, I know it. We need our privacy today, don't we, sister?" Gert asked.

"We sure do."

The door next to them closed, and they both turned with a start. A blond-haired woman they'd seen a few times in the last week nodded hello to them. They had noticed her going out with a dark-haired woman last night. "Hello," the twins greeted her sweetly.

"Hello," she answered politely.

Once inside their room, they looked at each other nervously.

"I'll be relieved when our special project is finished," Ev admitted.

"You said it. But we're about to cross the finish line."

Ev smiled. "And nothing's going to stop us."

17

The couple whom Regan talked to on the beach went to bed very late. When they got back to the room, they drank champagne. Then, when it was a reasonable hour on the East Coast, Carla got on the horn. She couldn't wait to tell her friends and family the good news about her engagement.

Carla's mother was greatly relieved. "It's about time!" she declared in a sleepy voice. "I thought he'd propose on your anniversary. All day yesterday I cried. I didn't like the idea of you living with him at such a young age and wasting your time. He's finally doing right by you."

"Thanks, Ma," Carla said. "I gotta go." She then called her sisters and her ten best friends. All of whom screamed with joy. All of whom she asked to be bridesmaids. All of whom said yes and said they'd have been insulted if she hadn't asked.

Jason was lying on the bed with his eyes closed while she squealed the news over and over again. When the phone was finally free, he called his parents, but they weren't home. He left them a brief message. "Carla and I got engaged. Talk to you. Bye."

"Aren't you going to call your friends?" Carla asked in disbelief.

"Why? I'll tell them when I get back."

It was very late when they finally went to sleep.

When they woke just a few hours later, they ordered room service. "I love it," Carla cooed as she admired her ring. "I love you. I love us. I am soooo happy."

"I hope the coffee gets here soon," Jason grumbled as he turned on his side. Two nights in a row he hadn't gotten anywhere near his full eight hours of rest, which was very important to him. Between the night Carla disappeared and all the phone calls last night, he was way behind on his rack time.

Carla wrapped herself in one of the blue and white cotton robes provided by the hotel and pulled open the sliding glass door to the balcony. She stepped outside, walked to the railing where Jason's beach towel was draped, and pulled it off. The hotel had specifically asked people not to hang their belongings over the railing. They said it made the place look like a flophouse. They also didn't want people's bathing suits and towels getting blown off and landing on other guests' heads. She sighed deeply. Sometimes Jason was in another world.

Their tower was set back from the beach. From their fourth-floor terrace, they could see people wandering in and out of the shops. Carla spotted the blond-haired woman who had been on the beach with Regan Reilly the night before. Exuberantly, Carla yelled down to her. "Hey!" she called, waving her arms.

Kit looked up, squinting her eyes. "Hi! How are you?"

"Great. I was thinking about what your friend asked me last night—you know, if I noticed anything odd on the beach the other night."

"Did you think of something?" Kit called.

"No. But it's on the tip of my tongue—or right off the top of my head, or whatever. I know there was something weird, but I just can't remember what it was. But tell her I'll think of it."

"I'll tell her."

"Okay. Have a nice day."

"You, too."

Carla went back inside where Jason was slowly starting to come to life. He had decided to make coffee using the little pot on the counter in the bathroom. He ripped open the envelope of coffee granules, and they scattered all over.

"Oh, forget it," he groaned and lay back down on the bed.

On the desk was a copy of the magazine called *Spirits in Paradise*. It had a sticker that read: "Please do not remove from the spa." Carla grabbed the magazine, propped a pillow against the headboard, and made herself comfortable. Skimming through the pages, she came across an article about the Big Island's version of graffiti. People collected coral shells on the beach and used them to spell out messages on the dark volcanic rocks lining the sides of the highways. Many people used the shells to express their love for each other.

"Cool," she said aloud.

"What?" Jason asked.

Carla pointed to the picture of the graffiti and explained it to Jason. "Why don't we go over there today?" she asked excitedly. "We'll go on the beach, collect the shells, and then write out Jason and Carla forever. And the date. And we'll take a picture we can show our kids years from now. It'll be in the collage at our fiftieth anniversary party."

"We're not even married yet. I can't believe you're thinking about our fiftieth anniversary. I thought you wanted to swim in the big dolphin-shaped pool today."

"They have gorgeous black beaches on the Big Island. We can go swimming over there. We're leaving Sunday and won't get this chance again."

"We might not get a flight," Jason said hopefully.

"Let's call and see. It doesn't take that long to get there. It says so in this article. And we don't have to pack a suitcase or anything."

"How are we going to get around?"

"They say you can rent a car at the airport. Why not? This is a very special occasion in our lives, Jason."

The doorbell rang. "Coming," Jason boomed as he jumped up and hurried to the door. While the room service waiter wheeled in a table full of breakfast goodies, Carla picked up the phone and called the airlines.

"A flight at eleven-thirty?" she repeated. "You have two seats left? Perfect!" She gave the credit card information and hung up the phone. "Two seats left, Jason. It was meant to be."

"How come we didn't think of this before?" Jason asked as he cut up his pancakes.

"Because you took so long to propose, that's why."

"The best things to do always come up at the end of a vacation," Jason muttered. "Things seem like they'd be even better than they really are when you have no time left to do them."

"Well, we do have time to do this, so hurry up and eat!"

Carla ran into the shower, thinking about the picture they'd take of their names written out in shells. She'd have it blown up and hung over their fireplace. It would mean good luck for them forever. It never occurred to her that this could turn out to be a very bad idea. A very, very bad idea.

18

Gert and Ev were settled in their seats at the front of the small plane that would soon be taking off for Kona on the Big Island.

"Ready to go," Gert declared as she fastened the seat belt around her.

"That's right." Ev stuffed a giant bag under her seat. It contained everything from suntan lotion to notebooks to an extra battery for her cell phone. She also had a couple of disposable cameras.

"We'll be taking off in a few moments," the flight attendant announced. "We're just waiting for two more passengers."

"Here we are!" a young girl's voice cried breathlessly. "We made it!" She stepped onto the plane, and a young man followed her. The flight attendant smiled but urged them to take their seats quickly.

"We will," the girl replied. As she turned to head down the aisle, she spotted Gert and Ev. "Hey there," she enthused. "Haven't I seen you two at the Waikiki Waters?"

"Maybe," Ev said in a tone that did not encourage further discussion—at least to most people.

"Don't you love it?"

"Ummmmm," Ev replied.

"This is my fiancé, Jason."

"Please take your seats," the flight attendant ordered. "We are striving for an on-time departure."

"Okay, okay. See you two later."

When the couple disappeared down the aisle, Gert and Ev looked at each other.

"Don't worry," Gert whispered to Ev. "We'll handle it."

In the back of the plane, as she pulled her seat belt tight around her, Carla turned to Jason. "I passed those two coming out of the ladies' clothing store at the hotel when I was going in. I heard the salesgirl say they're in charge of a tour group. Maybe when we land we can catch up with them and ask them where we should go for lunch. If they lead people on tours, they must know, right, honey?"

"Right. I just want to make sure we return to the airport in time to catch the plane back. We cut this too close."

"You worry too much."

"Usually with good reason." Jason closed his eyes and fell fast asleep.

19

On the way back to the hotel, Regan's cell phone rang. It was her mother calling.

"How are things?" Regan asked Nora.

"Still snowy. Our poor deceased skier's relatives are all at the hotel tearing up the joint. They've got cabin fever. The streets are still impassable, so the funeral has been postponed indefinitely. I think the family is spending all their time at the hotel bar having a little reunion. They're now convinced that old Ernest arranged the weather and is sending a message to them to get out and ski. But none of them are listening."

"You should put on your snowshoes and go over and take notes. I'm sure you'd get some interesting material for a new book."

"No doubt I would. It's a small hotel, and rumor is that they've already run out of gin."

"Nothing like a good snowstorm." Regan laughed as she gazed through her sunglasses at the clear blue sky.

"What's going on in sunny Hawaii?" Nora asked.

Regan looked out the window of the cab at the beach in the distance. "Well, Mom, I'm on the job again."

"What?"

"A hotel employee drowned yesterday. Her body washed ashore early in the morning. The police think it was an accident, but the hotel manager isn't so sure. And she was wearing a royal shell lei that had been stolen from a museum here over thirty years ago. The manager asked me to check things out."

"That's terrible. What did she do at the hotel?"

"She wrote and took pictures for their newsletter. Apparently she wanted to start her own gossip paper. She moved here from New York just a few months ago. She had written for several different publications back there."

"Oh," Nora said as she turned up the heat in the kitchen. "What's her name?"

"Dorinda Dawes."

"Dorinda Dawes!"

"Yes. Do you know her?"

"Regan, she interviewed me about twenty years

ago. I'll never forget that name. I really got burned by her."

"What do you mean?"

"She was young and aggressive and had the ability to get you to say things you normally wouldn't. I guess that's what a good interviewer does. Up until then I had never talked about the time when Dad and I were on our honeymoon and I got into serious trouble out in the water. We were down in the Caribbean. I was in the ocean and started getting pulled under. I waved to Dad on the beach. He waved back. I waved again. Finally the lifeguard realized I was in trouble. He rushed into the water and saved me. Dad didn't realize I needed help."

"He thought you were just being friendly."

"Regan!"

"Sorry, Mom."

"For some reason I started telling her the story. It didn't seem like a big deal. We had been talking for a couple of hours, and this was just before she left the house. It ended up being the headline of her story. 'MY HUSBAND ALMOST LET ME DROWN,' LAMENTED FAMED MYSTERY WRITER NORA REGAN REILLY."

"I don't remember that," Regan said.

"You were about ten years old. It was during the summer. I think you were away at camp."

"The article must have made Dad really upset."

"Not as upset as I was. All his friends teased him that he was looking for more business. It ended up being a funny story that our friends would tell at cocktail parties, though when it first came out, we weren't laughing. But, Regan, I find it hard to believe Dorinda drowned. The way she got me to open up about that story was because she admitted to me she was afraid of the water. She said she'd been at the beach right before a hurricane when she was a kid, got knocked over by a big wave, and pulled under. She told me that she hated going in the ocean from that day on, but she loved swimming in pools."

"She hated going in the ocean?" Regan repeated.

"According to what she told me that day. She said she never told anyone that story because it made her feel weak and vulnerable. The discussion started because she flattered me that a scene in one of my books where someone drowned was so real that it gave her chills."

"Then Will might be right. This wasn't an accident."

"It's hard to say. She could have been just trying to soften me up to say something stupid, which I did, but she was so convincing. Be careful, Regan. If she wasn't acting, the Dorinda Dawes I met all those years ago made it clear that she would never even dip her toes in the ocean alone, day or night. I wonder what happened."

"That's what I'm working on."

"And what was she doing with a lei that was stolen even before I met her?"

"I'm working on that, too."

"Where's Kit?"

"I think she's on the beach with the new guy."

Nora sighed. "I wish you were there with Jack."

"Believe me, Mom, so do I. I'll talk to you later." When Regan hung up the phone, she tried to absorb what her mother had just told her. One thing seemed certain: More than twenty years ago Dorinda was already writing stories that embarrassed people. Had she done that here and antagonized someone who wanted revenge? Regan was anxious to go back and read everything that Dorinda had written since she'd stepped off the plane in Hawaii three months ago.

20

Will shut the door of his office. He dreaded making the call, but he knew he had no choice. He poured himself another cup of coffee. It had that muddy look that comes from being on the burner so long a lot of the water has literally dried up. But he didn't care. He could barely taste a thing.

He sat at his desk, pulled the phone closer to him, and buzzed his secretary. "Janet, hold my calls."

"Whatever."

Whatever is right, he thought to himself as he dialed his sister's number in Orlando. Will's parents had gone there for Christmas and were staying for the month of January, taking side trips to other Florida cities to see their retired friends. He steeled himself for their reaction to what he had to tell them. The last thing he needed was for his parents to give him a hard time.

The owners of the hotel were already on his case. They were warning him that the "Be a Princess" Ball had better be a huge success, critically and financially. They weren't happy that an employee had drowned and then washed up on their beach. "It's all image," they told him. "We want the Waikiki Waters to have a happy, positive image. People come from all over the world to enjoy themselves at our fine establishment. They don't want to come to a place marred by scandal and overflowing toilets!"

Will swallowed as his sister, Tracy, picked up the phone.

"Tracy, it's Will," he began, attempting to sound cheery. He hated having to call his parents at her house. She'd be hanging on to every word of their conversation with him, sticking her nose into his business. She wouldn't miss one word despite the fact her three kids were screaming in the background.

"Hi, Will," Tracy answered. "How's it going out there? Any toilets overflow today?"

"No, Trace," he said, gritting his teeth. "I need to speak to Mom and Dad." Some *ohana* I have, he thought—*ohana* being the Hawaiian word for family.

"Hello, Will!" his mother chirped as she picked

up the extension. "Bingsley!" she yelled to her husband. "Pick up the phone in the bedroom. Will's on. Are you there, Will?"

"I'm here, Mom." Will could hear his father's breathing as he slowly brought the phone to his mouth.

"I'm on, Almetta," his father grunted. "Hey, big guy. What's up?"

"Hi, Dad. Trace, would you mind hanging up? I have something to discuss privately with Mom and Dad." He knew she'd hear about it anyway, but he wanted her off the phone.

The phone clicked in their ears. No more sounds of screaming kids.

"She's off," his mother said gaily. "What's going on, dear?"

"You know that lei you gave me when I moved to Hawaii?"

"My gorgeous shell lei?" his mother asked.

"That would be the one. Where did you get it?"

"Son," his father said, "you know that we bought it in Hawaii thirty years ago."

"I know in Hawaii, but where in Hawaii?" Will asked, trying not to sound impatient. "Did you buy it at a store or at a stand on the street?"

"I remember that day very clearly," his mother declared triumphantly. "Do you remember, Bingsley? We bought the bathing suits for the kids and then we saw that boy at the airport who sold us the lei. You wanted to buy a special present for me, but we hadn't found anything. Then right before we got on the plane to go home, I spotted that lei the boy was trying to sell! It was so beautiful. I have always loved and treasured it, and I just know it brought me luck. That's why I gave it to you, Will, so you would have good luck in Hawaii. If you had to move so far away, I wanted you to have something that would remind you of me every day. You promised to always keep it hanging on your living room wall."

Oh, brother, Will thought. He shook his head and sighed, careful to put his hand over the phone. Once his mother got on a roll, that was it.

"I remember that boy who sold it to us was only a teenager. He had a round baby face, a mop of unruly black hair, and was wearing shorts and sandals. Dear, do you remember he had the longest second toes we had ever seen?"

"I didn't get a look at them," Bingsley answered his wife. "I was too busy forking over two hundred bucks for the lei. That was a small fortune in those days, you know."

"Well, I told you about it many times afterward," Almetta continued. "I was just so mesmerized by his second toes. They looked as if they had practically been pulled out of their sockets. You know women have operations to shorten their toes now. They get them shaved so they can fit into crazy-shaped designer shoes with pointy toes and spike heels. Isn't that awful? But let me tell you, that boy was a perfect candidate for that operation."

Will calculated in his head as his mother babbled on. That kid must be in his mid to late forties now, so conceivably there is someone on this planet pushing fifty who had long second toes and who sold the stolen lei to his parents thirty years ago.

". . . I tell you I don't think they make leis like that anymore," his mother continued. "It is absolutely magnificent. Now what about it, dear?"

"Why did you call us in Florida to ask us about the lei?" his father asked skeptically.

"Well . . . I just found out that that lei was stolen from the Seashell Museum thirty years ago. It had belonged to a woman who was queen of Hawaii in the late 1800s. The kid sold you stolen property."

"I told you I always felt like a queen when I wore that lei!" his mother exclaimed. "Now it must really be worth something. It's so wonderful we have it in our family! And we came by it honestly!"

"I don't have it anymore."

"What?" his mother cried. "What did you do with it? I gave it to you for good luck!"

Some good luck, Will thought. He cleared his throat. "I lent the lei to a woman who worked at the hotel and was in charge of our newsletter. She wanted to photograph the lei and use the picture in the newsletter she was going to write covering the 'Be a Princess' Ball we're having this weekend.

I gave it to her the other night right before she left the hotel. The next morning her body washed ashore. She had the lei around her neck. The police identified it as the royal lei stolen from the museum thirty years ago."

"My word!" his mother cried.

"I haven't told anybody that it was our lei. I don't want them to think I had anything to do with the woman's death. And I don't want them to think that my parents stole the lei when they were on vacation in Hawaii."

"Of course we didn't!" his mother said indignantly. "You should never have let it out of your possession. That was a family heirloom!"

I wish *you* had never let it out of your possession, Will thought. "I just wanted to let you know what is going on. And to find out where you bought the lei in the first place."

"Where could that boy at the airport be now?" his mother asked.

"Good question. He's not a boy anymore. Maybe he's getting his toes operated on at this very moment. I may need a sworn statement from you both explaining exactly where and when you got the lei."

"Maybe we should go out there. Bingsley, what do you think?"

"Mom, that's not necessary."

Suddenly Tracy's kids could be heard screaming in the background.

"That's a great idea," Bingsley said with abrupt enthusiasm. "I'm logging on to the computer. I'm sure I can find us a bargain flight. Son, we'll be there as soon as we can."

"That ball sounds like such fun," his mother cried. "Can you get us tickets?"

Will put his head on his desk. His wife was coming home tonight. They hadn't seen each other in almost two weeks. Wait till she found out that Almetta and Bingsley were on the way. And why they were coming to Hawaii.

Why me? he thought. Why me?

21

As Gert and Ev's flight approached Kona on the Big Island, passengers were craning their necks to look down at the acres and acres of dark, rugged lava stretching endlessly below. It resembled the surface of the moon.

"I can't believe this is Hawaii," a woman in the front row complained to the flight attendant seated nearby. "That's not paradise. It looks like a bunch of burned-out rocks. Where are the pineapples and palm trees, for goodness' sake?"

"You'll see them soon," the flight attendant assured her. "You know, you are about to land on the island that is home to the world's largest active volcano. That's why it looks barren. But there are beautiful beaches, huge ranches, waterfalls, and pineapple plantations down there as well. And the Big Island gets bigger all the time."

"How's that?" the woman scowled.

"The volcano's eruptions have added twenty thousand acres of land to the island since 1983. Part of the airport sits atop a lava flow."

"Terrific."

"I promise you, you'll love it. Soon you'll want to live here forever."

Gert turned to Ev and smiled. "There's always one wet blanket in every bunch."

"Don't you know it," Ev replied. "At least one. We're stuck with two wet blankets in our group. Did you see the way Bob and Betsy sat there like stones this morning at breakfast? And they're writing a chapter on exciting relationships! That's like you and me writing about life as a supermodel."

Gert laughed, emitting a little snort. "And that Joy is a little troublemaker. That makes three wet blankets. She even had the nerve to ask if we give spending money to the group. She should be lucky she has that little butt of hers in Hawaii. Remember when we were her age?"

"I certainly do. The only time we got out of Hudville was to drive to the State Fair. Whoop-dee-doo."

"Now we're making up for it, sister."

"We are—all because we were sweet and kind to our neighbor."

"What luck he moved in next door."

"What luck his wife died."

The plane swerved from side to side and then bumped across the pavement a few times before it settled into a smooth glide down the runway. The airport was small, and the passengers disembarked down a set of portable stairs and onto the tarmac. Palm trees swayed in the breeze, and the luggage carousel was just steps away. Tour guides greeted groups of arriving passengers with welcome leis. Gert and Ev strode through the crowd and made their way to the curb where a young man in a beat-up all-terrain vehicle was waiting for them.

Carla and Jason hurried to catch up with the twins. "Ladies," Carla called to them as Gert opened the front door of the Jeep.

Impatiently, Gert turned to the couple. "Yes?" she asked, trying to sound civil.

"I heard you two were in charge of a tour group at the hotel. We wondered if maybe you knew of a good place to have lunch over here. It's a special day for us. We just got engaged last night." Carla proudly held out her hand to show off her engagement ring.

Gert briefly glanced at Carla's hand and was clearly unimpressed. "We don't know of any lunch places," Gert answered abruptly without complimenting Carla's treasure. "We're visiting friends."

"Oh, okay," Carla said dejectedly, stealing a

glance at the guy in the front seat. He hardly looked their type. He was young, sweaty, and had on old work clothes. The twins got in, slammed the doors shut, and the Jeep pulled away. "It doesn't look to me like they're going to high tea," she commented, staring at the departing vehicle.

"No, it doesn't." Jason took her hand. "Forget them. Let's go rent a car."

"Okay," Carla agreed, silently wondering where the twins had gone. She thought their actions seemed suspicious. Why couldn't they have asked their friend about a restaurant? It wasn't every day you got engaged. Something was up with those two not very nice people. They were downright rude for no reason. And worst of all, they didn't tell her what a gorgeous ring Jason and his mother had so carefully picked out for her. The woman had actually been dismissive of the one piece of jewelry Carla had been waiting for her whole life! What an insult! Carla's blood started to boil.

And after someone insulted Carla, she wasn't the type to let it go. Ever. Grudge was her middle name.

22

He stared at the picture of Dorinda Dawes and read the story of her death. He remembered everything about the night he broke into the museum and stole all those seashells. He had the Queen's lei around his neck when the cops chased him into the alley. That was almost the end for him. But when Dorinda Dawes wore that lei around her neck, it was the end for her.

Thank God he wasn't caught that night thirty years ago. It had been close. Why can't I resist a dare? he asked himself.

Sometimes he wished he'd been born with a larger capacity for coping with boredom. He envied people who were content to do the same thing over and over again.

"Till I'm blue in the face," as his grandmother

used to say. "I cook and clean till I'm blue in the face, and I'm still tickled pink that God gave me two hands."

Granny was some character, he thought, laughing to himself. He didn't get to see her that much growing up. He was an army brat. His family was always moving around. It was hard to make friends because his family never stayed in one place. And once kids got a look at his toes, they would torment him. He reacted by causing trouble and developing a tough exterior. He was eight years old when he started to steal kids' lunchboxes.

His family had spent the year in Hawaii when he was sixteen. What a year. His father was stationed at Fort de Russy, right on the beach in Waikiki. He was enrolled at the local high school but spent most of his time surfing and hanging around the hotel beaches, stealing whatever he could from unsuspecting tourists.

How did the lei that I sold to a couple about to get on an airplane to the mainland end up back here with Dorinda Dawes? he wondered.

I have to see that lei again, he thought. Now that it's back at the museum, maybe I should return to the scene of the crime. Lucky they didn't have face recognition software thirty years ago. But I had a pair of panty hose over my head. Maybe they have panty hose recognition software. "Look for the union label," he hummed as he turned the page of the newspaper.

I would love to hold the lei in my hands, put it around my neck again. Relive those thrilling moments when I outran the cops. Maybe I can steal it a second time. The thought was irresistible. They're making such a big deal about auctioning off the other royal shell lei at the "Be a Princess" Ball. If this lei disappears again, it'll really be a story!

He wondered if they had upgraded their security at the Seashell Museum. It wasn't exactly the Louvre, but they loved their leis.

I'm aching for trouble, he realized. And I've been like this since I was a little kid. He remembered the time he'd volunteered to make a milk shake for his sister's friend. He poured Ivory liquid into the blender. The shake came out so frothy that the girl took a big sip. The look on her face as she went running outside the house and spitting it out in the bushes was priceless. He'd never laughed so hard in his life. And while she was outside, he stole some change from her purse.

The start of my problems, he thought. From that day on he got such a thrill out of stealing and screwing things up for people. Why can't I just laugh at stupid jokes and movies that the rest of the world thinks are hilarious? I need more than that to keep me excited. I need to always be on the move. It's why I exercise like a maniac, he told himself as he turned the page of the newspaper.

The van stopped in front of a beautiful surfing

beach. Francie tapped him on the shoulder. "Ned! Look at those waves! They're monstrous!"

He smiled. "I told you."

"They look so dangerous!" Francie cried. "Are you sure you want to surf there?"

Ned turned to her. "Don't you see, Francie? That's what makes it fun."

23

When Regan got back to the hotel, she stopped in Will's office. Janet, his sturdy-looking secretary, was on the phone. Keeper of the gate, Regan dubbed her. Janet's glasses were resting at the tip of her nose, and she had that take-charge air of someone who had never experienced a nervous moment in their life. Nor a second of self-doubt. Regan guessed that she was probably in her fifties.

"Is Will here?" Regan asked quietly. Turned out it wasn't necessary to be discreet.

"No. I think he's a little stressed. He went out a little while ago," Janet practically bellowed. "Listen, hon," she yelled into the phone, "I've got to go." She dropped the phone into the receiver, looked up at Regan, and lowered her voice. "I know Will wants you to look into things around here."

"He told you?"

"Of course. If you can't trust your secretary . . ." Her voice trailed off. Temporarily. "Between what happened to Dorinda and all the problems since the renovation, Will has a full plate, I'm telling you that. The poor guy is a wreck." She picked a manila envelope off her desk and handed it to Regan. "In there are all the newsletters Dorinda wrote, the magazine article, and the list of problems and complaints since the renovation."

"Thanks."

"Excuse me, Janet," a male's voice said.

Regan turned. It was a guy in a bellman's uniform. She smiled at him.

"Is Will around?" the bellman asked politely, with a big smile.

"He'll be back in a little while," Janet answered.

"I'll catch him later then." He smiled again, waved, and exited the room, reminding Regan of a guy she knew in college who never stopped smiling. You could tell him your house was burning down, but nothing could wipe the grin off his face.

Janet gestured to the departing figure. "Will is Glenn's mentor. Will also started as a bellman, and for the last year or two he's been showing that kid the ropes. He thinks the guy will work his way up in this hotel." She paused. "Regan, you would not believe the morning we're having. People have been calling like crazy. With all the publicity about the royal lei around Dorinda's neck and the matching lei being auctioned off, half of Honolulu now wants to come to the 'Be a Princess' Ball. We're squeezing as many tables as we can into the ball-room, but we have to turn people away. Dorinda finally got us some business."

Regan's eyebrows raised. "I guess she did."

"Don't get me wrong," Janet continued quickly. "I feel bad she died. She was hired when the reno-vation was finally finished to jazz things up around here with the newsletter. All she did was get on everyone's nerves. But her death has certainly added spice to the Towers. Now everyone wants a ticket to the ball, and they want the lei that is being auctioned off. They also want to know what's going to happen to the lei that Dorinda was wear-ing when she died. If you ask me, people have been watching too many of those crime shows on tele-vision."

"I was just at the Seashell Museum. The owner hasn't decided whether to auction off the second lei or not."

"He should," Janet declared as she fluffed her short red hair with her pencil. "Some sick person would be willing to pay a lot of money for it. At least it's all going for a good cause."

"He told me he'll make the decision at the ball."

Janet shrugged. "More drama. Who knows? Maybe his big last-minute decision will drum up more excitement that night. I'm sure the auction-eer will milk it for all it's worth."

Regan nodded. "He wants to see how much the other lei goes for first."

"Naturally," Janet replied in her deadpan voice. "It all comes down to money, doesn't it, Regan?"

"A lot of things do," Regan agreed. "Nobody had seen Dorinda with the shell lei before, huh?"

Janet shook her head emphatically. "Nobody. People have been stopping at my desk, which I should rename Grand Central Station, to talk to me about Dorinda. Everyone remembers the floral leis she usually wore that matched the flowers in her hair. She thought she was Carmen Miranda. If you ask me, it got to be a bit much. She was always in costume with the 'tropical' outfits she wore. Always had to put on a show. Sometimes I just wanted to tell her to calm down and hang loose— we're in Hawaii, after all."

She's calm now, Regan thought. But I doubt poor Dorinda is resting in peace. It doesn't seem as if there's anybody who is too choked up about her passing. "She really hadn't been here that long," Regan commented.

"Long enough to make her mark. She started in the middle of October when the renovation was complete and the new Coconut Tower and Ballroom had just opened. Will thought it would be a good idea to start a newsletter for guests. Dorinda applied for the job, and the rest, as they say, is history."

"You said Dorinda got on people's nerves. Can you give me any examples?"

"Sure. To start, I'll tell you how she got on my nerves," Janet pronounced. "Pull up a chair."

"Yes, thanks," Regan answered as she obediently grabbed one of the chairs by the door and brought it closer to Janet's desk. She sat down and fished her notebook out of her purse.

"You going to take notes?" Janet asked.

"If you don't mind."

"Be my guest."

"Thank you. So you were saying . . ."

"Right. Dorinda. She was a piece of work. Some of the girls who work in the clothing store out there stopped by this morning. Now don't get me wrong. People are sorry she's dead. But nobody's going to miss her too much. For example, she'd breeze in here to see Will and treated me like I was the hired help. I guess I am the hired help, but what the heck was she?"

Regan nodded sympathetically.

"Who knows where she got her attitude?" Janet continued as she shrugged her shoulders. "The girls from the shop were saying that when Dorinda first got here, she acted friendly and asked millions of questions. She got together with them a few times for lunch and drinks. But then she'd break lunch dates at the last minute. And not return phone calls. It was as if she realized they couldn't do her much good. It seemed to be her pattern with people who worked at the hotel. She plied everyone for gossip and information about life around here and then dropped them when she'd gotten all she could out of them."

"Do you have any idea about her private life?"

"She was here a lot at night covering the parties and taking pictures. And I know she was always angling to get herself invited to parties and openings around town. I don't think she had any sort of boyfriend."

"A waitress in one of the coffee shops told me she was a real flirt."

"That she was. I saw the way she'd act with Will. She'd breeze past me and then saunter into his office with a big smile. I don't think he bought into it, but he was stuck. He'd signed a six-month contract with her and wanted to make it work."

"Did Will ever mention anything about firing her?" Regan asked quickly.

"No! But I know Will. He couldn't have been happy with people's reaction to Dorinda. He wanted someone to bring people together with the newsletter, not alienate them. I shouldn't be talking about Will. All I'm saying is *yes*. Dorinda was a flirt, and she was attractive."

Interesting, Regan thought. I've had the feeling all along that there's something Will is not telling me. "Did you read the article she wrote for the magazine *Spirits in Paradise*?"

"No. That reminds me: Now I have to find somebody else to take pictures at the ball." She jotted down a note on a Post-it on her desk.

Business is business, Regan thought. "Apparently Dorinda walked home every night. Did you know that?"

"Yes. Her apartment is not too far from here, in Waikiki. She took the path along the beach. When it rained, she was always looking for someone to give her a ride. I did once. She barely thanked me. And I live in the opposite direction."

"I wonder what the story is with her apartment now."

"Her cousin is on his way here to clean it out."

"Her cousin is coming here?" Regan repeated.

"Yes. He called after you left before."

"Where does he live?"

"Venice Beach, California."

"Oh, really. I live in the Hollywood Hills."

"Well, he's flying in today, and Will's parents will be here in the morning."

"Will's parents? He mentioned he was looking forward to his wife coming back this weekend."

"He was and she is. That's the problem. She's been gone since before Christmas, and when she gets back tonight, she'll hear all this good news. Like her mother-in-law will be arriving in no time flat. Not that Will's mom isn't a nice lady but . . ."

"I understand," Regan said quickly.

"I'm glad you do because I don't think Will's wife will." Janet laughed. "Poor guy. He has so much going on. He's got to get through this ball. He's going to put his parents up in a room here."

"Sounds like a good idea," Regan said.

"You wouldn't believe what a good idea it is. Of course that means I'll be dealing with Mama Brown. And I have to work this weekend at the ball."

"Things will be busy," Regan commented.

"They sure will."

"Janet, did you ever hear that Dorinda was afraid of the ocean?"

"No. But as they said on the news, she did like to sit on the jetty at night. It can be so beautiful and peaceful sitting in the moonlight. I told her more than once to be careful out there by herself. She never listened. She said it calmed her down after a busy day. The currents are strong. Maybe she slipped and fell."

"Maybe," Regan agreed as she jotted down a few notes. "Janet, you see a lot of what goes on around here."

"I hear it, too. I feel like the president of the complaint department."

"Do you know of anyone who would have wanted to hurt Dorinda?"

"Plenty of people felt like strangling her, but not killing her. I think you know what I mean."

"I suppose I do. Dorinda started working here just after the renovation was complete, and Will said that the problems around the hotel started soon after that. I know she's not here to defend herself, but I wonder if she could have had anything to do with the trouble at the hotel."

"Hard to say," Janet responded. "We hired a lot of new employees at that time."

"Could I get a list of those people?"

"Sure. I'll have that ready for you in a few hours. I really don't think Dorinda could have been behind the trouble. She would have had to sneak around, and she couldn't help but make her presence known. When Dorinda was in a room, you knew it. Some of the problems we had originated in the kitchen. Some in the public bathrooms. Some in the guest rooms. Whoever is behind it must have a master key. I suppose Dorinda could have gotten one. It'll be interesting to see if anything happens now that she's gone."

The phone on Janet's desk rang. She rolled her eyes. "I bet this is about the ball."

"I'll get out of your way." Regan closed her notebook and stood. "I'll take a look at everything in here." The manila envelope was in her hands.

"I'll be in all day. Give me a call or stop by if you need anything."

"Thanks very much," Regan said and walked out of the office and into the bustling open-air reception area. A poster for the Princess Ball was propped on an easel next to the concierge desk. SOLD OUT! was written across the top. ACCEPTING NAMES FOR THE WAITING LIST.

Oh, Dorinda, Regan thought. Maybe not the way you wanted, but you certainly have made your mark.

24

Bob and Betsy were in their room sitting together at the desk where their laptop computer was open and running. Handwritten notes were scattered all over the bed. A pot of room service coffee was at their side, and Bob had just proposed a way to do research for their chapter of the relationship book.

"I don't know," Betsy hesitated. "It doesn't seem that exciting to go out in the world and pretend to be Bonnie and Clyde."

"It doesn't?"

"Not at all."

Bob took off his glasses and used the bottom of his T-shirt to give them a good cleaning. It was something he did many times a day, more out of habit than the fact that his glasses were fogged. "I think it would help our marriage."

Betsy looked aghast. "What's wrong with our marriage?"

There was a pause. "Nothing," he muttered. "Nothing that can't be fixed with a little old-fashioned excitement."

"By acting like we're criminals?"

"Yes. If we're writing a chapter about how to keep a relationship exciting, then we should offer a smorgasbord of ideas to keep the fires burning. Pretending to be devilish is one of the choices."

"That's what Halloween is for," Betsy replied as her face developed a pinched look. She was beginning to think there was something seriously wrong with her husband. Ever since he'd gotten into a chat with that book publisher who wandered into town looking for a couple from Hudville to write a chapter for his book, Bob had started to go nuts. The publisher had traveled the country looking for couples from all different backgrounds to share the ways they kept excitement in their relationship. Bob had leaped at the chance for him and Betsy to represent the rainy states. The only problem was, he was not exciting in the least. Neither was she, but that was his fault. He'd made her boring.

As Betsy looked down and folded her hands, she thought longingly of her college boyfriend Roger. Where was he now? If only they had ended up together. If only he hadn't met that other girl who got her hooks into him during a semester at sea. Betsy couldn't go because she got seasick. Roger said he'd go for five months and get in enough cruising for a lifetime. Huh! I should have gone and taken Dramamine, Betsy reflected. Her mother had tried to comfort her by singing "Que Sera Sera," but it only made things worse. Then she'd heard that Roger and Nautical Nancy had had their reception on a boat.

If I'd married Roger, she mused, I wouldn't be living in depressing, soggy Hudville. If I were vacationing with Roger in Hawaii, we'd be out on the beach with a mai tai in our hands instead of sitting in the hotel room thinking about ridiculous ways to liven up other people's lives. Roger and I would have paid for the trip ourselves instead of having to win a lottery to get here. If only . . .

How had she stood thirty years with boring Bob? It was impossible to believe. He'd had the same menial job for twenty-eight years in a store that sold drain pipes. Business was brisk in Hudville. The book publisher had spotted the store when he was driving through town, and the rest, as they say, was history.

Now Bob put his hand on her thigh. Inwardly she cringed.

"Itsy Bitsy?" he whispered softly, using his nickname for her.

"What?"

"It's important that we write this chapter."

"Why?"

"It'll make our lives more exciting. When the

book is published, we'll travel with the other
couples in the book. It could change our lives. But
most important, it's a gift for our children."

"Our children?" Betsy's voice went up an octave.
"How is it a gift for our children?"

"Our children are wonderful, but they're a little
dull. I don't know how they got that way. I just don't
understand it. They'll need this guidebook. They
are both married, thank God, but if they don't
liven up, I'm afraid their spouses will leave them."

He must be on drugs, Betsy thought. That's the
only answer. "Jeffrey and Celeste are wonderful
people," she cried indignantly.

"You never hear a peep out of them."

"Yes, but they have deep thoughts."

"Deep thoughts don't get you anywhere unless
you share them." Bob patted her thigh again.
"Now, I was thinking. Little Joy says there are
problems going on around the hotel. Why don't we
walk around the hotel today and pretend we're the
criminals? Let's just see what trouble we might be
able to find."

"Around the hotel?"

"Yes. The hotel is having problems. If we think
like criminals, maybe we'll figure out what's going
on. It's called role-playing. Who knows? We could
end up being heroes. It's just a little game."

At this point Betsy felt it was useless to protest.
"All right," she relented. "But only if we start at
the bar."

25

Regan passed the sign for the Princess Ball, with Princess Kaiulani smiling down on the hotel guests, then went over to the house phone and dialed her room. There was no answer. She then pulled out her cell phone and called Kit's cell. Kit answered after three rings.

"Regan, I'm out on a boat!"

"Where?"

"In back of the hotel. I met some people after breakfast who were going out for a quick sail. I'll be back in a little while. Steve is coming over at lunchtime. Let's meet in the bar by the big pool at noon."

"Sounds good."

Regan walked out to the smallest of the Waters' five pools and took a seat in the shade of a

large striped umbrella. Elvis was crooning "Blue
Hawaii" from poolside speakers. Regan pulled
out the newsletters from the envelope Janet had
given her and retrieved the notebook from her
purse.

Well, it was clear enough that Dorinda Dawes
could make enemies. Regan couldn't believe that
even her mother had an unpleasant experience
with her. Regan clicked her pen and started jotting
down a few notes.

Dorinda had started working at the hotel in
mid October. The problems at the hotel had
started around that time. I'm sure Dorinda would
have loved to expose the culprit on the front page
of the newsletter, Regan thought. She unfolded a
sheet of legal paper that was behind the newsletters. It was a handwritten list of the hotel's
problems.

Regan's eyes scanned the offenses. Leaky pipes.
Toilets overflowing caused by foreign objects not
meant to be flushed, such as full tubes of suntan
lotion. Oversalting of food. Complaints from
guests that small convenience items were missing
from their rooms: toothpaste, body lotion, the
coffeemaker. A faucet turned on in an empty room
that caused a flood. Jars of bugs opened and left in
guests' rooms. Complaints from numerous guests
that one of their sandals or sneakers went missing
from their room.

A thief who steals one shoe. Regan pondered

what that meant, if anything. The Waikiki Waters
had a phantom who was clearly out to annoy.

How does someone get away with this for three
months without being discovered? Regan wondered. Maybe there's more than one phantom.
This could be the work of several people.

A tan young waitress in a short, flowered shift
approached Regan. "Can I get you something to
drink?"

"An iced tea, please."

"Certainly."

Could Dorinda Dawes have stumbled onto
something? Regan wondered. Did someone murder her because she found out who was causing
trouble at the hotel? It was certainly possible.

The big Princess Ball was tomorrow night. If
someone was trying to tarnish the reputation of
the hotel, the Princess Ball was a perfect target.
With all the press that would be there, as well as
more than five hundred people from all over
Hawaii, anything negative that happened would
be written about, discussed, and rehashed for days.

She picked up the Waikiki Waters newsletter
that had been published in early January, the last
one Dorinda had worked on. Pictures of parties
held at the hotel in the month of December filled
the pages. The men looked great, but the pictures
of most of the women were very unflattering.
Everything from wide-open mouths to messy hair
to clothing somehow out of place. One photo in

particular caught Regan's eye. A woman was laughing with her head thrown back. The camera seemed to have been pointed up her nose. She was standing next to Will. Regan read the name below.

It was Kim, Will's wife.

The newsletter had been printed when Will was on vacation, Regan realized. Dorinda's photo captions included descriptions like "only twice divorced," "recently slim," and "planning marriage number four." She glanced through the rest of the newsletters, and they all seemed fairly tame—obviously Will's influence.

Oh, Dorinda, Regan thought. It does seem that you had a talent for striking a nerve—a lot of nerves. But did you get someone upset enough to kill you?

Every instinct told Regan that the answer was yes. But who? And what did the shell lei around Dorinda's neck signify?

26

Jazzy awoke in one of the downstairs guest rooms at Steve's house. It was ten-thirty. She and Steve had stayed up until nearly four o'clock shooting the breeze. She got out of bed, wrapped herself in a luxurious white terrycloth bathrobe, and went into the spacious marble bathroom that was bigger than many people's bedrooms.

First she brushed her teeth with the toothbrush she now left in residence at Steve's house, and then splashed water on her face. "That helps," she murmured as she patted her face dry with an Egyptian cotton towel. Staring at herself in the mirror, she again analyzed her cute, almost tomboyish reflection. She knew that guys didn't feel threatened by her and were comfortable having her around. Work it, baby, she told herself.

Her cell phone rang in the bedroom. She hurried over and checked the caller ID. It was her employer, Claude Mott.

"Good morning!" she answered.

"Where are you?" Claude asked. Jazzy could picture Claude with his wispy goatee and head of thinning gray and black hair. He was slight in stature but had been a powerhouse at buying and selling companies. Now he wanted to stretch the left side of his brain by designing Hawaiian shirts, bathing suits, and muumuus. His first line would debut in the gift bags at the "Be a Princess" Ball, the ball that Claude Mott Enterprises had helped to underwrite.

"I'm at Steve's house. I stayed here last night, and today I'm going over to the Waikiki Waters to do some work on the gift bags. How's everything in San Francisco?"

"It's a business trip. Business is business is business. Deals, deals, deals. That's why I have my house in Hawaii, so I can get away from it all and design my Hawaiian clothing."

"I know, Claude, I know."

"You know, I know, we know. As we speak it becomes apparent to me that you have not yet read this morning's papers."

"What do you mean?"

"I spoke to Aaron. He's at the house. He told me that there's an article today about the dead woman that focuses on the royal shell lei around her neck. I hope this doesn't mean that people will get disturbed and not want to wear my clothes with the same beautiful shell lei design."

"That won't happen, Claude," Jazzy assured him. "The chairman of the 'Be a Princess' Ball committee called me last night to report that all this attention has helped ticket sales."

"Really?"

"Yes."

"What else are you putting in the gift bags?" he asked in a grumpy tone.

"A bunch of junk so that your items will be the big treat."

"What kind of junk?"

"A key ring with a miniature plastic palm tree, pineapple soap that smells like ammonia, and a small bag of macadamia nuts that will have people running to the dentist. Believe me, your Hawaiian shirts and muumuus will stand out."

"Good. That's good. Because you know, Jazzy, I think that's where my true genius lies."

"I agree, Claude. I am doing my best to make sure everyone in Hawaii takes notice of Claude's Clothes. The shell lei you drew for the fabric is so beautiful, so intricate."

"Well, how many days did I go to that Seashell Museum to study the royal lei they're auctioning off? How many? You think that idiot Jimmy would have trusted me with the lei. I could have taken it home and done an even better replication. But no."

"After the robbery all those years ago, I guess he was afraid to let it go."

"He's not a good businessman."

"I don't think many people would accuse him of that."

"I should say not. If I showed up at a meeting with bare feet, I don't think people would want to do business with me."

"Claude," Jazzy began in her most comforting tone, "the 'Be a Princess' Ball will be a huge success for us. You will get the attention you deserve."

"I hope so. I'm flying in tonight. Will you be there to pick me up at the airport?"

"Of course."

"Did you get me a room at the Waikiki Waters for the weekend? I want to be there and make sure my clothes are in those bags."

"I booked you a suite."

"What would I do without you?" Claude wondered aloud.

"I don't know," Jazzy answered.

After she hung up the phone, Jazzy went upstairs where Steve was reading the sports section of the paper and sipping coffee.

"Where are the guys?" she asked as she helped herself to a cup of delicious Kona coffee.

"They went out to the beach."

"You didn't go?"

"No. I'm going to spend the day with Kit at the hotel."

"That's where I'm heading. Can I grab a ride with you?"

"Sure. I have to be there at lunchtime."

"Perfect. We can all have lunch together," Jazzy said breezily.

Steve looked up from the paper. "That should work." At least I hope it will, he thought. He liked Kit and was hoping that they could spend some time alone today. Her friend Regan was around but didn't seem like the type to get in the way. Not like Jazzy.

"So," Jazzy cooed as she took her first sip of coffee. "You seem to like this Kit. Maybe you should bid for the princess lei for her."

"I don't know." Steve handed her the paper with the article about Dorinda Dawes. "These leis must have a curse on them. What is it they say about lava from the Big Island? If you take a piece of it home with you, you're in for trouble. Something tells me it's the same story with the two royal leis. They originally belonged to a queen who was forced to abdicate her throne and a princess who died young. Who would want them?"

"Well, don't spread that word around," Jazzy replied a little testily. "Claude will have a fit. He wants everyone to love those leis. It's the signature of his fabric."

"And we don't want to upset Claude," Steve muttered with a tinge of sarcasm.

"No." Jazzy laughed. "We certainly don't."

27

Regan and Kit hoisted themselves onto two of the stools at the hotel's outdoor bar and ordered lemonade. Fliers for the hotel's hula classes were piled on the bar. Kit had her wet hair pulled back and smelled of suntan lotion.

"It was fun out there, Regan. I wish you had been with me."

"It sounds like fun. I'll go for a swim later in the afternoon. Who were you with?"

"I went for a walk on the beach and ended up talking to some people who were going out for a quick sail on the hotel catamaran. They invited me, and I thought why not? Everyone is so friendly around here."

"Don't you know you're not supposed to talk to strangers?" Regan said with a laugh.

"If I didn't talk to strangers, my social life would be the pits." Kit looked around, then lowered her voice. "But there are two strangers over there whom I'd be wary of talking to. That couple is staring at us."

Regan glanced over at the middle-aged man and woman a few seats down from them. He was graying and thin. She was, too. In an odd way they looked alike—like couples who had been together for years. It also helped that they both had on black oversized sunglasses and matching hats in a jungle camouflage print. Where in the world did they get those? Regan wondered. The woman caught Regan's eye and raised her glass.

"Cheers," she toasted.

"Cheers," Regan responded in kind.

"Where are you gals from?" the man asked.

"Los Angeles and Connecticut," Regan answered. "And you?"

"A place where it rains a lot." The man laughed.

That might explain the hats, Regan mused.

"Are you gals having fun?" the man continued.

I hate being called a "gal," Regan thought. But she smiled gamely and said, "How can you not have a good time here? What's not to like?"

The woman rolled her eyes. "We're with a tour group. Sometimes the others get on my nerves. We're spending a lot of time alone." She took a gulp from the martini glass in front of her.

That's strong stuff for this time of day, Regan thought. And under this hot sun.

The woman put down her martini glass. "I'm Betsy, and this is my husband, Bob."

Regan noticed that ever so briefly Bob looked at Betsy with an annoyed expression. What's that about? she wondered. "I'm Regan, and this is my friend Kit."

Regan could tell that Kit had no interest in talking to these people. Her mind was on Steve. She couldn't blame her. And these two looked as if they wanted to chat.

"What do you do for a living?" Bob asked Regan.

Here we go, Regan thought. The question she didn't always feel comfortable answering. And now that she was on the job, she definitely didn't want to tell the truth. "Consulting," she answered. It sounded vague, and people usually didn't pry. It was often a term used by someone who was out of a job. "And you?"

"We're writing about how to keep the excitement in your relationship," Bob boasted.

I guess it's by wearing matching hats, Regan decided. "Oh," she answered. "How interesting."

"You must be in a relationship," Betsy said. "I can see you're wearing a beautiful engagement ring. Where is your fiancé?"

They're jewel thieves, Regan thought wryly. She knew the game plan of couples who cozy up to people at bars, ply them with liquor, and then rip them off. "My fiancé is in New York," Regan answered then changed the subject: "Are you going to the Princess Ball?"

"Those tickets are expensive," Bob noted. "I kind of doubt it. The leaders of our tour group are cheapskates. We're on an all-expenses-paid vacation, and the ball isn't part of the package."

"Now they're sold out," Regan informed them.

"I guess we have no choice then," Bob said with a laugh.

"They're accepting names for a waiting list," Regan offered.

Kit poked Regan in the ribs. "Regan," Kit whispered. "Steve is coming. Look who's with him. I don't believe it."

Regan turned and spotted Steve and Jazzy walking around the pool and heading toward them. Jazzy started to wave.

"How does she do it?" Regan asked.

"I wish I knew," Kit answered.

"Remember," Regan cautioned Kit, "not a word about my checking things out for Will."

"My lips are sealed," Kit promised.

Regan turned to Betsy and Bob as she and Kit got up from the bar. "Nice talking to you."

"Hope to see you gals again," Bob said with a wave of his martini glass.

"Hi, girls," Jazzy cooed as she and Steve approached. "I have so much to do today with packing the gift bags for the ball, talking to the manager of the hotel's secretary to make sure everything is in place, and who knows what else. But Steve invited me to join you for lunch. I hope you don't mind."

"Of course not," Kit answered without much conviction.

They secured an outside table for four that had a large umbrella and was also shaded by a large banyan tree. Kids were splashing in the pool, and the smell of suntan lotion was in the air. The beach spread out endlessly in front of them, and the sun was directly overhead. It was high noon in Hawaii, and people were relaxed and enjoying themselves.

It was hard for Regan to believe that the East Coast was still caught in the grip of a blizzard. People there are hunkering down in their long underwear while we're sitting here in bathing suits and summer clothes. Jazzy had on a sundress that would work at a cocktail party, and it looked a lot like the dress she was wearing last night. Regan had the feeling that short low-cut flower print dresses were her uniform of choice.

Regan glanced at Steve's handsome profile. I hope he turns out to be a nice guy, she thought. Though it's a little suspect that he thinks Jazzy is good company. And he did seem terribly impatient with that girl at the bar last night.

They ordered drinks and sandwiches from a waitress wearing white shorts, a pink top, and a lei made from pink carnations and white plumeria.

"It feels good to sit," Jazzy announced. "This is going to be a busy day!"

"How did you get involved with the ball?" Regan asked.

"My boss is very charitable. He's helping to underwrite the ball."

"How generous of him."

"And he's donating Hawaiian shirts and muumuus that he designed for the gift bags."

"He's a designer?" Kit asked.

"He's just getting started with his line of Hawaiian wear."

"Is he coming to the ball?" Regan asked.

"Of course. I've organized a couple of tables for him."

"Where does he sell his clothes?" Regan asked.

"Well, as I said, he's just getting started," Jazzy replied in a tone one might use correcting a child. "He hopes the ball will attract publicity for his line, Claude's Clothes." She shrugged. "We'll see. He's a very successful man, so if it docsn't work out, I'm sure he'll be on to the next venture."

"Of course he will," Regan answered, trying not to sound too sarcastic.

Over lunch the conversation was light. Steve admitted he didn't want to be completely retired and that he was looking for new investments. How about Claude's Clothes? Regan wanted to ask but refrained. Steve intended to spend half the year in Hawaii and then have a second home somewhere else. He just wasn't sure where yet.

A nice way to live, Regan thought. But what about Jazzy? Surely she wouldn't be happy to house-sit forever—not after she had been a lawyer in New York.

When the check came, Regan was relieved. She was eager to get up to the room and make a few phone calls but told the group she was heading to the spa. Steve insisted on paying for lunch, which Jazzy seemed to expect. The group disbanded with Kit and Steve heading down to the beach alone. Jazzy made a beeline for Will's office. I'll stay away from there for now, Regan decided. She walked back to the room and spotted Betsy and Bob down the hall. They had just emerged from the employee supply room.

What are those two up to? she wondered.

"Hey, Regan!" Bob called to her. "We're on this hallway, too. They never seem to give us enough towels no matter how much we complain." He laughed. "So we took matters into our own hands." He held up several towels that they'd obviously taken from the unguarded room.

"You can never have enough towels," Regan agreed as she quickly opened the door to her hotel room and gratefully slipped inside. What a morning, she thought. Now she wanted to call the man Dorinda had interviewed for *Spirits in Paradise*. Then she'd take a walk around the hotel. She also wanted to find Will and tell him that she'd like to meet Dorinda's cousin. Who knows what she might find out from him?

Regan sat down on her bed and pulled the cell phone from her purse. "First things first," she said to herself as she dialed Jack's number. She hadn't had much of a chance to talk to him yesterday. This morning he had been in a meeting when she called, and she told him she'd call back later. When he answered the phone, he said, "Finally!"

"Hi!"

"I'm sorry I couldn't talk this morning. How's it going out there in paradise?"

"Fine. I'm actually working for a living out here. You know, a lot of people would love to work in Hawaii, and I got a job without trying."

"What?"

"I know Mike Darnell told you a female employee drowned here at the beach in front of the hotel. The manager thinks she may have been murdered. And strange things have been happening at the hotel. He wants me to see what I can find out."

"Where's Kit?"

"On the beach with the new guy."

"Oh, boy. It sounds as if she doesn't need you."

"I'm glad she's having a good time. And now I'm occupied."

"Did you speak to Mike about the manager's suspicions?"

"No. He joined us for drinks last night. I wasn't hired until Kit and I came back to the hotel and the manager asked if we'd join him for a drink."

"How did he know you were a private investigator?"

"Kit told him earlier in the evening when we ran into him in the lobby."

"Kit doesn't waste time, does she?"

Regan smiled. "Not lately. Anyway, according to Mike the police believe that the woman drowned. There were no signs of struggle. But, get this: the woman was from New York and had interviewed my mother years ago. She turned out to be a piece of goods. She burned my mother with the article she wrote about her."

"Maybe Nora arranged the hit."

"Very funny, Jack." Regan laughed. "I'm telling my mother you said that."

"She won't mind. She thinks I'm going to be a wonderful son-in-law."

"I know she does. According to her, you're capable of doing no wrong."

"Your mother has good taste," Jack pronounced with a laugh. "But seriously, Regan, why does the manager think she was murdered? He must have some good reason."

"That's the $64,000 question. All he said was that when she was leaving the other night, she told him she was going straight home."

"That's it?"

"That's it."

"There's got to be more to his story."

"I know. I think I'm going to have to talk to him again."

In his office, Jack shook his head. "I guess it's why I love you, Regan. You do manage to find yourself in these situations more often than not. I've said it before, and I'm sure I'll say it at least a thousand times more: Be careful, would you please?"

Regan thought of Jimmy standing over her this morning. It was uncomfortably close. Then that weird couple with the camouflage hats admiring her ring. "I'll be fine, Jack," she insisted. "Besides, I don't like to sit in the sun all day. I'll take a swim later, but this gives me something to do."

"I'd prefer you with a sunburn."

Regan laughed. But she had to admit to herself that things at the Waikiki Waters were a little "off." And probably destined to get worse.

28

Even though the waves were great and the scenery magnificent—with the mountains serving as a backdrop and the cloudless blue sky, turquoise ocean, and white sand beach—Ned could barely concentrate on his surfing. He had taken Artie to a cove where the waves were smaller than out on the open sea. Ned demonstrated how to paddle out, place your hands on either side of the board, and jump to your feet. They practiced on the sand, and then Artie went out by himself, eager to catch a wave. All Ned could think about was the fact that the lei he had stolen years ago was back at the Seashell Museum. How was it possible? What happened to that couple who bought the lei from him at the airport?

As Ned paddled through the water on top of his board, he thought about the story he'd heard of a kid who threw a bottle in the ocean with a note stuffed inside asking whoever found it to get in contact. How many years did it take before the bottle finally washed ashore? At least twenty years, Ned remembered. Lucky the kid's parents were still living at the address in the bottle—not like his parents who moved so much they never once finished unpacking their boxes. They schlepped them from house to house to house. When Ned's dad finally retired and they moved to a condo in Maine, they ended up throwing out most of the stuff they'd carted around for years. It made Ned crazy.

If any of Ned's old classmates had ever tried to find him, it would have been an impossible task. But that was the way Ned liked it. He didn't want anyone from his childhood to come knocking at his door. Keep the past in the past, he often thought.

But the lei. When he sold it to the people at the airport, he was sure he would never see it again, and that was fine with him. The couple was on their way to God knows where. He remembered that the wife kept calling the husband by some weird name. What was it again? I can't possibly expect to remember, he thought, but it was un-usual, and it made him laugh at the time. And now the lei was back in Hawaii. Back at the museum. And he was back after having moved away with his family all those years ago. After Ned separated from his wife, he wanted to get as far away from her as possible. So he moved from Pennsylvania to Hawaii. What a coincidence that both he and the shell lei had found their way back to paradise. It must mean something, he thought. I've got to see the lei again.

"Hey, Artie," he yelled, "that's it!" Ned was amazed to see that Artie actually got up on the board and was riding a wave. He even looked happy. On the shore, Francie was cheering. Ned was relieved that she had opted against surfing. It was difficult enough to teach one person to surf, and after reading that newspaper article, Ned had a lot on his mind. But he was glad Francie was along. She could watch him show off on the board. This is what he craved—attention. People listening to him. People who didn't think he was a geek.

Artie had on a wet suit, but Ned thought they were for wimps. The Pacific Ocean felt good on his body. All he wore besides his bathing suit were rubber shoes. He told the others that the broken shells in the water could be fierce when you're trying to get in or out and that he had a bad cut on the bottom of one foot. He did a song and dance about how coral cuts could lead to serious infections. Of course he really wore the shoes to cover up those stupid toes of his.

When he thought about it, he couldn't believe

there was ever a time in his life when he wore sandals. As a matter of fact, he realized, the last time he had worn sandals was in Hawaii all those years ago. First that lady whose husband bought the lei couldn't take her eyes off his feet. It was as if she was in shock. Later that night he got in a fight at a bar with some drunken freak who made fun of his toes. After that he vowed he'd never let them be exposed again. Tough work for an athlete who loved water sports. Somehow he managed.

I look cool in these seaweed-colored shoes, he thought. It's all in the attitude. He tried to teach that to the kids he worked with at the hotel—especially the ones with no natural athletic ability. If I didn't have such a taste for crime, I could have been a really swell guy.

He steadied himself and got up on the board as a wave was coming in. He stood and balanced himself, riding the wave and feeling the thrill. He could feel his endorphins kicking in as his surfboard glided through the water. It was an exhilarating feeling.

But it wasn't the same high as stealing.

He was laughing when the ride ended, and he and Artie together carried their boards to the shore.

"That was great!" Francie cried. "I should try it again one of these days!"

"I have to admit it was fun," Artie said as he caught his breath.

"I'm getting hungry. Why don't we go back and grab a late lunch?" Ned suggested.

"Then we can hit the beach," Francie suggested.

"Sure," Ned agreed, but he had no intention of going to the beach again this afternoon. He had business to take care of at the Seashell Museum.

On a black sand beach north of the Kona air-port, Jason and Carla walked hand in hand, only letting go of each other to pick up coral shells. They had already filled two shopping bags.

"Will we always be this happy?" Carla asked Jason as they put their shopping bags down, walked to the water's edge, and let the ocean swirl around their feet.

"Hope so." He paused. "But the odds are against us."

Jason laughed as Carla poked him in the ribs. "You're not very romantic."

"I was just kidding! And I am romantic. I was waiting for a moonlit night to propose. I should have checked the *Farmer's Almanac,* and then I would have known it wasn't a good idea. My best intentions just got me in trouble."

Carla kissed him on the cheek. "I still can't believe I was walking on that beach at the same time Dorinda Dawes was floating around in the water."

"You gave me a good scare. I wake up at three in the morning, and you're gone."

"It was scary on the beach at that hour. Something out there struck me as weird, but I was a little tipsy so I don't remember what it was. I really want to think of it so I can help that girl Regan."

"What do you mean weird?" Jason asked.

"Like I saw something strange. Not a murder weapon or anything, but something was out of place."

"You usually forget nothing, especially what I do wrong."

Carla laughed. "I know, but we'd been drinking piña coladas by the pool all afternoon and had wine at dinner. And then I grabbed a couple of beers from the mini bar before I went on the beach. I'm surprised you didn't smell it on my breath."

"What did you do with the bottles?"

"I threw them into the ocean when I was finished."

"Litterbug."

"I made a wish on each one."

"What did you wish?"

"Well, one wish came true. You finally proposed."

"What was your second wish?"

"That it doesn't rain on the big day. Or else my hair will frizz, and I'll go nuts."

"Some people say rain brings good luck."

Carla smiled at him sweetly. "With you I don't need any more luck. I'm not greedy."

Jason hugged her. He wouldn't let himself think too much about the fact that this girl he loved was walking around on the beach when, quite possibly, a murder was being committed—all because it was cloudy and he hadn't proposed. There's no question, he thought, that Regan Reilly is asking questions because they don't think it was a simple drowning. "I think we have enough of these shells to write out the Gettysburg Address," he finally said. "Let's get in the car and find a good spot to declare our love for each other to anyone who bothers to read Hawaiian graffiti."

"Are you kidding? It's a tourist attraction. Everyone on the highway to and from the airport will read it. And people flying above can look down and see it."

"Only if you're flying in a plane six feet off the ground or you happen to own a pair of supersonic spy glasses." He picked up the shopping bags off the sand. "Let's go."

They ambled up to their rental car that was parked on a cliff overlooking the turquoise water and marveled that there was no one else on the beach. The setting was gorgeous, complete with a waterfall and coconut palm trees. Everything was postcard perfect except the dent on the left back door of the car. Tiny traces of yellow paint lingered. The rental agent had presented the damaged vehicle to them without batting an eye. Jason immediately called on his bargaining skills and received a ten percent discount.

"More money to spend on our honeymoon," Carla had trilled. "You are such a smart businessman."

The sun was blazing, and inside the car it was hot. Jason turned on the air conditioning which promptly blew even hotter air in their faces. "Come on, baby," he urged. "Let's cool down."

Carla pulled down the visor and inspected herself in the mirror. She was starting to sweat, and her mascara was running. "After we do the shells, let's go swimming to cool off and then find a place for lunch. My stomach is grumbling."

"You want to eat now? It'll take energy to arrange the shells."

"Good idea."

They pulled out onto the highway and drove north. On their left the Pacific Ocean stretched out endlessly. On their right were coffee-covered mountain slopes.

"This is awesome," Carla said. "I read somewhere that the Hawaiian Islands are the most isolated island chain in the world."

"I read the same magazine. It's back in the

room. It also said that the Big Island is the size of the state of Connecticut. Too bad we don't have time to drive down to the big volcano."

"The most active volcano in the world."

"I know. Like I told you, I read that magazine."

"When did you read it?"

"When you took two hours to get ready last night."

"Oh. Well, maybe we should come back to the Big Island on our honeymoon. It's rural and romantic. There are rain forests to explore, and we can horseback ride, kayak, hike, snorkel, swim . . ."

"Maybe."

Carla settled back in her seat. She looked out the window as Jason turned on the radio. A song was ending, and the DJ started to speak: "Well, that was a song for lovers. And for all you lovers out there, have you tried eating at the Shanty Shanty Shack? It's right on the beach in Kona, and it's a great place to gaze in each other's eyes at breakfast, lunch, or dinner. Turn off the highway at—"

"Look!" Carla exclaimed. "It's a sign for the Shanty Shanty Shack! Make a left two hundred feet ahead. Let's try it! It was meant to be."

Jason shrugged. "Why not?" He put on the blinker, and they turned off the highway at the next sign for the restaurant, which had a big arrow pointing toward the beach. They went down a poorly paved narrow road that curved around a grove of banana trees and ended in a little cove with a small parking lot. The restaurant was perched on stilts overlooking the water. It was connected to a sweet, quaint hotel.

"What a discovery! Now this is Hawaii!" Carla exclaimed. "I'd love to stay here. You feel so close to nature!"

"Let's go inside and check out the food," Jason said practically.

They got out of the car and stepped onto the restaurant's rickety wooden deck. The water lapped below. "Smell that salty air!" Carla urged. "It smells not only like salt but flowers, too!"

"I smell it, I smell it. Let's keep moving. I'm hungry."

"Oh, look, Jason!" Carla pointed to a treehouse in the distance. In front of it was a big sign with large yellow lettering that read PRIVATE PROPERTY—KEEP OUT! AND I MEAN IT!

"Jason, can you stand it!" Carla laughed. "I'd love to meet whoever lives there."

"Yeah, well I don't think they want to meet you." Jason held open the restaurant door for his fiancée. They stepped inside. The dark wood walls, large vases of tropical plants obviously cut from the lush gardens outside, and sweet cool air immediately soothed customers—not that many people in Hawaii needed soothing, but plenty of tourists who hadn't yet unwound did. It was already late for lunch, and the restaurant was quiet. There were three people sitting at a corner table.

Carla's happy-go-lucky mood quickly evaporated. "I knew it!" Carla whispered to Jason. "Look over there! They're not eating at a friend's house! Those two rotten ladies lied to us!"

Gert and Ev looked up from their seafood salads. Ev inhaled sharply when she saw the couple they had ditched at the airport. Gert turned to her and calmly put her hand on her sister's. "I love this hotel. It's charming, but there aren't enough activities for our group."

Ev looked blank, then smiled. They couldn't have heard what we were talking about, she realized. They just walked in a second ago. "You're absolutely right, Gert. We'll never book any rooms here for our group. But they do make a mean seafood salad," she exclaimed in a loud voice.

For a moment the young man at their table looked at them quizzically, but he had learned not to ask any questions. Boy oh boy would he be glad when this project was over.

When Regan hung up the phone with Jack, she once again looked quickly through the newsletters. There were ten of them, the last one with all the unflattering pictures and question-able captions published just two weeks ago. Regan couldn't find anything that would make someone want to *murder* Dorinda Dawes. Of course some would argue that merely publishing bad pictures could be grounds for murder, espe-cially lousy pictures of Hollywood stars. But there weren't any stars in the newsletters. If they were staying at the hotel, they would have avoided the camera.

Regan looked again at the picture of Will and his wife, Kim. She was very pretty and had a dark tan, long, straight black hair that almost reached

her waist, and large brown eyes. Regan wondered
if she was Hawaiian. She also wondered if she had
seen this photo yet. Probably not if she's been away
for several weeks. So Kim is coming back to her
mother-in-law, an embarrassing photo in the
newsletter from her husband's place of employ-
ment, and a husband who's afraid he may lose his
job. Swell. Welcome home, honey.

Regan was anxious to talk to Will, but not while
Jazzy was around. She picked up the *Spirits in Paradise* magazine, which she had only gotten a chance
to glance at before lunch. Dorinda had profiled a
guy named Boone Kettle, a cowboy from Montana
who had moved to Hawaii a year ago. Regan
turned to the article. A picture of fifty-two-year-
old Boone, handsome and rugged and perched
atop a horse, filled the page. He had a job leading
horseback riding tours on a cattle ranch on the Big
Island.

The piece was several pages long. It talked
about how the winters in Montana had gotten on
Boone's nerves. He came to Hawaii on vacation
and decided that this was where he wanted to live.
It was tough, but he managed to get a job at a cattle ranch and was now celebrating his first anniversary in Hawaii. The worst thing about
moving, he said, was leaving his horse. But his
nephew brought the animal to live on his farm,
and Boone planned to visit Misty at least once a
year.

Regan dug out the interisland directory from the drawer of the night table and looked up the number of the ranch where Boone worked. She pulled out her cell phone and made the call, hoping she might catch him in. The girl who answered told Regan to hold on, that he had just gotten back from a ride. *"Boooooone!"* she screamed. *"Boooooone!* Phoooooonnnne!"

For a moment Regan held the phone away from her ear, afraid that if Boone didn't hurry, the girl would scream again. Then she could hear the girl saying, "I have no idea who it is."

"Aloha, Boone Kettle here," he said, his voice sounding gruff.

Regan considered how incongruous it sounded for this Montana cowboy to say "aloha." She brushed that thought aside. "Hello, Boone. My name is Regan Reilly, and I'm doing some work for the Waikiki Waters Resort where Dorinda Dawes worked writing their newsletter—"

"It's such a dang shame about her," Boone interrupted. "I couldn't believe it when I read the story in the paper. But I do think she had a thirst for danger. She was a bronco that needed to be broken."

"What do you mean?" Regan asked.

"Who did you say you are?" Boone inquired.

"Regan Reilly. I'm a private investigator working for the manager of the Waikiki Waters Resort. I wanted to know if maybe she talked to you about what was going on in her life—"

"I get it. You mean if there was anything she said that would indicate someone might want to off her."

"Something like that. What makes you think she had a thirst for danger?"

"She told me she felt a little frustrated. When she was hired by the manager, she thought it was to liven things up at the Waikiki Waters. But as it turned out, if you're writing a newsletter about a hotel and their guests, everything in it has to be hunky-dory. The hotel doesn't want gossipy things written about it, and the guests don't want 'spicy' tidbits written about them. So Dorinda's hands were tied, and she was a little bored. She was even a little worried that they might not want to continue the newsletter when her contract was up. I know she was worried about making enough money to live in Oahu. She said she was going to be writing one profile a month for the magazine but was intent on starting her own gossip sheet—something with the word 'Oahu' in the title. Truth be told, she hinted that she wanted to get into something a little juicier."

"Juicier?" Regan prodded.

"Something with a little more bite. She wanted to find out what's going on behind all the fancy hotels and the private homes. She felt the newsletters were puff pieces. The profile she did of me was good. Did you read it?"

"Yes. It was great."

"Yup. Good picture, huh?"

"Very good picture, yes. Boone, did you spend much time with Dorinda?"

"She came up here three times. I took her out on a horseback ride. She was a pistol. Whew-ee! She wanted me to take her on the most difficult trails. I obliged. We had fun and then went to dinner."

"What did she talk about at dinner?"

"You know, I think she was lonely because she never stopped talking about herself. Maybe that's because we'd been talking about me all day. She told me a little bit about her life back in New York. Oh, I remember one thing she talked about that might be of interest. She said that she was trying to decide who would be the subject of her next profile, and there was a guy who kept bugging her to write about him but she didn't want to."

"What did he do?"

"Something with Hawaiian clothing."

"What about Hawaiian clothing?" Regan asked quickly.

"He was designing them or something. But Dorinda felt he was too much of a capitalist. He had a lot of money, so it wasn't like he had to succeed at a second career in Hawaii. He never has to work again if he doesn't want to. So she didn't think he was a good candidate for the *Spirits in Paradise*. Neither did the editor of the magazine. But they liked old Boone!"

Regan couldn't believe it. Could Boone be talking about Jazzy's boss?

"It sounds like Dorinda opened up to you," Regan commented.

"I'm a good listener. I guess it's from all those years sitting around the campfire."

"Uh-huh." Regan quickly wound up the conversation. She promised to get up to the ranch for a little "giddyap" when she visited the Big Island, secured Boone's home and cell numbers, and hung up. She immediately dialed Will's direct line.

"Is Jazzy there?" she asked.

"No."

"I'm coming over. I really need to talk to you."

"I'll be waiting," Will said wearily. "I really need to talk to you."

31

Joy had rented a beach chair, slathered on suntan lotion, and parked herself on the sand close to the lifeguard stand, but not too close. Zeke was up there keeping an eye on the masses, and she enjoyed stealing a glance at him every few minutes. She knew that he was checking her out, too, but she pretended to be engrossed in her magazine.

I can't wait until tonight, she thought. Maybe we'll really click, and he'll ask me to move in with him. Then I can get out of Hudville. Now that I've won this vacation, there's nothing left worth staying for in that puddle-ridden boondocks. Since you can't win this junket twice, I'm never going back to any of those stupid Praise the Rain meetings. Joy couldn't believe that her parents didn't mind living there. Her mother believed Hudville was the perfect place to live if you wanted to avoid wrinkled skin. Better than Botox, she always told Joy. Joy had other ideas.

Bob and Betsy, wearing slacks and camouflage hats, walked past Joy down to the water's edge. Those two are so weird, she thought. Didn't they say they had to stay in today and write about their exciting relationship?

What a tour group. Joy shook her head. It's unbelievable. We have almost nothing in common. Gert and Ev leading Artie, Francie, Bob, Betsy, and me. The twins are the only ones who get to go to Hawaii every three months. What a waste. They never take advantage of what Hawaii has to offer. All they do is prance around the hotel in their muumuus and chaperone our meals. Tonight I'll have dinner with them and then take off. That's the only way to eat for free. They've been such penny-pinchers, encouraging us to lay off the appetizers. They even invited us to their room one night for cheese and crackers and cheap wine so they wouldn't have to pay for the expensive tropical cocktails that came from the blender. I don't think that's what our benefactor had in mind.

And that Francie. She drives me nuts asking about my love life every night. I don't want to talk about it with her. She's older than my mother! She confessed to me last night that she had a crush on Ned. Well, at least they're around the same age.

Joy watched as Betsy and Bob kicked water at each other. Bob looked as if he was really getting into it, almost in a mean way. I hope he falls over backward, Joy thought. She looked up at Zeke who had told her last night that he was a people person. Maybe I should go over and talk to them and let Zeke see that I love people, too. Joy hoisted herself out of the beach chair and, knowing full well that Zeke was watching, did her best sexy strut over to the water. Bob and Betsy had their backs to her, facing the sea. They didn't realize she was right behind them.

Joy could barely overhear what they were saying. Are they calling each other Bonnie and Clyde? she wondered. These two are definitely from the twilight zone.

"Hi." Joy announced her presence.

The two of them spun around. "Joy! What are you doing here?"

"I was sitting on the beach and saw you walk down to the water. What are you two doing here? You're not exactly dressed for the occasion."

"We're taking a break from our writing," Bob explained. "We wanted to get a little fresh air."

"Too bad you have to work when you're on vacation," Joy opined.

You're not kidding, Betsy thought.

"This book is going to help a lot of people," Bob

told Joy. "You are young and can't imagine that a relationship could get dull. But believe me, it can. We all need help."

Joy stole a quick glance at Zeke. He looked awesome. There was no way things would ever get dull with him. She was sure of that.

"Things can really get dull. Dull as dishwater," Betsy agreed wholeheartedly. "Have you talked to your mother since you've been here?"

"Yes."

"How is she?"

"Fine. She said it's raining."

"So what else is new?" Betsy sighed.

"What else is new is right," Joy echoed. I don't want to get stuck in Hudville and end up like these two, she thought. Their brains are waterlogged. "Well, I'm going to sit and relax. I'll see you tonight."

"Are we having drinks in Gert and Ev's room?" Bob asked.

"I hope not!" Joy cried.

"We have only a couple of days left. I thought I heard them saying something about using up the wine they bought."

"That jug was so huge, it'll never be used up. It's the least expensive swill you can get. I think they're cheating us."

"You do?" Betsy and Bob asked in unison.

"I do. A friend of mine who went on this trip three years ago got spending money and said his group was free to do as they pleased except for breakfast and a few dinners. With us, if you don't eat with the twins and if you don't want to pay for your own meals, you starve."

"Don't you like eating with the group?" Bob asked, sounding hurt.

"It's all right. But I wish I had more money to go off and do my own thing. I'm finishing school, so I don't have extra cash."

Bob pulled out his wallet, much to Betsy's horror. He produced three crisp twenty-dollar bills and offered them to Joy. "Go out and have some fun tonight."

"Nooooo. Thank you, but no."

"I insist."

Joy hesitated. Briefly. "Well, okay." Joy took the twenties, said her thanks, and walked up to the lifeguard stand.

"Hey there," Zeke greeted her. He was twirling the cord of his whistle around his finger.

"Hey. I'm buying drinks tonight," she cooed.

"Did that strange guy just give you money?"

"Yeah. He's from Hudville. He's an old guy, but he likes to flirt. He gave me cash because our tour directors are so cheap."

"Someone from the last Hudville group told me that."

"Who?" Joy asked quickly, afraid it was some girl she didn't know about.

"A guy I got friendly with when a bunch of us

went surfing out here. He mentioned that it was great to win the trip, but the group had nicknamed those two women the Scrimp Sisters."

"You're kidding! Why didn't you tell me that last night?"

"I wasn't thinking about the Scrimp Sisters last night," Zeke said softly. "I was only thinking about you. I'll see you later." He turned and stared out at the water, his whistle twirling and untwirling around his finger.

Joy walked on air back to her seat. Zeke really really seemed to care. She sat down, lay back, and closed her eyes. She made a decision. She was going to get everyone in the group together for a little powwow. Everyone except Gert and Ev. It wasn't right if they weren't getting the trip they deserved. Sal Hawkins had wanted them all to enjoy these trips. He wanted them to bring sunshine back to Hudville. Who can bring back sunshine when you feel as if you just spent a week in budget boot camp?

Joy was taking a workshop at college about being assertive and getting involved in causes. I'll make this my first cause, she decided. Joy versus the Scrimp Sisters. She couldn't possibly have guessed how dangerous it could be for anyone to go up against that dynamic duo.

32

"Okay, Will," Regan began. "Why don't you tell me what's really going on?"

"I don't know where to start."

"How about at the beginning? You know what they say?"

"No, what?"

"The truth shall set you free."

"I wish."

"Give it a shot."

They were in Will's office, the door was shut, and Janet had once again been ordered to hold all calls. If possible, Will looked worse than he had a couple of hours ago. He folded his hands as if in prayer. He is about to confess something, Regan thought.

"I didn't do anything wrong," he started to explain. "But things could look suspicious."

Something made Regan want to cover her ears.

"The night Dorinda Dawes died"—Will hesitated, looked at Regan as though he'd seen a ghost, and continued—"she came into my office just before she left the hotel. It was late because she'd been taking pictures at the parties and restaurants and bars. With the ball coming up, all the talk had been about the lei that was going to be auctioned off. I had told her I had an unusual shell lei at home that my mother and father bought in Hawaii years ago. She asked if she could take a picture of it for the newsletter she'd be writing about the ball. I brought the lei into work and gave it to her, then she left. That's the last time I saw her alive."

"The lei she was wearing when she was found dead was yours?" Regan asked in astonishment.

"Indeed."

"Your parents bought it in Hawaii how many years ago?"

"Thirty."

"It was stolen thirty years ago."

"I'm well aware of that now, but I swear I had no idea . . ." Will stared off into the distance, unable to complete his thought.

"Where did your parents buy it?"

"At the airport from a kid who had long second toes."

"What?"

"I spoke to my mother on the phone this morning. She said the kid was wearing sandals, and his second toes were much longer than his big toes. It was all she could focus on."

"A lot of people have unusual feet," Regan commented. "It's not the worst affliction in the world. It's better than having bunions. They're painful."

"Yes, but my mother said his second toes were unusually long."

"That kid, if he's still alive, is now thirty years older. Couldn't she remember anything else about him?"

"No. Wherever he is, I'm sure he looks different. But dollars to doughnuts his feet are still identifiable."

"So that kid may be the one who stole the lei?"

"Yup." Will sighed heavily. "Don't you see, Regan? I can't tell anyone that lei was in my family for the last thirty years. It makes me look bad for a lot of reasons."

"It sure does."

"Regan!"

"Sorry, Will. Although it might look suspicious that your parents had a lei that had been stolen from a museum, I'm sure they had no idea the lei was stolen when they bought it."

"Of course they didn't! They bought the lei, boarded the plane, and never looked back. My mother wore it at all the big occasions at home. She said it made her feel like a queen."

"She must have ESP."

"She's got something," Will agreed wearily. "But, Regan, this could all look very bad for me. Dorinda was wearing my lei—a stolen, valuable lei—when she died. That could place me at the scene of the crime."

"The police believe she accidentally drowned. Whether she was wearing your lei or not, they don't believe a crime was committed. But, Will, you are the one who wanted me to start investigating. Why? If you're worried about the finger being pointed at you, why didn't you just let the whole thing go?"

Will inhaled deeply. "When I handed the lei over to Dorinda, I immediately got a bad feeling. The lei had meant so much to my mother. I realized that it was probably not a good idea. Dorinda told me she was going straight home. I asked her if she could take the picture right away, and I'd pick up the lei on my way home. I still had a bit more work to do."

"What did she say?"

"That she'd go straight to her apartment. She was going to put the lei on a piece of dark felt on her kitchen table, set up the proper lighting, and take the picture. She suggested we have a glass of wine when I picked it up. I didn't want any part of that. I knew it wouldn't look good with my wife away. But I didn't want to leave the lei with her overnight, and once I had handed it to her, I felt foolish asking for it back. So I said maybe a quick nightcap. I knew I wouldn't be able to sleep if I let her keep the lei overnight."

Oh, boy, Regan thought.

"Dorinda was a bit of a flirt, and my wife couldn't stand her."

"Did your wife see the newsletter with her picture?"

"Not yet. In any case, I drove over to Dorinda's apartment after work and rang the bell. It was late, and she didn't answer. I waited in my car and tried to call her a few times, but she didn't pick up. Finally I went home. The next morning I come to work and her body washes ashore. And she's wearing that lei around her neck. I gave the lei to her in a special pouch and asked her to please be careful with it. The minute she walked out of here, she must have put the lei around her neck. But, Regan"—Will paused—"Dorinda intended to go straight home. She liked my company and knew I was coming over. She wouldn't have stopped to sit on the jetty that night. And now I keep thinking that someone might have seen me sitting outside her apartment on the night she died."

Regan sat there thoughtfully. "From everything I've heard about Dorinda, she was impulsive. Maybe she did just decide to go out on the jetty for a few minutes."

Will shook his head. "I just don't believe it. Someone must have lured her down to the water."

"She was wearing the lei. Maybe she decided to show it off to someone on the beach."

"Could be. But to whom? And did that person

intentionally hurt her? Will he or she harm some-one else? Regan, I don't want anyone to find out about my involvement in all this. But I do believe that someone killed Dorinda and should pay for it."

"You know, Will, in years past, supposedly she burned a lot of people. Even my mother was not happy with an article Dorinda wrote about her years ago. And that last newsletter . . ."

Will put his head in his hands.

"I heard that some guy who wanted Dorinda to interview him was bugging her. He designs Hawai-ian clothing. Do you know if that's Jazzy's boss?" Regan asked.

"Yes. Claude Mott. He wants to bring attention to his line of clothing and was pushing to get Dorinda to profile him, but she told me she didn't want to do it."

"Jazzy never mentioned this to me when she was telling me what a terrible person Dorinda was."

"That's Jazzy for you."

"I think I'd better have a chat with her. I'd also love to talk to Claude."

"He'll be here tonight in one of our best suites."

"Good. Another thing: I met a couple out at the bar at lunchtime. They're with a tour group from a place where it rains all the time."

"Oh, yes. The Praise the Rain Club."

"What?"

Will filled her in on the history of the club and the tours. "They've been coming for three years now."

"I want to keep an eye on this couple. They're very strange. I caught them coming out of the supplies closet. The guy insisted they were just grabbing some extra towels. But with what you say has been going on around here, I don't know."

"It's the first time that couple has stayed here. They may be strange, but they probably don't have anything to do with the troubles we've been having. But I'll be glad when that group is gone for good. The two women in charge have been badgering me to lower their room rates. I already have many times. I've decided I'm not making any more deals with them. If they want to come back, they'll have to pay a fair price. I already give them way too much attention and too many perks, and they're just not worth it."

Regan smiled. "Especially if their group members are stealing your towels."

Will chuckled and rubbed his eyes.

"When are your parents arriving?" Regan asked.

"Tomorrow."

"And your wife?"

"Tonight, thank God. It'll give me a little time to help her get used to the idea of their being here. And then the lei . . ."

Regan stood. "I'm going to see if Jazzy is around. I understand Dorinda's cousin is coming by later. Could you please call me when he gets here? I'd like to talk to him. Maybe he'll let me take a look at her apartment. There might be something there that will be helpful . . ."

"Okay."

"And don't worry, Will. You're doing the right thing. I would love to find that kid who sold the lei to your parents."

"They'll be here tomorrow. I'm sure my mother will be happy to describe his toes to you."

Regan smiled. "I can't wait to meet her."

"I think I inherited ESP from my mother," Will said, his face very serious. "I know it sounds crazy, but I have a very strong feeling that the person who killed Dorinda and the thief who stole the lei are among us."

"I'm doing my best to find them," Regan said as she walked out the door. The storm of the century in New York City would have been a lot easier to handle than this, she thought.

33

When Ned, Artie, and Francie returned to the hotel after their surfing expedition, Ned felt as if he was being propelled by a jet engine toward the Seashell Museum. He was desperate to see the lei that he had worn around his neck ever so briefly thirty years ago. And he wanted the lei to be his. He knew it would give him a feeling of power if he stole it again. He also knew that was kind of pathetic. He hadn't spent ten years in therapy for nothing, but he didn't care.

It was three o'clock when the van dropped them off at the hotel.

"Shall we get a bite to eat and then go to the beach?" Francie asked.

"I can't," Ned replied quickly.

"But I thought you said you were hungry," Francie protested.

"I am. But I'm going to take a shower and then check in at my boss's office. He loves you guys, but he might want me to pay attention to some of the other hotel guests. I'll have a drink with your group later."

Francie made a face. "Then maybe I'll go to the spa and see if I can get a lomi lomi massage and a seaweed wrap."

"I feel as if I just had a seaweed wrap," Artie commented. "Getting knocked over by a couple of those waves made me feel like I was one with the ocean."

"But you liked it, right?" Ned asked.

"I suppose," Artie agreed begrudgingly.

Back to his friendly old self, Ned thought.

The two of them walked to their room, and Ned jumped in the shower. Artie pulled a bottle of chilled water out of the mini bar and went out on the lanai. They had a nice view of the beach, and it was pleasant to sit and relax as the heat of the day and the strength of the sun started to fade. It was as though the world were mellowing out.

But not in the shower. Ned soaped up as fast as he could, rinsed his muscular body, and turned off the faucet. He grabbed a towel and dried off. Back in the room, he pulled a pair of shorts and a shirt from his drawer and quickly dressed. He slipped his feet into a pair of worn Top-Siders, glancing at

the pair of sandals he'd bought on a whim in one of
the hotel clothing stores. I should make myself
wear those, he thought. Who cares what people
think of my toes? But not now. He didn't want to be
conscious of his feet at a time like this, even
though it would be fitting. The last time he stole
the lei was the last day he ever wore sandals. For a
brief moment he considered that wearing the sandals might bring him luck.

But he decided against it.

And what am I thinking wearing these Top-
Siders? he mused as he kicked them off. I might
have to do some running. He picked a pair of socks
out of the drawer, sat down on the bed, and put
them on. He slid his feet into his sneakers. I could
use the PF Flyers I had when I was a kid, he
thought with a smile. He always loved their com-
mercials. Kids could run and fly and help people in
danger. Ned always thought of the ways he could
get into trouble if he could fly. And I blame that on
my childhood. I can't help it. Always being made
fun of doesn't exactly lay the groundwork for a
healthy, well-adjusted adult. But I've stayed out of
trouble these past few years. Now this lei! The
thought of it made him move faster.

He dashed over to the terrace door. "See you
later," he called to Artie.

Artie spun around. "Come down to the beach
when you're free. Francie's going to join me there
after her spa treatment."

"Yeah, sure," Ned said and waved his hand. He turned, grabbed a baseball cap and his empty knapsack out of the closet, and hurried out of the room before Artie tried to make any more plans. No two ways about it, Artie was a strange agent. His late-night walks on the beach. His constant flexing and unflexing of his hands. His total lack of savoir faire with women. Ned had seen him in the bar trying to make time with a couple of the ladies. No one was interested. When Dorinda Dawes took his picture, he tried to flirt with her. Even though she was a world-class flirt, she moved on quickly. First Bob had hit on her and then Artie. She must have had some opinion of the Lucky Seven. Poor Dorinda. To think we both started working here at the same time.

Ned walked out of the room and called information from his cell phone for the address of the Seashell Museum. He hadn't been there in a while. He bought a map in the store that sold newspapers, postcards, and travel guides, and pinpointed its location.

In the front of the hotel he jumped in a cab and gave an address several blocks from the museum. He didn't want any taxi driver saying he had brought a guy from the Waikiki Waters to the museum. They took off, drove for several miles, and finally stopped along a stretch of lonely road in front of the beach.

"This it?" the driver asked.

"Yes."

"Nothing much around here."

"I want to take a quiet walk."

After fifteen minutes of strolling along the sand, the museum was in sight. His pulse racing, Ned remembered the feeling he'd had thirty years ago. He had been a kid; now he was older, but it made no difference. He felt the same excitement, the same pounding in his heart. But everything was quiet. There was no one on the beach, and the museum was set off on its own. He wandered over, approached the steps to the museum, and noticed that off to the side there was a picnic table. A guy with a toga was sitting there facing the westward-moving sun, his back to the table. It looked as if he was meditating. His eyes were closed and his palms outstretched, facing up. Is that the guy who made such a stink about the robbery thirty years ago? Ned had seen him on TV the day after the theft. He seems to be wearing the same outfit, Ned thought.

As Ned got closer he could see the two historic shell leis lying on the table. He was astonished. There they were, just feet away. Do I dare? he wondered.

Of course. How could I not? So close and yet so far. He could always say he was only taking a look.

Ned crept over as quietly as he could. With his index fingers he picked up the leis just as the meditator opened his eyes, smiled contentedly, and started to turn around. Before he knew what hit him, the large man was shoved violently and fell headfirst onto the pavement.

The pain in the meditator's head was tremendous, but it was only when he pushed himself to his feet, turned around, and saw that the leis were missing that he began to scream. Jimmy's ungodly howls could be heard for miles.

34

Regan walked around the hotel and spotted Jazzy sipping coffee and going over papers in the coffee shop where Regan had eaten breakfast. She decided to go in and have a little chat with the queen of the gift bags.

"Mind if I join you?" Regan asked.

Jazzy looked up. She had reading glasses perched on the bridge of her nose and was looking very efficient. She tossed back her mane of blond hair and urged Regan to sit down. "Things are a little hectic getting ready for the ball. It's really going to be exciting."

Regan nodded and ordered a cup of tea from the waitress who had served her breakfast. "You're still here?" Regan asked.

"Another kid called in sick," Winnie noted matter-of-factly. "I guess the surf's pretty good today. Oh, well. If my feet hold out, I'll be fine. More money for my eventual retirement."

Regan smiled and turned to Jazzy. "I understand the ball is sold out."

"It's crazy and a little strange. People are intrigued by the auction. All the press about Dorinda and the antique lei has sparked a lot of interest in the whole evening."

"Here you go, honey." The waitress placed Regan's tea on the small table. "Drink it in good health."

"Thanks." Regan picked up the metal container of milk and poured in a few drops, added a touch of sugar, and stirred.

"How come you're not down on the beach?" Jazzy asked. "You're on vacation. Steve and Kit surely wouldn't mind having you join them."

"Oh, I know. Steve seems like a nice guy," Regan answered evasively.

"He is a nice guy. I'd get a little bored being retired at such a young age, though."

You've got to be kidding me, Regan thought. House-sitting on the Big Island for a rich guy isn't exactly like being part of the labor force.

As if Jazzy could read her thoughts, she continued, "I know I'm no longer working as a big-city lawyer, but that's okay. I like working for Claude. It's much less stressful than being an attorney. And getting his Hawaiian clothing business off the ground is really important to us."

Regan couldn't help but wonder what the "us" meant. Maybe that explains why Jazzy hadn't zoned in on Steve. She certainly is an operator. "This whole Dorinda thing," Regan said, "is so puzzling. I spoke to someone today who had been interviewed by her years ago and said that Dorinda really burned her."

"Was that your mother?" Jazzy asked coolly.

"My mother?"

"Your name is Regan Reilly," Jazzy said quickly. "Her name is Nora Regan Reilly. Even though you have dark hair, you look a lot like her."

"You're quite a sleuth, Jazzy."

"And so are you."

"Dorinda did interview my mother. She didn't exactly endear herself to her with the article, but my mother actually felt sorry for her."

Jazzy waved her hand at Regan. "She had her whole journalist act down pat. I'm telling you, she manipulated people. She was talking about interviewing Claude for the magazine *Spirits in Paradise*. Then she backed off. Then she thought she might. Then she said that she decided he was too rich, that he didn't need a second career out here because he had enough money to live no matter what happened. She wanted to focus on go-getters who had the courage to leave their safe jobs on the mainland and try to make it in Hawaii. Please! Claude would have been a wonderful interview subject. He had the courage to try something different. Just because he had been successful, it shouldn't be held against him. And the last thing Claude needs is to be embarrassed if his business flops. After all, doesn't everyone just love to see someone fail in a new career when they've been so very successful at something else?"

Not everyone, Regan thought. She raised her eyebrows and sipped her tea. Well, I guess she answered my question about her boss—and I do think their relationship runs a little deeper than just business. "Did Dorinda ever meet with Claude?"

"We had a big outdoor party at the house at Christmastime and invited her. This was when she said again that she was going to interview Claude. She was so nosy, it was unbelievable. She was snooping around everywhere." Jazzy laughed. "Inside and out. She was even wandering through our woods, taking pictures. I put glass marbles in Claude's medicine cabinet because I'd heard how meddling people can be at parties. Well, wouldn't you know, it was Dorinda who used the bathroom at the end of the hall in the master bedroom. She opened the cabinet, the marbles went rolling, and they broke all over the bathroom floor. I was nearby and got the broom. She claimed she had a headache and was looking for aspirin."

It sounds like Dorinda and Jazzy were birds of a feather, Regan thought.

"That's when I knew she was trouble," Jazzy continued. "You know how sometimes you just get an instant reaction to a person? And it's often right?"

"I sure do," Regan said. And my instant reaction to you was hardly positive. What kind of person puts glass marbles in their medicine cabinet that might potentially mortify one of their guests? The same kind of person who will write lousy things about people.

"I mean, she had a stolen lei around her neck. What does that tell you?" Jazzy asked.

"There could be a lot of explanations for that," Regan answered quietly.

"Which we probably will never hear. She took that secret to her grave." Jazzy looked down at her paperwork for a moment, then looked back up at Regan. "You and Kit will be at the ball, right?"

"Yes."

"I told Steve he should bid on the princess's lei for Kit. Wouldn't that be romantic?"

"I guess it would."

"He really seems to like her." Jazzy leaned in toward Regan as though she were about to divulge a big secret. "Let me tell you something: A lot of the ladies on this island are circling around him," she whispered. "He is a catch with a capital C. I'm surprised some girl hasn't nabbed him already. It makes me wonder what he's waiting for. Whoever lands that big fish is going to be one lucky girl."

Regan smiled. "And if he lands Kit, he'll be one lucky guy."

Jazzy threw back her head, laughed, and waved her hand. "Of course he will. In any case, we'll all have fun tomorrow night. I can't wait to see how much money that shell lei brings in at the auction. And if they auction off both—wow! This place will be in a frenzy!"

"I'm sure it'll be interesting," Regan agreed, wondering if there would be a moment of silence for Dorinda Dawes. Somehow she doubted it.

35

Ned stuffed the leis in his yellow nylon knapsack and ran as fast as he could from the grounds of the Seashell Museum. Everything happened in a blur. He never expected to see the leis sitting right there on the picnic table, and the second he spotted them, Ned knew there was no time to hesitate. He waved down a taxi and asked to be taken into the heart of Waikiki's shopping district. He didn't want anyone to trace him back to the Waikiki Waters, just as on the way out.

Luckily the cabdriver seemed oblivious. He was playing loud music and grunted when Ned gave him his destination. In the back of the car Ned's pulse was racing. He'd given that guy a shove when he started to turn around. Boy, could he scream.

You'd think after meditating it would have taken him a minute or two to get so worked up.

Ned got out of the cab on Kalakaua Avenue at the Royal Hawaiian Shopping Center in Waikiki and started to walk. He blended in easily with the Japanese and American tourists who were wandering in and out of the stylish shops. It was now four o'clock, and Ned's mind was racing. What am I going to do with these leis? he wondered. How can I bring them back to the hotel room? What if Artie sees them? I have to hide them somewhere until Artie and the tour group leave. Then I'll figure out a permanent spot for them.

Ned ducked into a stationery store and bought a box, sexy gift wrap depicting hula girls in action, adhesive tape, and a small pair of scissors. He went out and walked until he found an alley on a side street, which he ducked into and began to wrap his gift.

"How sweet," mumbled an old guy who walked by.

"You have no idea," Ned muttered as he secured the final pieces of tape. He put the box in a shopping bag and picked up his knapsack. He had inadvertently placed it in a damp patch of oil on the ground. The side of it was sticky and black. Ned threw it back on the ground, stood, and headed back to the Waikiki Waters.

As he walked down the crowded street, he regretted that he wouldn't have a chance to really look at the leis until Artie left. He didn't dare take them out in the room. He couldn't wait to examine the delicate shells. I'm sure I can find a buyer who will spend a lot on them, he thought.

The reception area of the Waikiki Waters was abuzz: Guests and hotel personnel were discussing the latest Waikiki news bulletin.

"Ned, did you hear what happened?" one of the bellmen asked him. Glenn was a young guy who had been on the job for a couple of years. He had a slightly Stepfordish look. Behind his back employees called him the "Will wannabe." He was a favorite of Will's and was clearly being groomed to move up the hotel ladder.

"No," Ned answered, holding tightly to his shopping bag.

"The royal leis for the Princess ball were stolen from the Seashell Museum. It's all over the news. Now there's nothing to auction off at the ball."

"You're kidding!" Ned exclaimed. "Poor Will. I know he's counting on the ball's being a big success."

"He's not a happy camper," Glenn admitted and shrugged as he glanced down at Ned's bag. "Wild wrapping paper."

"Huh?" Ned looked down. "Oh, yes."

"What have you got in there?" Glenn asked, still smiling.

"A friend of mine asked me to pick up a gag gift for her for a party she's going to. I told her I'd leave it at the bell desk. She should be by later today to pick it up. Can you take it for me?"

Glenn stared at Ned with his affable, yet slightly vacant look. "Sure. What's her name?"

"Donna Leggate."

"I just love gag gifts. What did you get for her?"

This guy is always so nosy and in the middle of everything, Ned thought with irritation. "Just some crazy toys," he answered offhandedly. "You know, juvenile stuff. It's her friend's bachelorette party, and she didn't have time to shop." Ned felt as if he was beginning to babble.

Glenn slapped him on the shoulder and grinned knowingly. "I'll be sure to take good care of your precious package. It sounds like something you don't want to lose! Oh, here's a customer." He took the bag out of Ned's hands, hurried over to a taxi that had just pulled in, and opened its back door to usher out two arriving guests who were wearing big floral leis.

"Welcome to the Waikiki Waters!" Glenn said cheerily. "We're so glad to have you stay with us!"

Ned turned on his heel and started to walk past the reception desk. Did I do the right thing? he wondered. Maybe I should have risked bringing the leis to the room. One of the girls at the desk called out to him. "Ned! Will wants to talk to you."

"Now?"

"Yes."

"Okay." He went behind the desk and through the door to Will's office.

Janet was at her post. She looked up and pointed with her thumb. "He's back there."

Ned walked through Will's door. Will waved to Ned to sit down, gestured to a chair, and hung up the phone.

"Ned, we've got trouble."

"I heard the leis were stolen."

"Even worse. My parents will be here tomorrow."

Ned laughed, relieved that they weren't going to be discussing the goodies in the bag that was now mixed in with all the suitcases going in and out of the Waikiki Waters hotel.

Will laughed, too. "I can't believe I'm even making a joke right now." It felt good for him to let go of at least some of the tension. All hell was breaking loose now that the leis were missing. But Will liked Ned. He seemed like a guy's guy. "My parents are arriving tomorrow morning. I know they'll be tired, but I know they won't stay in their room and rest. I need to keep them busy, or my mother will drive everyone crazy while we're trying to set up for the ball. Could you take them out on the beach for a couple of hours? Maybe take them for a sail tomorrow afternoon?"

"Sure, Will. No problem."

"How's everything with the Mixed Bag Tour group?"

"Okay. I took a couple of them surfing today. You probably want to know that Gert and Ev said they were going hotel shopping to see if they could find better deals."

Will waved both his hands in disgust. "Those two have been harping at me for the last year for bigger discounts. I've had it with them. I even have you sharing a room so they save money."

Ned rolled his eyes. "I know."

"You're a good sport, Ned. I won't do that to you again. At this point I say let them go someplace else. When they first came here, they spent money and enjoyed themselves. Now those two women are stingy with their group. I think they're leaving Monday—not a day too soon."

"The guy I'm sharing a room with is a very strange agent."

"That bad, huh?"

"And the couple in the group who are writing a chapter of a book on exciting relationships—they are not to be believed. And so dull! The young girl in the group had a few things to say at breakfast today about what's going on around the hotel."

"What?" Will asked quickly.

"She heard this place isn't safe and there's a rumor Dorinda Dawes may have been murdered."

"Those kinds of rumors can hurt us very badly. We have had a few problems around the hotel, but we're doing our best to make sure they don't happen again. As for Dorinda, the police believe that she drowned. So . . ." Will stood.

Ned jumped up. "You seem okay about the stolen leis."

"Very much to the contrary, Ned. If I got my hands on whoever took them, I think I'd strangle him."

Ned nodded. "I don't blame you. But who knows? They might turn up before tomorrow night. I'm looking forward to meeting your parents. Mr. and Mrs. Brown?"

"At this stage they like to be called by their first names. It makes them feel young."

"What are their names?"

"Bingsley and Almetta. Unforgettable, huh?"

Ned gulped. "You b-bet," he stammered. "Have they been to Hawaii before?"

"Many times since I've lived here. They fell in love with the place thirty years ago when they took their first trip to Oahu. They had such a great time, they've been coming back ever since."

"How wonderful. I'll do my best to keep them entertained."

"You've got your work cut out for you," Will joked. "My mother is a handful."

36

Local and national newspeople had all gathered at the Seashell Museum to interview Jimmy. He was in the museum lobby, holding an ice pack to his forehead, surrounded by cameras and microphones.

"Jimmy going to kill whoever stole my leis. Kill them!"

"What were you doing sitting outside like that with the leis?" a reporter asked.

"I was thanking God for bringing the queen's lei back to Jimmy. Then this happens! Now they're both gone."

"Do you have any idea who could have crept up behind you and then viciously shoved you to the ground?"

"No. If Jimmy knew, he'd be out looking for him

right now. But the miserable thief was strong. It takes a lot to knock Jimmy over."

"Can you identify him in any way?"

"Jimmy has been concentrating very hard. He saw a flash of yellow."

"Yellow what?" a reporter from the back of the crowd called.

"Yellow something. When Jimmy was shoved, he thought he saw something yellow fly by his face."

"That's all you remember?"

"What do you want from Jimmy? Jimmy could have been killed. It's something! Cops should figure out what to do!"

"Is there anything else you'd like to tell us, Jimmy?"

Jimmy looked straight into the camera. "Whoever did this will have very bad luck, especially if I get my hands on them. Those royal leis were stolen many years ago from the women who made them right before they were to be given to Queen Lili-uokalani and Princess Kaiulani. They found the thief and chased him into the ocean. Yesterday one of those royal leis was found around the neck of the lady who drowned at Waikiki Waters. To whoever took both my leis today, I hope the sea swallows you up! There is a curse on those leis!" He paused. "Jimmy needs an aspirin."

The reporters closed their notebooks, and the cameras were shut off.

"A flash of yellow," one of the reporters muttered. "This guy should be easy to find."

37

Jason and Carla were seated at a table by the window, across the room from the twins. Carla couldn't help looking over at the older women every two minutes.

"Relax and eat," Jason told her more than once.

"I can't. I'm so mad. They thumbed their noses at us and this beautiful ring." She held out her hand.

"Forget it!"

She tried to eat her ahi burger but didn't feel hungry. What was it about those two that was different today? She glanced over at them again. They were wearing beige slacks and long-sleeved beige shirts. Carla squinted her eyes and recalled seeing them at the hotel wearing garish muu-muus.

A waitress walked by and refilled their water glasses as Carla remained deep in thought.

"Carla," Jason said, "you're ignoring me."

"That's it!" she whispered to him. "Now I remember what I saw the other night when I took my walk on the beach."

"What?"

"Those women's muumuus were hanging over their railing. Their lanai is right on the beach. I remember seeing them and thinking that the hotel doesn't want people hanging things out to dry like that. It makes the place look like a flophouse. The muumuus were soaking wet!"

"So?"

"So that's the night Dorinda Dawes drowned. Maybe *they* killed her. How else does your muumuu get all wet like that?"

"How do you even know who the muumuus belonged to, Carla?"

"They were two big ugly muumuus! I know they were theirs. I was tipsy, but I remember thinking that I had seen them before. One was hot pink and the other purple, and otherwise they were identical. They practically glowed in the dark."

At the other table the twins called for their check.

"Get our check," Carla ordered Jason.

"Why? I'm not finished."

"I want to follow them and see what they're up to."

"What?"

"We have to. They could be murderers. It's our duty."

Jason rolled his eyes. "You're crazy," he muttered as he signaled their waiter. "There's no law against hanging your muumuu out to dry."

"No, there isn't," Carla agreed. "But I still think they're no good."

"I guess we'll find out." Jason sighed.

They certainly would.

38

Regan wandered down to the beach to look for Kit. She spotted Steve and Kit under a large umbrella near the edge of the ocean.

"We've been waiting for you, Regan," Steve announced as he jumped up. "We have a seat right here with your name on it!"

"Thanks." Regan plopped down and kicked off her sandals. It felt good to dig her toes into the warm sand. Kit and Steve were in bathing suits, and their hair was wet. It was after four, and already many of the sunbathers had retreated from the beach. Empty beach chairs dotted the sand.

"How's it going?" Kit asked.

"Fine."

"You're not a beach person?" Steve asked.

"I love to swim, but I can't sit in the sun for very long. No matter what I put on, I get burned," Regan explained.

Steve laughed. "There are a lot of different ways to get burned."

"I suppose," Regan answered. Their eyes met for a second, but he looked away quickly. Funny, Regan thought. All of a sudden he looks older than thirty-five. And last night he seemed much more wholesome. Right now he has the aura of someone who's been to one too many singles parties—slick and tired.

"Kit tells me your fiancé is head of the major case squad in New York City."

"Yes, he is."

"And you're a private investigator?"

"That's right."

Steve smiled. "No one can get away with much when the two of you are around."

"I can't wait to see what their kids are like," Kit said with a grin. "I'm the godmother of your first—right, Regan?"

"I'll be the godfather," Steve volunteered.

Kit looked at him with an expression of pure joy.

Oh, Kit, this guy is too smooth, Regan thought. He seems to be the type who promises too much too soon and doesn't mean a word of it. He had already given Kit the line that he couldn't believe they had so much in common. And Kit loved it! But Regan silently warned herself not to become one of those women who gets in a good relationship and then loses patience for their single friends' dating problems. "Let's see if we're lucky enough to even have kids," she answered.

"I want to have a houseful of children," Steve declared.

And I want to trust you, Steve, Regan thought. Don't make it so hard. Those classic lines you're feeding Kit are just too much. Regan had heard them all and much to her regret, had too often believed them. I should say a prayer right now thanking God for Jack. Regan watched as Steve reached over and patted Kit's knee. Kit smiled and reached out her hand. He clutched it for a moment and then brought it to his lips for a little kiss.

I feel a wave of nausea, Regan thought. This Romeo is getting phonier by the minute. Her cell phone rang. Saved by the bell. She reached for it in her bag and pulled it out. The caller ID had the Hawaii area code.

"Hello."

"Regan, it's Janet. We've got a problem. The leis were stolen from the museum, and Dorinda's cousin is on his way from the airport. He should be here in about fifteen minutes."

Regan stood. "Thank you. I'll call you right back." She closed her phone and turned to Kit and Steve. "I have some business to take care of."

"Dinner at my house tonight," Steve proclaimed. "We'll cook up some tuna and mahimahi, with a little Italian bread. It'll be great. Same group as last night."

I'd rather stick pins in my eyes, Regan thought. "Sounds wonderful," she said with a smile. "Kit, I'll see you back at the room later."

"I'm going to take off soon and go food shopping," Steve announced. "If you two don't mind taking a cab to my place, I'll of course get you home."

"Do you need help?" Kit asked.

"No," Steve answered quickly. When he saw the dejected look on Kit's face, he added, "You girls have a little time together. My buddies are back at the house. They'll help me get the dinner ready."

"I have to get back to this caller," Regan explained. "Kit, I'll see you by six at the latest." She turned and headed toward the hotel. She couldn't believe that both leis were stolen. Dying to hear how it happened, Regan rushed to Will's office.

Janet was sitting at her desk, glasses perched on her nose, phone to her ear. A little television was on in the corner of the office. The station was replaying Jimmy's press conference.

"Can you imagine?" Janet asked.

"No," Regan answered as she listened to Jimmy threaten the thief. "How could this have happened so fast?"

"I'll tell you one thing," Janet said when Jimmy was finished. "I think he's right. There must be some kind of curse on those leis. They're certainly creating chaos with our ball."

"Someone just walked up behind Jimmy and stole the leis?" Regan asked.

"Just like that."

"And the only lead is that the thief may have been wearing or carrying something yellow?"

"That's all Jimmy remembers."

"Is Will inside?"

"He's just finishing up with someone."

Just then the door to his office opened. "Hi, Regan," Will said. "Say hello to Ned. He works here at the hotel, helping people get in shape."

"I could use a little exercise," Regan joked as she reached out her hand.

Ned shook Regan's hand firmly, so firmly that she had to resist the impulse to massage her thoroughly squeezed palm. He's a strong, athletic-looking guy, Regan noticed. I guess he can't help himself. Though he does seem a little distracted and fidgety.

"Nice to meet you. Talk to you later, Will," he said and was gone.

"He's a big help," Will explained as he shut the door. "I've had him spending time with that tour group we were talking about before. He's been great with them. He has a lot of patience."

He didn't strike me as the patient type, Regan thought as she sat in what by now felt like her chair. "Will, what happened to the leis?"

"Janet told you they were stolen."

"I just saw the press conference. I can't believe it. What is with those leis? It's as if they're taking on a life of their own."

"And just when my parents are coming to town. With my luck someone will offer to sell them to my mother again."

"What effect will this have on the ball?"

"It's hard to say. The fund-raising committee is trying to figure out what else they can auction off that will get people excited. People have already paid for their tickets. We have to make sure they don't try to cancel."

"No matter what, you're getting a lot of publicity."

"If I live through this weekend, it'll be a miracle."

The buzzer on Will's desk rang. Janet informed him that Dorinda's cousin had arrived.

"This should be interesting," Will commented with a raised eyebrow as he got up from his desk and walked over to open the door.

Regan turned and was shocked at the sight of Dorinda's closest kinfolk. Maybe because he lived in Venice Beach, California, she expected a young muscular skateboarder. But this guy was about seventy and had brownish-red shoe polish hair. He was wearing a loud print shirt, tan pants held up by a white patent leather belt, and white patent leather shoes. His bushy eyebrows and sideburns looked as if he'd made an attempt to match them

with the shade of his hair but hadn't quite succeeded. He was medium height and medium build
with a protruding stomach that struck Regan as
the steering wheel for his body. But he seemed an
affable sort as he put down his carry-on bag on the
floor and greeted them.

"So pleased to meet you," he boomed to Will.
"I'm the cousin."

The cousin? Regan thought. That's a good one.
The cousin of the deceased.

Will introduced himself and Regan.

"Hello, Regan," he boomed. "I'm telling you
traveling these days is getting tougher and
tougher. The lines at the airports are just terrible.
I need to sit down."

"Please." Will quickly indicated the other chair
in front of his desk. "Your name is?"

"Oh, yes. Well I'm a Dawes. Dorinda's father
and my father were brothers. Dorinda's father got
married much later in life. They said they never
thought Uncle Gaggy would tie the knot, but he finally did. That's why there was a little bit of an age
difference between me and Dorie."

Uncle Gaggy? Dorie? And I'd say there was
more than a little bit of an age difference. Your last
name is Dawes. And your first name? Regan wondered.

The cousin sat down and crossed his legs,
extending his left leg. The pointy toe of his shoe
was inches from Regan's thigh.

"Can I get you anything?" Will asked.

"I'm telling you I could use a mai tai. But right now I'll settle for a cup of that coffee you have over there." He pointed to the pot on a side counter. "Is it that fancy Hawaiian coffee that Dorinda liked? She had champagne tastes I'm telling you."

Will jumped up and poured a cup. "Dorinda did like this Kona coffee," he mumbled.

"Thank you," the cousin said as he stirred his coffee and added three sugars. He cleared his throat. "Now as I was saying, Uncle Gaggy married later in life. Dorinda's mother was no spring chicken, either. They had one child, Dorinda. Her parents have been dead about ten years. I was an only child as well. But we didn't grow up together. My parents have passed on and I'm Dorie's only relative, but she didn't seem that interested in getting together much. We spoke occasionally." He paused to take a sip.

My God, Regan thought. I never met Dorinda, but from what I gather she wouldn't have found you to be her speed. And you were her only relative. I'm sure she wouldn't have introduced you to her friends because she wanted to project a more chic image. Regan was about to ask him a question when he started talking again.

"That's good coffee. Hawaii produces good coffee," he pronounced, then started to laugh and slap his knee. "I still haven't told you my name. I'm Gus Dawes."

Regan smiled. "It's good to finally know your name, Gus."

"Now I don't mean to be rude, but who are you?" he asked as he wiped his mouth with the paper napkin Will had offered him.

Regan looked at Will and decided to let him answer the question. She didn't know how much Will wanted to tell Dorinda's only relative about his suspicions relating to her death. She needn't have worried.

"Regan is a private investigator who is staying at the hotel. I met her the other day and asked her to look into Dorinda's death," Will stated.

Gus uncrossed his leg, much to Regan's relief, and crossed the other one. At least there's no one sitting in the direction of his other shoe, she thought. Gus leaned forward and grabbed the sole of his left loafer. "I'm not surprised. With that acid pen of hers, I wouldn't be surprised if a lot of people wanted to kill her!" He chuckled. "Even when she was a kid, she was a brat," he reminisced. "I remember being at a family party. She had her little camera and was going around taking pictures of people's behinds." He started laughing, then coughing, then gained control of himself. "She enjoyed making people look stupid."

Clearly he's not grief stricken, Regan decided. Will's expression, she realized, was one of horror. He's probably wondering why he ever hired her.

"I think that's a good idea to check out her

death," Gus continued. "I've also been thinking about that lei she had around her neck. She always managed to get herself into trouble."

"That lei has been stolen again," Will informed him and gave the details of what he knew.

Gus slapped Will's desk. "You're kidding! Well, I'll tell you."

"When's the last time you saw Dorinda?" Regan asked.

"Three or four years ago."

"You live in California?" Regan asked.

"Yes. I love the sun. It's wonderful."

"Do you have any other family?" Regan asked.

"A few distant cousins on my mother's side, but they're strange."

"How long are you planning to stay in Hawaii?" Will asked.

"I figured as long as I'm making the trip and have a place to stay, I may as well make the most of it. I figure about ten days. I want to see the Dole plantation and do some sightseeing. Hey, I hear that a few months back thousands of pounds of bananas were stolen from a farm up north. I hope those thieves acted fast. After a couple of days what are you going to do with them? They start to smell and they attract flies." His eyes crinkled as he laughed. "I say they should check and see if there's a cereal convention going on around here. That's the most likely spot for all those bananas!"

Will smiled trying to be polite. "So you will clear

Dorinda's things out of the apartment when you leave?"

"Oh, yes. I spoke to the woman at her apartment in New York. She has Dorinda's apartment for a few more months. Then I'll take a trip to New York and clear things up there. It's a good thing I love to travel. It's good to get away. Who knows? Maybe I'll stay here until Dorie's lease is up."

"Gus," Regan began, "I was wondering if I could go with you to Dorinda's apartment. I want to see if there's anything there that might be helpful in figuring out what might have happened . . ."

"Be my guest," Gus said. "I was told I could get a set of keys from the superintendent. Do you want to come with me now? Because, let me tell you, once I get in that bed and fall asleep, I'll be out for twelve hours. But tomorrow I'll be ready to rock and roll." He turned to Will. "I see you're having a big ball tomorrow night. Any chance I could get a ticket? I love to party."

"I'm sure we could arrange that," Will said.

"Grand! Let's go, Regan. I'm dying to get out of these clothes."

Will looked at Regan and smiled.

"I'm ready," Regan said, winking at Will. Wait till Jack hears about this, she thought.

39

Ned went back to his room, not quite believing that the people he had sold the lei to thirty years ago could be Will's parents. How is it possible? he wondered. But how many other people could be called Bingsley and Almetta? It was thirty years ago, and I still remember being surprised by their names. And he remembered how intently Almetta had stared at his feet. Maybe she had forgotten. Not that it mattered. He had no intention of exposing his feet to them even though Will wanted him to take them swimming and boating tomorrow.

When he got to the room, he was grateful that Artie was nowhere in sight. He flipped on the TV. A reporter was talking about the theft of the shell leis.

"In broad daylight a brazen criminal went up and grabbed them off the picnic table outside the Seashell Museum, but not before brutally shoving the owner to the ground. . . ."

"It wasn't that hard," Ned protested to the television.

". . . The owner did not get a look at his assailant but says he's sure he saw a flash of some sort of yellow. It's not a lot to go on, but the police are determined to track down and put the coward who perpetrated this horrendous act behind bars."

Ned went white. My yellow knapsack. I left it in the alleyway. Did it have anything in it that would identify me? He raced out of the room and, too impatient to wait for the elevator, took the stairs to the main floor two at a time, and once again jumped into a cab. I can't get caught, he thought. No matter what, I can't get caught.

40

Will arranged for a driver from the hotel to take Regan and Gus to Dorinda's apartment. It was located several blocks from the beach in a two-story pink building with a small parking lot right in front.

"Not exactly glamorous," Gus declared when the car stopped, "but the price is right."

This guy is classic, Regan thought. He's about to enter the apartment where his dead cousin has been living for the past couple of months, and all he's thinking about is that he can stay for free. The driver offered to help with Gus's bag, but Gus had a suitcase with wheels and seemed pleased to cart it himself. He rang the super's bell and identified himself as, once again, the cousin.

The super handed over the keys and shut the door.

"She lived on the second floor," Gus proclaimed cheerfully.

There was no elevator, so he lifted his suitcase, and Regan followed him up the steps. On the second-floor landing Gus turned and announced, "Here we are!" He unlocked the door to 2B and pushed it open. He reached for the light switch and flicked it on. A small but cozy living room lay in front of them. Straight ahead a round dining-room table was pushed up against a bay window. The table was covered with papers. A desk against the wall was also overflowing with clutter. Photographic equipment was scattered around.

"From the way it looked out front, I expected worse," Gus declared, "but this place is kind of cute."

"It is," Regan agreed, wondering if the bright blue couch was a Bernadette Castro special. A multicolored area rug, two beige overstuffed chairs, and a coffee table filled with Hawaiian knickknacks filled the room. Framed prints of various sunsets covered the walls. Regan glanced briefly in the bedroom, which was tiny. The bed was made, but some clothes were thrown on a chair. In the bathroom, toiletries filled the shelves. A compact kitchen was located just off the dining area. The place was clean but messy. Dorinda had clearly made her mark.

Gus walked around. "I have to say it is a little depressing to think that Dorinda is dead. Now that

I see her things, I wish we'd seen each other a little more."

"I can understand. I'm sorry." Regan walked over to the desk and looked at the framed pictures. One was a group shot obviously taken at a party. A beaming Dorinda was gazing up with adoring eyes at a tall guy in a tuxedo. Regan picked it up, inspected it closely, and was shocked to realize that the guy Dorinda was gazing up at was Steve! I can't believe it, she thought. She looks like she's in love with him.

"No family photos," Gus commented as he looked around. "Well, everyone except me is dead, and Dorie was hardly the sentimental type."

"You don't mind if I go through a few of the things on her desk?" Regan asked.

"It's all the same time to me. I'll bring my suitcase into the bedroom and start to get settled. I'm going to need to lay down soon."

"I won't be long."

"Take your time," Gus practically ordered in his booming voice. He took out his handkerchief and heartily blew his nose. "I get so stuffed up on planes," he commented. He waved his handkerchief around and then crammed it back in his pocket.

He must have driven Dorinda nuts, Regan mused. She turned and picked up the photo once again and looked at Steve and Dorinda. He obviously knew Dorinda but hadn't said much about her. Regan sat down and sorted through the papers that were all over the desktop. There were scribblings on various sheets of paper. Notes to do errands and take pictures. She pulled open the top drawer where she expected to find a jumble of pens and paper clips. Instead there was a lone tan file marked PROSPECTIVE DIRT. Regan's heart skipped a beat. She opened it. The first thing she saw was a last will and testament of someone named Sal Hawkins.

Who's that? Regan wondered as she started to read.

"I, Sal Hawkins, being of sound mind and body, do hereby leave all my earthly possessions, including cash and the proceeds from the sale of my house, to the Praise the Rain Club for future trips to Hawaii."

That's the group at the hotel, Regan realized as she read on. He'd left two sisters in charge of the money with instructions to lead five others to Hawaii every three months. Sal Hawkins had left an estate valued at $10 million. That should cover a lot of trips to Hawaii, Regan imagined. She looked at the date of the will. It was only four years ago. If he died soon after, there should be money for trips for years to come. But Will had been talking about how cheap the tour organizers were.

Regan found a blank piece of paper and took a few notes. She looked through the rest of the file and almost missed another picture of Steve, this time by himself. She turned the photo over. The caption read, "Retired from WHAT?" Oh, boy, she thought. What's this all about? He was standing in a bar smiling at the camera. Regan wasn't sure whether it was a bar at the Waikiki Waters or not. So what's the prospective dirt on him? A newspaper clipping about Claude Mott Enterprises was also in the file. It was one paragraph long and said that he was attempting to launch a line of leisure clothing. Stapled to the back of the article was a picture of Jazzy.

Well, Regan thought, she really seems to have zoned in on that group. But why? Did Steve spurn her advances? Regan could certainly understand why Dorinda and Jazzy wouldn't have gotten along; they were too much alike. And what about this tour group?

"How are you doing, Regan? Did you find anything interesting about my cousin?" Gus reentered the room. He was drying his face with a hand towel. "It feels so good to freshen up. I can't wait to get a swim tomorrow. Now that will really feel good."

"There are a few things here, Gus. Do you mind if I take this file with me?"

"Go ahead. It looks like it's going to be some job sorting through Dorinda's things. I'll probably give most of it away to whatever Hawaii's version of Goodwill is."

"I know you want to rest, so I'll get out of your

way. If you don't mind, I might give you a call tomorrow."

"I'd be delighted. And I'll see you at the ball tomorrow night, right?"

"I suppose so."

"Marvelous. Shall I call you a cab?"

"I'll head out and start walking. I could use the exercise. I'm sure I'll be able to hail one on the street."

"Be careful out there, Regan. This doesn't appear to be the best part of town."

"I'll be fine."

Two minutes later Regan was out on the street. She walked toward the beach and decided to take the route to the Waikiki Waters that she had been told Dorinda had taken many times. The route Dorinda was supposedly taking a couple of nights ago, the night she didn't make it home.

As Regan walked, she wondered at what point Dorinda had steered from this path. When Regan approached the jetty, she stared out at the rocks. A couple, hand in hand, emerged from the base down at the very end, out by the water. They started walking slowly back toward the beach. Oh, Dorinda, Regan thought. Was this where you met your fate? Regan shrugged. I'm afraid it's something we might never know.

41

" I just got out of a relationship," Francie declared to Artie as the two of them meandered along the beach. "He always had me on the back burner. I don't think of myself as back burner material, you know?"

"Sure," Artie answered absentmindedly. He was thinking about the way Ned had run out of the room today. All of a sudden Ned seemed to have something important on his mind, and it was obviously distracting him.

"I'd really like to meet a guy," Francie admitted. "And I'm sick of being hit on by men who just want a little fun on the side. If you can believe it, that Bob tried to put the moves on me the other night. Can you stand it? His wife had gone to bed, and he's writing the chapter in the book about how to keep a relationship exciting. If his wife catches him, it will really be exciting. She'll throw a vase at his head."

"He made a pass at you?" Artie asked.

"I'd have to say yes. He said that his wife was really boring and wished he could have a little extra fun in Hawaii."

"What did you say?"

"Dorinda Dawes came up behind us and snapped our picture. Bob got upset. End of conversation."

"And now she's dead."

Francie stopped in her tracks and grabbed Artie's arm. "Do you think there's a connection?"

Artie shrugged. "You never know."

"The Mixed Bag Tour group would never be the same."

"Who cares?" Artie answered as he picked up a stone and threw it into the water. "Gert and Ev are nothing but two big cheapskates. It's hardly fun. Can you believe that I have to share a room with Ned?"

"He seems nice," Francie said coyly.

"You like him, don't you?"

"Well, at least he's the right age. But it doesn't matter. We're leaving in a couple of days anyway."

Joy was approaching them from the opposite direction. She was jogging.

"Here she comes," Artie grunted. "Little miss lifeguard chaser."

"She's just a kid," Francie said. "I wish I were her age again. Sometimes."

Huffing and puffing, Joy ran toward them. She finally stopped a few feet from them and struggled to catch her breath. "Gert and Ev called my cell phone," she said. "They're not going to make it back for cocktails or dinner."

"They're not? How many hotels could they be looking at?" Francie asked.

"I don't know. They never let me ask questions." Joy wiped her brow with her hand. "They said the five of us should go to dinner together in any of the restaurants here at the hotel and sign it to their room."

"Let's all order caviar and champagne," Artie suggested, "and then move on to prime rib and lobster."

"Did you tell Bob and Betsy?" Francie asked.

"I called their room, but there's no answer. I left them a message."

"It's so unlike Gert and Ev not to be here breathing down our necks and watching everything we order," Artie commented. "Something's up with them."

"Let's make the most of it," Francie cried gleefully. "We'll eat, drink, and spend money."

"When are our fearless leaders going to be back?" Artie asked.

"Later tonight. They plan to be on the morning beach walk tomorrow."

"You know, it seems that everyone is going to the ball except us," Francie noted. "I think we should order tickets for the group and charge them to their room, too."

"They're sold out," Joy declared. "I don't want to go anyway."

"Well, I do," Francie said. "They're going to have hula dancers, two bands, dinner, and dancing. I don't want to just sit through another boring group dinner. I feel like Cinderella." She turned to Artie. "What do you think?"

"If I don't have to pay for it, I'll go."

"Well, you don't," Francie said with conviction. "I'm sure Sal Hawkins would have wanted us to have some fun. Let's go to the manager's office and see if we can order tickets. Joy, you're sure you don't want us to get one for you?"

"Positive."

"What about our exciting couple?" Artie asked.

"Let them fend for themselves. We'll get tickets for you and me."

"I can't wait to see the expressions on Gert and Ev's faces when they find out you charged expensive tickets to their room," Joy said mischievously.

"I don't care," Francie declared. "Artie, let's go. Joy, how about if we meet at the pool at seven for cocktails and then we'll go eat?"

"Fine."

"Where could Gert and Ev possibly be?" Artie asked as he and Francie headed for the reception area.

Francie laughed. "Maybe they got lucky."

42

"Why did you have to follow us?" Ev asked Jason and Carla. "Why? You should have known that that was a very bad idea."

Jason and Carla were tied up in the basement of Gert and Ev's newly built, nearly finished home on the Big Island. The smell of sawdust was still in the air. The house was up in the hills, twelve hundred feet above sea level, nestled in a rural wooded section of the island. Gert and Ev planned to move in lock, stock, and barrel by early summer. They figured they'd have lots of privacy on their six-acre lot. The next-door neighbor could only be reached by taking an overgrown path through the woods. But Gert and Ev could stand on their deck and see the Pacific Ocean way off in the distance. They had a large swimming pool and a hot tub for cold mornings in the mountains. It was their dream home purchased with Sal Hawkins's money that should have been spent on waterlogged Hudville residents.

"You couldn't mind your own business, could you?" Gert asked. "You followed us out of the restaurant and thought you were being sneaky. Or did you just happen to come up this way? Our long, winding driveway is not exactly a busy thoroughfare."

"You were so rude to us at the airport," Carla snapped.

"Since when is being rude a crime?" Ev retorted. "Gert, did you know being rude is a crime?"

"No, sister. I certainly didn't."

"Then what crime *did* you commit?" Carla asked with more bravado than she felt. "Just because we drove up your driveway, you don't have to hold us against our will. You could have just told us to get lost."

"You were getting into our business," Ev declared. "And now you've made us miss our flight back to Oahu. We're not happy about that."

"I hate missing my dinner," Gert said as she blew on the pistol she had in her hands. The sight of the pistol was the only reason Jason did as he was told.

"Let us go," Jason implored. "Let's just forget we ever ran into you."

Ev shook her head. "I don't think so. We know that you'll go and tell everyone about our hideaway. Right, Gert?"

"Sure enough, sister."

"Then what are you going to do with us?" Carla asked, practically choking on her words.

"We have to figure that out. But I don't anticipate a very pleasant outcome for you. Gert and I have a lot to look forward to, and we don't want anyone to ruin our plans."

"So do we," Carla cried. "We just got engaged. I want to get married!"

"Gert can marry you. She's an online minister."

"I'd rather die!" Carla spat.

"Maybe you will, my dear," Ev answered. "Let's go, sister. We have to see if we can get a later flight back to Oahu. We have to be there first thing in the morning or else our tour group will start to wonder."

"Are you just going to leave us here?" Jason asked. His hands were tied behind his back, and they ached. Ev had tied them so tightly, his circulation was being cut off.

"We'll be back to take care of you tomorrow night when it's dark and no one is around. But first we have to make sure you don't try to make too much noise." Ev pulled some torn sheets from a bag on the floor. "Here, sister." She nodded to Gert.

Quickly the two of them tied gags around Carla and Jason's mouths.

Gert pointed the gun at the couple. "Don't try anything funny. You'll be sorry if you do." She turned, followed her twin up the steps, and flicked off the light.

43

Glenn the bellman took a quick break shortly after Ned had handed over the shopping bag. He went into a tiny staff lavatory off the package room where they stored all the suitcases, packages, surfboards, and golf clubs that were waiting to be delivered to guests' rooms. It was a Friday afternoon, large groups of people were checking in, and it was a madhouse. Glenn was sure he could slip away for a couple of minutes and not be noticed since there were several other bellmen on duty.

The bathroom rated high on the gross-out scale. In fact, gas station latrines were more inviting.

But Glenn didn't care. He'd chosen it because of that. He knew that he'd have more privacy here. Girls wouldn't come within ten feet of this place, and even the guys preferred to use the decent bathrooms down the hall from the bell station, as opposed to this little box that had somehow escaped the renovation process. It also seemed to have escaped attention from any maid for the last twenty years.

Glenn's conversation with Ned had sparked his curiosity. Ned had seemed nervous. What exactly was in the box? What kind of toys was he talking about? It looked like a pretty sloppy wrapping job. He was sure that he could take a peek at the box's contents, reseal it, and leave it for Ned's friend to pick up.

He locked the door and flicked the seat cover down on the toilet. It landed with a bang. He sat down and pulled the box out of the shopping bag. The hula girls on the wrapping paper were smiling at him, as if they knew what he was up to. Glenn shook the box. It rattled.

A piece of tape had become unstuck, and the wrapping paper that had covered a side of the box spread open. Glenn laughed. "This is too easy."

Glenn was something of an expert at fishing around people's bags and packages, and at slithering in and out of rooms at the hotel. He was able to appear and disappear without people taking much notice, and if they did, he could say he was doing something for Will. He had really pulled the wool over Will's eyes and used it to his great advantage. Will thought that he was Glenn's mentor. Huh! I could mentor him on a few things, Glenn thought.

Glenn rested the box on his knees. Carefully he pulled another piece of tape off the wrapping paper, trying not to destroy the image of the hula girl. He slid the box out and dropped the paper in the shopping bag. He lifted the top off the box and placed that in the shopping bag as well. He then turned his full attention to the contents of the box. He couldn't believe his eyes! There were no toys inside. Glenn slowly lifted two exquisite shell leis into the air.

"Oh, my God!" he whispered. "These are the stolen royal leis. I can't believe what a liar Ned is!" He unhooked his cell phone from his belt and made a call. "You are not going to believe what I have in my hands!" Quickly he recounted his story. Then he listened. "Yes! That's a wonderful idea. Better than anything we've done so far! Don't worry. I'll take care of it."

Glenn turned off his cell phone, returned it to his belt, wrapped up the now empty box, and placed the leis at the bottom of the shopping bag. He returned to the storage room, found another shopping bag, and slipped the leis into it. He scooted out to the garage and placed both bags in the trunk of his Honda. Then he hurried to one of the hotel shops where he knew they sold newspapers, magazines, and cheap shell leis. He purchased two of the leis, went back to his car, put the new leis inside the box, and resealed the wrapping paper. He left the valuable leis in his trunk. Then he returned to the bell station, slid the shopping bag Ned gave him under the counter, and told the captain that it would be picked up by a friend of Ned's, one of the hotel's trainers.

Glenn couldn't wait until his dinner break. It wouldn't be long. Then he'd get a chance to have a little fun with the royal leis. Let Will try to explain this one, he thought gleefully. Just another day at the Waikiki Waters Playground and Resort.

44

Regan decided to stop on the beach for a few minutes before going back to the room. She sat on the sand, pulled out her cell phone, and called Jack. Quickly she filled him in on what she had found in Dorinda's apartment, as well as the fact that the leis had been stolen again.

"Stolen again? What's going on out there, Regan?"

"That's what I'm trying to figure out. And I've got to tell you, this guy Kit has hooked up with seemed iffy, but then to see his picture in Dorinda's 'Prospective Dirt' file is really disturbing. On the back of the photo, Dorinda wrote, 'Retired from WHAT?' "

"What's his name again?"

"Steve Yardley."

"I'll run a check on him. Maybe you should try to get his fingerprints on something."

"They're all over Kit."

"He's really putting on the moves, huh?"

"I'm afraid so. And Kit is falling for it. Maybe he's all right, but now I just don't trust him. We're invited to his house for dinner tonight. Don't you think trying to get his fingerprints is a little extreme?"

"Nah. See if you can nab something small with his prints. I'll ask Mike Darnell to process them. Then I can find out if he has a criminal record. It's not a big deal to check him out."

"I feel a little guilty," Regan admitted. "Kit really likes this guy. He might be just fine, but my gut tells me he isn't. I may be paranoid but seeing him in Dorinda's file . . ."

"You remember what happened with Kit's last suitor," Jack reminded her. "He wasn't a criminal, but he was a liar. You didn't go with your gut then because Kit's your friend, and she ended up getting hurt. You obviously won't tell her your suspicions. If this guy checks out, then all the better. We'll be relieved, and Kit will never know."

"Okay. If Steve weren't in Dorinda's dirt file, I might let it go, but there he is along with a few of the other suspicious characters around here. Maybe I'll give Mike a call later and ask him if they have any leads about the leis. That's not my problem, but Will, the hotel manager, is worried that they have nothing interesting to auction off at the Princess ball. There's no hook for the event, so to speak."

"I'll just be glad when you're back," Jack said. "And when we're on our honeymoon, I'm not going to let you take on any cases."

"As if." Regan laughed. "If I can help Will out at least a little bit, I'll be happy. If the ball is a success, then that will be good for him. And if I can find any leads about how Dorinda ended up in the water the other night, then that's all to the good. But I don't see how I can do that and figure out the source of the problems at the hotel in just a couple of days."

Jack, who always was so calm, reassured her— "Regan, I know that no matter what, you'll end up helping Will. I'm sure he feels better just having you around. I know I always do."

"And I feel much better when you're around." Regan smiled. "Oh, Jack, you'd get such a kick out of Dorinda's cousin. He's a trip. I can't believe he's her only living relative. Even though she had a bad rep in a lot of ways, I'm sure one thing she never worried about was embarrassing her family."

"Are you going to see him again?"

"He managed to score a free ticket for the ball tomorrow night."

"Well, don't be too much of a princess at that ball. I don't want some guy sweeping you off into the night."

"If there's anything that I'm sure of in this world, it's that that won't happen." When she hung up, Regan looked at her watch. It was 5:15. The beach was peaceful, mellow, and nearly empty. I think I'll pay a quick visit to Will, she decided. Then it's off to dinner at Steve's with Kit.

Somehow she had no appetite.

45

At 5:15, Glenn went on his dinner break. As he left the lobby area, he saw Will standing and talking to the concierge. They looked as if they were deep in discussion. I've got to make this quick, Glenn thought. He quickly headed to his car, took the bag with the leis out of the trunk, and snapped it shut.

He hurried out of the garage and up onto the circular driveway where the cars pulled in and out of the reception area. His destination was Will's office. He planned to gain access through the sliding glass doors that looked out onto a small garden of lush tropical vegetation. It was an isolated area that you could only get to from the main path where hotel guests strolled to the shops and different towers. The solid brick wall of the ladies' clothing store was right across the little garden. If I can just slip into that area without being seen, he thought, then I can be in and out fast.

Once on the main path, Glenn ducked into the narrow grassy area that led to Will's own private little garden. He was sure no one had seen him. He stayed close to the building, and when he reached the door, he hid behind a shrub and took a quick peek into Will's office. There was no one there. The screen of the sliding glass door was closed. Glenn inched forward and quickly pulled on it. The screen door slid open easily. Glenn took the leis out of the bag and placed them on the floor so they couldn't possibly be missed. He then turned and dashed off. When he was in the clear, he called his contact and told them to call the police.

Within minutes, the police received an anonymous tip that the stolen leis from the Seashell Museum were in Will Brown's office at the Waikiki Waters Playground and Resort.

46

"Will, there you are," Regan said as she approached the concierge's desk.

"Hi, Regan. This is Otis, our concierge. He tells me that people are still looking for tickets to the ball."

"That's good news. It's nice to meet you, Otis."

Otis had a thin mustache and seemed very efficient. His expression indicated that he was overly pleased with himself. "You, too," he said to Regan almost dismissively. "Mr. Brown, I am doing my best to accommodate everyone. But a couple of people from the tour group from Hudville are insisting that we find them tickets for the ball. I told them they should have made reservations days ago. I told them I would put them on the waiting list and consult with you."

"They want to buy tickets?" Will asked. "I'm surprised. They usually don't want to spend money. Are the twin sisters the ones requesting the tickets?"

"No, sir. A woman and a man from the group were asking," Otis said primly.

Lighten up, Otis, Regan thought. This is the land of aloha. And this might be the Princess Ball, but we're not talking Buckingham Palace.

"Were they planning to pay for the tickets themselves?"

"No, sir. They said if we were able to procure tickets, we should charge them to the sisters' room."

Will whistled. "That's a new one. How many tickets do they want?"

"Two. Possibly four."

"If they're finally going to start spending money, I'll have to find them some seats. Tell them they can have the tickets."

"Very well."

"I hope that we don't get too many cancellations for tomorrow night now that the leis are off the menu," Will said.

"Sir, it appears that the interest in the ball has waxed rather than waned."

"Glad to hear it."

"Will, could I speak to you in your office?" Regan asked.

"Sure. Let's go."

Regan followed him through the reception area, which as usual was bustling. They went behind the desk where people were checking in and entered the inner sanctum.

Janet was at her desk. She handed Will a piece of paper. "The head of the auction committee called. She just got word about the leis being stolen. She wants to know if you have any suggestions about what they can auction off in place of the leis."

"How about my head on a platter?" Will muttered. He took the paper with the phone number on it and entered his office. He stopped short so fast that Regan almost bumped into him. "Oh, my God!" he exclaimed.

"What?" Regan asked. Quickly she moved aside and looked down. The two beautiful shell leis she had seen just this morning at the Seashell Museum were lying on the floor. The sliding screen door was open.

Will went over and picked them up.

"The royal leis," Regan said, her voice incredulous.

The color was draining from Will's face. He looked at Regan in bewilderment. "What am I going to do?"

"We'll call the police."

Janet was standing in the doorway. "There's no need. They're already here."

47

The cab dropped Ned off in front of the old movie theater on Kalakaua Avenue, the main street in Waikiki. By now he was perspiring. It's just a knapsack, he told himself over and over. Even if there's something of mine in it that identifies me, that doesn't mean I stole the leis. The cops don't even know it was a yellow knapsack. It could have been a guy in a yellow shirt.

He crossed the street, darting around the traffic, and headed straight for the alley where he'd done his gift wrapping. It was narrow and dark, but he could tell immediately that the knapsack was gone. Ned ran down the alley looking for it. Nothing. He checked in a garbage can. It wasn't there. What could have happened to it? he thought frantically. He was trying to remember if there could have been anything inside it that would identify him. Was there a bank slip? A receipt from the ATM machine? Ned just wasn't sure.

He emerged from the alley and noticed a vagrant with a hangdog expression sitting on the sidewalk, his butt smack on the middle of Ned's yellow knapsack. Ned was sure it was his. He could see the oil stains on the side.

"Excuse me, buddy," Ned said, "but I think you're sitting on my bag."

The vagrant ignored him.

"Come on, man," Ned pleaded as he leaned down and started to pull on one of the straps. It turned out not to be the greatest idea.

The formerly silent vagrant went nuts. *"This is mine!"* he screamed. *"Leave me alone! Help! Police! Hellllpppppp!"*

His noisy protests had the intended effect. Passersby started to stop and murmur the way people do when some drama is unfolding. In an instant Ned realized that it was far better to get the heck out of there and risk whatever might be found inside the bag, bank slip or no bank slip. He hightailed it down the block, crossed the street, and did his best to disappear into the Friday night crowds.

That's the second time today I ran off serenaded by the sounds of someone squawking in my wake, Ned realized. But this was too much of a close call. People had seen him. All I need is to be caught in a tug-of-war over a dirty yellow knapsack with a guy who lives on the street. Then they'd really have cause to lock me up.

Ned's heart was beating so fast, he decided to walk back to the hotel to calm himself. It wasn't that far. What have I gotten myself into? he wondered. I've got to get that package back from the bell station, he decided. It's not worth leaving there. I'll take the chance that Artie isn't as nosy as I was when I was a kid, going through my mother's closets and peeking at the wrapped Christmas presents.

When Ned got back to the hotel, there was more excitement. A police car was parked in the driveway, its lights flashing. The first person Ned saw was the ubiquitous Glenn.

"What's going on?" Ned asked.

"The stolen leis were discovered in Will's office. An anonymous tipster called the police."

Ned tried not to flinch. "The stolen leis?"

"That's right."

"Will must be happy," Ned said carefully.

"I don't know about that. It doesn't look too good for the hotel that stolen property is found in the manager's office."

"Oh, give me a break, Glenn. Will obviously had nothing to do with it."

"I didn't say he did."

Ned's head was spinning, but he was doing his best not to let his discomfort show. Now he really had to get his box with the hula girl wrapping paper back. "Do you know if my friend came to pick up the package I left for her?"

"If she did, I didn't see her," Glenn answered cheerily and efficiently. "But let me go check." He stepped away while Ned stood in the reception area trying to absorb what was going on. In two seconds flat Glenn was back. "No. Ms. Leggate didn't pick it up after all. The package is still behind the desk, safe and sound."

"Great. You know, on second thought, I think I'll drop it off at her place tonight. Could I have the bag, please?"

"Sure! She sounds like a good friend. You go shopping for her and then deliver the goods to her doorstep." Glenn waltzed off, retrieved the bag from behind the desk, sauntered back, and slowly handed it over to Ned. "I don't need a tip," he joked with a big smile. "We're both working stiffs at this grand resort."

"Right, thanks." Ned took the bag and started to walk back to his room. When he went around the corner and was out of Glenn's sight, he lifted the box and shook it. He was glad to hear a rattling sound, as if the shell leis were still in there. Is Glenn messing with my head? he wondered. If he is, he'll be sorry. I can't wait to open this box. He silently prayed that Artie wouldn't be in their room. But he had barely put the key in the door and was pushing it open when Artie called out to him.

"Hey, Ned."

Ned cringed. "Hi, there," he said as he entered the room.

Artie jumped up from his bed where he'd been lounging. "It's time to meet the others for drinks. Are you going to join us?"

"Maybe in a few minutes," Ned replied. He sat down on his bed.

"What have you got in the bag there?" Artie asked, his eyes looking down into the bag.

"A present for my mother," Ned answered quickly.

"That's sexy wrapping paper for a mother."

"My mother has always liked crazy stuff."

"Not my mother. She's prim and proper. She'd have me committed if I handed her a present with that paper on it. She prefers paper with rainbows and shooting stars and cutesy teddy bears."

Ned thought he was going to scream. Instead he shut his eyes, took a deep breath, and wiped his forehead.

"Are you all right?" Artie asked.

"Yes. Why?"

"You seem a little preoccupied."

"I'm fine," Ned insisted. "I'll join you downstairs for drinks in a few minutes. I want to call my mother. She hasn't been feeling well. That's why I bought her this crazy present."

"That's nice! If she were here, I'd give her a free massage. What crazy present did you get her anyway?"

Ned almost choked. Once you start lying, it truly

becomes a tangled web. "I just got her a couple of muumuus and a Hawaiian bathing suit."

"Where does she live?"

"In Maine."

Artie laughed. "I can just picture it. Someone walking around in a muumuu on the rocky coast of Maine."

Ned looked up at him and couldn't contain a flash of anger. "She goes to Florida in the winter. Women wear muumuus in Florida."

"I'm sorry, Ned," Artie apologized. "I was just trying to have some fun. Listen, old Gert and Ev aren't going to be back until late. Who knows what they're up to. Maybe they met a couple of guys. Anyway, the five of us are eating on our own and are planning to spend a lot of Sal Hawkins's money. We're starting with expensive drinks down by the pool. We're going to take in the hula show. I hope the girls look as good as they do on your paper there. Come down after you talk to your mother, and give her my best wishes. I hope she feels better soon." He quickly disappeared out the door.

Ned sat there for what felt like an eternity, sure that Artie would burst back in at any moment. When he was finally satisfied that enough time had passed for Artie to be sipping his first piña colada of the night, Ned went over and bolted the door—just in case. It would be hard to explain if Artie came back and couldn't get in. But Ned had to take that chance.

He laid the box on the bed and noticed that a tiny piece of the wrapping paper near where it was taped was white. Part of a hula girl's lei had come off and was stuck to a piece of the tape. How appropriate, Ned thought. Is this an indication that someone was tampering with the box? He pulled off the wrapping and lifted the cover. He gasped. Inside were two shell leis that looked as if they cost about a dollar each.

"Who did this?" Ned exclaimed. "Was it Glenn?" What can I do? he thought frantically. What can I do? Ask him if he took the leis I stole and put them in Will's office? Maybe he wasn't the one. Maybe someone followed me today and saw that I handed the bag to the bellman. But how did they get the package? Anything could have happened. And there's absolutely nothing I can do! Am I being set up?

Ned went into the bathroom and splashed cold water on his face. He grabbed a towel and held it up to his skin, closing his eyes as if that would provide a barrier from all his cares and woes. But when he opened his eyes and put down the towel, his reflection in the mirror looked grim. "And I still have to deal with Will's parents tomorrow," he reminded himself. "If I get out of this one, I'm going on the straight and narrow. And I have to get out of this one. I have to." He quickly brushed his teeth and then hurried out the door, craving the relief he'd feel after his first sip of a double scotch.

48

The first officers at the scene checked out the area outside of Will's office. Nothing had been dropped in the grass. There didn't seem to be any visible footprints.

"Do you have any idea who could have done this?" one of them asked Will.

"I wish I did."

When Mike Darnell walked into the office a few minutes later, he was shocked to see Regan. He smiled at her. "What are you doing here?"

"I'm helping Will out," Regan answered.

"Well, this is some story. It went out over the police scanner. There are lots of reporters outside who would like to talk to you, Will."

Will looked weary. "What am I supposed to say?"

"Some people think this whole thing might have

been a prank to drum up publicity for tomorrow night's auction."

"That's ridiculous."

"I agree. Especially since Jimmy could have been killed today. I just spoke with him. He's one happy guy, although he has an Excedrin headache. He asked me to keep these leis under lock and key until tomorrow night."

"Believe me," Will said, "I don't want to be responsible for them. Take them with you. Bring them back in an armored car right before the auction. It'll make my life a whole lot easier."

"Mike, who called this in?" Regan asked.

"We don't know. The call was made on one of those temporary cell phones where you buy a certain amount of minutes and then throw them out."

"So whoever did it is obviously someone who planned in advance and didn't want his calls traced."

"That's right."

"It just doesn't make sense."

"None of this has made sense," Mike commented. "Hey, Will, how many people around here wore yellow today?"

Will rolled his eyes. "Hundreds."

The phone on Will's desk rang. "It must be important if Janet put it through," he noted as he answered it. It was his wife, Kim, calling from the airplane.

While Will was on the phone, Regan talked

quietly to Mike. "I know that what I'm about to ask you has nothing to do with all this, but Jack told me that if I got something to you with someone's fingerprints on it, you could—"

"I can. Jack called me after he talked to you. You want to check out this guy your friend is seeing?"

"Yes. It might be silly. But I just have a feeling about him . . ."

"No problem. If you get me something tomorrow morning, I'll take care of it right away." Mike looked over at the screen door. "So whoever deposited these leis in here just opened the door, then ran off. The question is, why would they risk stealing them if they're just going to hand them over?"

Will had just hung up the phone. "Someone is out to ruin the good name of this resort," he answered Mike. "I asked Regan to look into it this weekend and see what she could find out. People who say this is a publicity prank don't realize that this kind of publicity is bad for the hotel. Are we happy that the leis are back and at least one of them will still be auctioned? Yes. But with an employee drowning the other day wearing the lei that was stolen from the museum, and now after it's stolen again it ends up back here, it all doesn't look or sound good. People are going to be afraid to set foot in this place. They're going to think the Waikiki Waters is cursed just like the royal leis." Will threw up his hands.

Mike looked at him thoughtfully. "I understand."

"Now I'm really afraid of what might happen at the ball tomorrow night," Will continued. "If someone goes to all the trouble to fool around with these leis like this, who knows what else they might try."

"I'll get some undercover guys to come to the ball to keep an eye on things."

"I'd appreciate it," Will said. "I'll be glad when these leis are gone for good. But until then I have to worry about the security of the hotel guests and my employees."

Mike turned to Regan. "And you thought you were coming here for a vacation?"

Regan smiled and shrugged.

"I'm heading out," Mike declared. "Call me if you need me, Regan. Will, do you want to talk to the reporters outside?"

"Do you really have to ask?"

"Then I'll make a statement that the leis are back, and we're investigating."

When Mike left the room, Will shut the door behind him. He sat back down at his desk and rubbed his eyes. "Regan, you know that guy?"

"He's a friend of my fiancé's. I met him when we were out last night."

"You're not going to tell him that I was the one who gave Dorinda the lei the night she died, are you?"

"No. That's client privilege."

Will sighed. "I have to pick up my wife at the airport. I'm sure she'll be thrilled by all the news I have to share with her."

"First I'd like to tell you about what I found at Dorinda's apartment."

"Should I cover my ears?"

"It's not bad for you personally."

"Miracles will never cease." Will clenched his hands together and looked up at the ceiling as if in prayer.

"Dorinda had a file, which I have in my bag here. It's marked 'Prospective Dirt.' It contains a few pictures, newspaper articles, and the last will and testament of Sal Hawkins."

"Sal Hawkins?" Will asked incredulously.

"Yes."

"He left a million dollars to the Praise the Rain Club I told you about. Ned, whom I introduced you to before, took a couple of them surfing today. The tours are run by the two older ladies who are twins. They're the group Otis was just talking about."

"Did you say one million dollars?" Regan asked.

"Yes."

Regan quickly produced the file. She opened it and pulled out the will. "It says here he left ten million dollars."

"Ten million?" Will was aghast. "To spend on trips to Hawaii?"

"Apparently so."

"And they're always poor-mouthing."

"It sounds as if they might be lying to the people in their group about how much money there is. Those weird people I met at the bar said their tour directors were cheap. Dorinda was certainly onto something with them. How long are they here?"

"Until Monday."

Next Regan showed him a picture of Steve. "This guy has been making a play for Kit. He's in this file, which doesn't bode well. What can you tell me about him?"

"Steve Yardley. He comes around to the bars here sometimes. All I know is that he retired young and supposedly has a fortune."

"Do you think he's legit?"

"I don't know, Regan. He's one of those guys who gets around town. He seems to be a real ladies' man. But I've noticed him talking to a lot of the businessmen at the bar."

"There was a group picture on Dorinda's desk taken at a party. Dorinda was gazing up at him with a big smile."

"Dorinda gazed up at a lot of men with a big smile. If she had something on him, I don't know what it could be."

"Okay. How about our dear friend Jazzy? There's a small article in here about her boss Claude's clothing line."

"He's always trying to get publicity. The guy is an extremely successful businessman who now wants to be famous. He wants to be in the middle of the action. As far as I know, that's not a crime."

"No, it's not. But Jazzy works for him. Who knows what she's capable of?"

"I told you. She's like dandruff. Wait till you see her in action tomorrow night. The guys love her. It's hard to stomach but I think she's harmless. Anything else, Regan?"

Regan handed him a couple of clippings about restaurant openings and parties around town. "Do these mean anything to you?"

Will glanced at them and shook his head. "They have no significance to me." He handed them back.

Regan shut the file. "I have to meet Kit and go to dinner at this guy Steve's house." She paused. "One more thing. There was a young couple I spoke to on the beach last night. She had gone for a late-night walk the night Dorinda drowned. She thinks she saw something unusual but couldn't remember what it was. She said she'd let me know. I haven't heard from her today, but I'd like to give her a call. Problem is, I didn't take their number."

"What are their names?"

"Carla and Jason. They just got engaged last night. The other problem is that I didn't get their last names, but I know they're staying in the Coconut Tower."

"I'll have someone run a check on the computer. They should be easy to find."

"Great. Are you going straight home from the airport?"

"Yes. And I'm not coming back until tomorrow. You can always reach me on my cell phone."

"I hope I won't have to."

"No more than me, Regan, no more than me."

49

"What are we going to do with them?" Gert asked Ev. They had taken a taxi to the airport and were waiting for a flight back to Honolulu. The airport was open and breezy and small. In spite of the unexpected development, Gert and Ev sat on a bench enjoying the beautiful evening.

"For one thing, we've got to come back tomorrow and get rid of them somehow, ya know?"

"Sure do. But how? We can't ever let them talk, or else we'll end up like those ladies in the prison movies." Gert laughed. "I can't believe we've turned into such bad girls."

Ev looked at her. "We deserve to have some fun in life. We took care of our parents. We took care of Sal Hawkins. I've stepped in too many puddles in

Hudville. That life is almost over. Now's our time, sister. It's Gert and Ev's time to have fun."

"I'm going to cry," Gert sniffled. "I'm so lucky to have you."

"We're lucky to have each other. We make a good team."

"I never thought we'd be partners in crime."

"Get used to it!" Ev laughed. "I've been thinking about those two jerks up in our house. I'm sorry they had to ruin it for themselves, I really am. And now they're going to cost us more money running back and forth. We've got the flight back here tomorrow afternoon. I figure we'll rent a car with a big trunk. Then when it gets dark we'll get them in there and drive to the other side of the island. There are lots of places where you can just give someone a good shove and away they go, down the cliffs into the deep blue sea."

"You're a genius."

"No, I'm not, sister. It's common sense. Luckily our ma taught us all about that."

"She didn't teach us how to kill people."

"There was no one worth killing in Hudville. Given half a chance I bet she could have done it in a heartbeat."

"I suppose. But how are we going to get back to Honolulu in time for our early morning walk on the beach Sunday? The group is really going to know that something's up if we're not there for that."

"We can tell them we have to go to church, to a special sunrise service that will take all morning. It'll be our last full day, so we'll go to the special Sunday brunch with them. And then we can say good riddance to these tour groups."

"I just thought of something."

"What, sister?"

"What about that couple's car? What are we going to do with that?"

"It's actually kind of perfect. Tomorrow you follow me in their car. We park it by the cliff. Everyone will think the lovers committed suicide for some dumb reason or other."

"One problem, Ev."

"What's that?"

"I don't drive."

"Sure you can. It's easy. You just never got your license because you know I like to drive. That's because I like to be in charge because I'm older."

"Only by five minutes and twenty-two seconds."

An announcement came over the loudspeaker that the flight to Honolulu was now boarding. The twins gave each other a quick hug, as they always did before they boarded a flight. When the plane finally took off, they looked down at the Big Island.

"Pretty soon we'll call it home," Gert said.

"Home sweet home," Ev agreed.

Off in the distance, in the basement of Gert and Ev's dream house, Jason and Carla were frantically trying to loosen the ropes around their hands.

Carla was sobbing. Her chest started to heave, and the piece of torn sheet they'd tied around her mouth gagged her.

"Calm down," Jason pleaded as he attempted to make himself understood through the sheet stuffed in his mouth. "We'll ... make ... it," he said, trying to assure this woman who, he realized now more than ever, was the love of his life. Please, God, he prayed. Let someone find us. He closed his eyes. Regan Reilly came into his mind. She was investigating Dorinda Dawes's death, which he was now sure was a murder. I can tell you who did it, Regan. Come find us, he prayed, before those two psychos get back.

He was sure they were capable of anything.

50

There was no denying it. Kit was in deep, deep like. When Regan got back to the room, Kit's clothing was all over her bed.

"Regan, I can't decide what to wear. How are things going?"

Regan explained that the leis had been stolen and then found in Will's office.

"This place is crazy," Kit commented as she held up yet another silk top before the mirror. "I have to find something to wear to the ball tomorrow night. When I came out here for the conference, I certainly didn't pack a glittery outfit."

"There's a huge shopping center down the street," Regan reminded her.

"I know. Steve is taking me there tomorrow. He wants to buy me a dress to wear."

"Are you going to let him?" Regan asked cautiously.

"At first I said no, but he really wants to. You don't think that's a good idea?"

"Ahhh," Regan began. She didn't want to dampen Kit's enthusiasm. And maybe Steve was a good guy. "It's just so fast," she said.

Kit sat down on her bed. "Regan, I know it sounds crazy, but I think this guy could really be the one."

"There's nothing I'd like better than if this worked out," Regan replied honestly if ambiguously. She didn't add that she thought that was a long shot.

"Wouldn't it be great if I got married not too long after you? Then we could have kids at the same time." Kit started to laugh. "You probably think I have sunstroke."

Regan smiled. "I don't think that. But being your friend, my advice is to take it a little bit slower. We both know how relationships that move so quickly have a tendency to crash and burn."

"Regan, don't worry. I'm having fun. I think he's really great. But let's face it, we're leaving on Monday. The true test will be after that. It's a long way to Hartford."

Her words reassured Regan. "It is, Kit. Have fun this weekend and then see what happens." But I'm still getting his fingerprints, Regan thought.

"You're so lucky you found Jack. Of course your

father had to get kidnapped for that to happen," Kit joked.

Regan smiled. "My father considers himself a real matchmaker. He loves to tell everyone that story. I can't wait until he grabs the microphone at our wedding reception. I'm sure he'll just happen to mention it again."

"I don't think my father would be willing to get kidnapped to help me find a guy, but I'm sure my grandmother would." Kit started to fold her clothes. "I can't believe everything that's happened to those leis. Will is lucky you just happened to be here."

"I don't know about that." Regan frowned. "I just hope I can make a dent in these cases before we leave on Monday."

"Anything new on the Dorinda front?"

"I went to her apartment with her cousin. It was interesting. There are a few things I'm looking into. I want to talk to that girl we met on the beach last night."

"You were sure she'd call you," Kit reminded her.

"She still might, but I don't want to wait for that. Will is going to find out what room she and her fiancé are in so I can contact them."

"They're probably still celebrating their engagement."

"You may be right. She was pretty excited."

"I'd be excited, too, after ten years." Kit paused.

"Can you imagine if Steve took ten years to propose? I shudder at the thought."

"Don't go there, Kit," Regan warned.

"I know, I know."

"By the way, has Steve said anything about Dorinda?"

"No. The other night, at the bar, she whispered something in his ear, and he rolled his eyes. She seemed to be annoying a lot of people."

Kit looked at her watch.

"I'll jump in the shower," Regan said.

A half hour later they were in a cab and on their way to Steve's.

"You're carrying a big purse," Kit commented.

The better to hold something with Steve's fingerprints, Regan thought. I might need room for a kitchen knife. "You know me," Regan answered. "I carry my notebook and cell phone in case I have to get back to work. Will is certainly hoping that won't happen tonight. He's picking up his wife at the airport and needs a little peace."

"And you deserve the night off. Regan, this is also your vacation. Let's just have fun."

Regan smiled at her best friend. Tonight is anything but a night off, she thought. She patted her buddy's arm, the buddy who'd been such an important part of her life for the last ten years. "I'm sure it'll be interesting."

51

Jazzy and Claude were in a stretch limo driving back from the airport. Claude liked to be seen in a certain light, the light that emanated from luxury cars, fine clothing, and upscale surroundings. His home on the Big Island made his heart swell, but as it turned out, that wasn't enough. He was now trying to find the meaning of life through his Hawaiian clothing line.

As the car glided along the highway, Jazzy poured champagne for Claude and herself. They clinked glasses and sipped the bubbly, content in the knowledge that people who saw their vehicle were probably wondering who the important people riding in the back were. They pushed away the thought that if they rolled down the windows and their identities were revealed, nobody would care.

"Are you tired, Claude?" Jazzy asked solicitously.

"I work very hard, Jazzy. I was stuck on an airplane for hours. Of course I'm tired."

Jazzy made the appropriate cooing sounds of sympathy. "Well, the ball is going to be a big success for us. I just know it."

"I think women are going to be thrilled when they put on my muumuus. You know why? Because they're sexy. Not too many muumuus are sexy. But I know how to design. I know what women want. And the men are going to love my Hawaiian shirts. Any word from *GQ*?"

"No."

Claude scowled.

"What I mean is, not yet," Jazzy hastened to add.

"I can't believe they're not interested. It would make a great story about how I, Claude Mott, will make it hip to wear Hawaiian shirts no matter where you live."

"I know you can do it, Claude."

"Of course I can. I thank God that those leis have been recovered."

She clinked his glass. "So do I. It will make everything so much better tomorrow night."

"I wonder if the discovery of the leis in Will Brown's office will cause him trouble."

"It can't be good. The reports I heard on my way to the airport said the police are investigating and they have no suspects. There's a private investigator named Regan Reilly staying at the hotel.

She's smart. I have the feeling that she's working for Will."

"Her name is Regan Reilly?" he asked with one eyebrow raised.

"Yes."

"That name sounds familiar."

"Her mother is a mystery writer named Nora Regan Reilly. She's well-known."

"Of course. The woman next to me on the plane was reading one of her books. No wonder it rang a bell." He sipped his champagne. "So, Jazzy, tomorrow night you will be modeling my sexy muumuu."

"I'll go around to every table and make sure they all get a good look. They'll love it."

Claude smiled for the first time in about three weeks. "You know, Jazzy, I've been studying the history of great designers. They all made their mark in different ways. For me it's about bringing the lei to the world. Leis are all over my clothing. I think leis should be worn to black-tie events in New York City. I say that everyone should have leis in their wardrobe. They should wear my clothing when they are casually dressed and real leis when they dress up. I think that is my mission in life: leis for everyone."

Jazzy held up her glass and smiled with satisfaction. "Here's to leis everywhere."

They clinked glasses and sipped Dom Perignon as the limo sped toward the Waikiki Waters Resort.

52

Down by the pool, Francie, Artie, and Joy were sipping piña coladas. The hula girls were getting ready to swivel their hips, and the musicians were testing the sound system. Ned approached and took a seat.

"How's your mother?" Artie asked.

Ned almost said "Huh?" but made a quick recovery. "She's feeling better. Thanks for asking."

A waitress came over, and Ned ordered his double scotch. Before she walked away, Bob and Betsy arrived and placed their orders for mai tais.

When the whole group was seated and served and sipping, Joy decided to open up the floor to a discussion of the twins. "You all know that Gert and Ev are being stingy with Sal Hawkins's money.

I say that when we get back to Hudville we ask to
see his will and the accounting records."

Bob's eyes lit up. "You think they're like Bonnie
and Clyde?"

"What?" Joy asked.

"Bonnie and Clyde."

"I don't think they're going around shooting
anybody. But for all we know they could have spent
the day shopping at Ala Moana Center with Sal
Hawkins's money and had everything sent back to
Hudville. It's not right. I know someone who went
on one of the first trips, and she said it was fantas-
tic. They were taking helicopter rides and sunset
cruises and doing fun things that cost bucks. Now,
if it cost money to go swimming in the pool, I think
those two would point us to the ocean."

Ned almost choked on the scotch that he was
drinking too quickly. "Could they be embezzling
funds?" he asked as he wiped his mouth with a napkin. "That's unbelievable. I know they drive a hard
bargain with Will."

"Of course they could!" Francie cried dramati-
cally, waving her arm in the air. "They are denying
us our right to enjoy Hawaii to the fullest!"

"At least we scored four tickets for the ball,"
Artie announced. "Wait till they get a load of
that."

Glenn the bellman waved from the walkway.

"He's everywhere," Joy commented.

Ned's central nervous system was on red alert.

He took another sip of scotch. When he saw Glenn approaching, he wanted to get up and run.

"I hope you all enjoy the hula girls," Glenn said, smiling broadly. "I know Ned has a fondness for hula girls, right, Ned? You folks should see the wild wrapping paper he had on a present he bought today."

"I saw that paper. Can you believe he's giving that package to his mother?" Artie laughed.

"That's not what he told me!" Glenn smiled.

Ned tried to laugh it off. "Give me a break. The store wrapped the present." He waved his hand dismissively.

Glenn clapped his hands once. "Well, I'll be off. Enjoy the show!"

I'm going to kill that guy, Ned thought. He's playing with my head.

"So," Joy said, "are we all in this or what?"

"All in what?" Betsy queried.

"Are we all going to go back to Hudville and find out what's up with the funds?"

Artie didn't answer. He knew he was moving out of Hudville as soon as possible, and he just didn't care. This Joy was annoying him. She made him feel old and uninteresting.

"Count us out," Bob said. "Betsy and I are too busy with our literary pursuits."

"What about you, Francie?" Joy asked.

"What worries me," Francie began, "is that

Hudville is such a small town. If we start some-thing and the twins are innocent, we'll look like a bunch of ingrates. Things might get a little awk-ward."

"Awkward?" Artie practically snorted. "I wouldn't want to run into Gert and Ev in a dark alley if I'd stirred up trouble for them."

"They don't scare me," Joy said dismissively as she stirred her drink with a straw. "It's something to think about."

"Misuse of funds is very common," Ned opined. "Power goes to people's heads, you know? They start to think that they deserve the money."

"Ned, where did you get your psychology degree?" Francie laughed. "You sound like you understand the criminal mind all too well."

To Ned's relief, at that moment the band decided to strike up, as they say. With big smiles the hula girls started to sway their hips, and their fingers fluttered through the air like little fishes. As Ned watched the scantily clad girls, all he could see was the hula girls on the paper that he had so carefully wrapped around the box of antique shell leis.

Who had their hands all over his paper hula girls and took the leis? he wondered. It had to be Glenn, he decided. Who else could it be? But why? How can I get back at him? While staring at the dancing girls he pondered the thought of

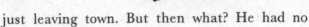

just leaving town. But then what? He had no place to go.

No, I'm staying, he told himself. Glenn must be up to something, and I intend to find out what it is. He's not going to beat me at this game.

Because I always play to win.

53

Steve's party was better than Regan had thought it would be. There were a lot more people there than the night before, and a lively, amiable atmosphere enveloped his home. Hawaiian music was coming from the stereo speakers, the blender was whirring with tropical drinks, and the grill was sizzling with fresh ahi, ono, mahimahi, and hot dogs and hamburgers. Members of Steve's softball team were there as well as a handful of his neighbors.

Steve couldn't have been more charming. He was the ultimate host, introducing people, refilling drinks, supervising the dinner, and paying a lot of attention to Kit. Regan and Kit sat at a large table on the deck, eating, socializing, and having a few laughs.

I've never seen Kit look so happy, Regan thought guiltily as she kept an eye out for an opportunity to grab something with Steve's fingerprints. But I'm only doing it for your own good, Kit, Regan mused. Lines from the song "That's What Friends Are For" ran through her head. And if you're best friends with a private investigator, there are certain drawbacks that come with the territory.

Regan was happy that Steve seemed to genuinely care about Kit. Maybe I'm wrong, she thought. Maybe Dorinda had him in her dirt file because he spurned her advances. Maybe Steve is what Jazzy proclaimed: "a good catch."

When Regan and Kit were alone for a moment at the table, Kit turned to her. "Isn't he great? I can't wait for Jack to meet him. I bet they will really get along."

"I hope so," Regan answered.

"As we've always said," Kit noted with a smile, "we'd better end up with guys who like each other."

Regan grinned. "That would help." Out of the corner of her eye she saw Steve take a sip and then give a little shake to his beer bottle. Clearly it was empty. He started to go inside.

Now's my chance, Regan thought. She had purposely chosen to drink the same beer as Steve. She didn't much like it, and even Kit had commented that she was surprised Regan had a beer. But she'd made a plausible excuse about how it felt good to drink beer in hot weather, nursed it, and now her bottle was empty. Regan leaned down to grab her purse. "I'm going to run to the ladies' room. Be right back." With the beer bottle in one hand and her purse in the other, she made her way around all the people standing on the deck and into the house where more guests were milling in groups of three or four. She watched as Steve put his empty beer bottle on the kitchen counter and then turned to talk to someone who announced he was leaving.

Regan took a deep breath. She slowly ambled past the counter, put down her bottle, and picked up Steve's. Two seconds later she was in the hallway heading for the bathroom. She passed the bedroom where Mark and Paul were staying. "Can you believe crazy Stevie has all this? I wish I'd gotten kicked out of college," Mark joked as he stepped out into the hallway.

Regan slipped into the spacious, luxurious marble bathroom and shut the door behind her. She carefully locked it, then put her purse on the counter. Exhaling a sigh of relief, she pulled a dark plastic bag out of her purse, dropped the beer bottle into it, and then carefully put it back inside. She combed her hair, freshened her lipstick, and figured out a game plan. Any reservations she had about checking out Steve Yardley had vanished.

Back out on the deck, she sat with Kit for a few

minutes and then said, "I'm kind of tired. It's been a long day. If you don't mind, I'll call a cab and head back."

"Regan, are you sure?" Kit asked with a look of concern.

"Yes. Definitely."

"I feel a little guilty that we're not spending time alone."

"Kit, it's fine. I was working today anyway. You have fun. I'll see you later."

Steve came up behind them.

"Regan's leaving. Can you call her a cab?"

Steve put his arm around Regan, his hand brushing the side of her bag which was still over her shoulder. "Aren't you having fun?" he asked with a twinkle in his eye. He looked down at Kit. "Doesn't your friend like me?"

Regan smiled. "It's jet lag. I'll go home and get my beauty sleep so I can stay up late at the Princess Ball tomorrow night."

"We're going to have a good time at the ball," Steve predicted. "Kit's going to be my princess." He leaned down and gave her a kiss. Standing back up he looked into Regan's eyes. "And I can't wait to meet your prince."

"He can't wait to meet you, either." More than you know, Regan thought.

Fifteen minutes later Steve escorted her outside. The cab had just pulled up.

"Have a good night, Regan." He held the door of

the car open for her. "And don't worry. I'll take good care of your friend."

"She's the best," Regan said. "See you tomorrow night."

"Put on your seat belt."

"I will."

"You can never be too safe." He laughed as he pushed the button down to lock the back door of the vehicle.

As the driver pulled away, Regan waved to Steve who stood in the driveway and watched her depart. She then patted her purse, reassuring herself that his beer bottle was still there. Kicked out of college, she thought. Why? What else are you hiding?

54

Kim stared at the spot on the living room wall where the shell lei had hung ever since they moved into the house. "Your mother will never cease to amaze me," she declared. "Only she could get her hands on a royal Hawaiian lei that had been stolen and manage to set these events in motion thirty years ago."

Will hugged her. "I know."

Their son, Billy, was asleep down the hall. Will and Kim had enjoyed a quiet dinner. It was now nearly midnight. They were sitting on the couch sipping an after-dinner drink and catching up. He explained everything that had happened, and Kim actually took it quite well.

"I knew Dorinda Dawes didn't like me. I can't

wait to see the newsletter with my terrible picture. But you were smart to leave it at the office."

Will looked at his beautiful wife, with her long dark hair and almond-shaped eyes. They'd met five years ago when they'd both been alone on line to buy a movie ticket. On a whim each of them had decided to take in a five o'clock show. They got to talking, sat together, and from that day on they were a couple. Now, every year on the anniversary of the day they met, they would always go to a five o'clock movie even if there is nothing they really want to see. He loved her and their son and the life that they shared. He never wanted to jeopardize it. But of course he had—by giving the stupid lei to Dorinda Dawes.

"Do you think your mother is really going to be able to keep her mouth shut tomorrow at the ball? How is she going to keep it a secret that the lei was in your family all this time?"

Will shook his head and rested it on her shoulder. "I don't know. But she has to."

"Just wait till she sees the lei, Will!" Kim exclaimed. "When it goes up for auction, she'll be jumping out of her seat."

"Jimmy hasn't decided whether it will be auctioned off or not."

"But didn't you say he was going to wear both leis to the ball?"

"That is his plan."

"Can you imagine when your mother meets him? Wearing *her* lei?"

"I don't want to think about it." He snuggled closer to her. "My head is spinning with everything that's going wrong around the hotel."

"And now Bingsley and Almetta will be checking in."

"I asked Ned to take care of them tomorrow afternoon. With any luck he'll tire my mother out. Then we have to get through the ball. I hope someone buys the leis and takes them far, far away from here. Then maybe we can move on from all this trouble."

"So this Regan Reilly is on the case."

"Yes. She has to leave Monday, but she has already done a lot. I'm glad she'll be here for the ball. One of the detectives in town is a friend of her fiancé. He's sending over undercover cops tomorrow night to keep an eye on things."

"The 'Be a Princess' Ball was supposed to be all about making the night a fairy tale. It's turned into a nightmare."

The phone on the table next to the couch rang. Startled, Will leaned over to answer it. "I hope this is nothing bad," he said under his breath. "Hello."

"Hi, darling!" Will's mother cried. "We're at the airport having a cup of coffee and a cinnamon bun before we board the flight. I can't believe how early it is! But your father managed to find some crazy airline that flies out at the crack of dawn. I just wanted to say hello and tell you we'll be there soon!"

"That's great, Mom."

"Anything new with our lei?" she chirped.

"They found it today," Will replied, failing to mention that it was located in his office.

"Oh, my goodness! That lei certainly gets around, doesn't it, dear?"

"That it does."

"Don't worry. It's our little secret. But will I get to see it?"

"At the ball. They might auction it off."

"I'll have to talk to your father. Wouldn't it be wonderful if he bid on it for me? We could have it back in our family where it belongs—unless some millionaire decides to spend a fortune on it."

That's all I'd need, Will thought. He looked at the hook on the wall where the lei had been hanging for years. As if his mother had ESP, she said, "You could hang it right back in that lovely little house of yours. It's too bad you don't think there's enough room for us to stay there."

Will ignored the last remark. "If Dad buys the lei for you, I insist you keep it," he said, "and I mean *insist*."

His mother considered this. "Well, I did feel like a queen when I wore it. Ohhh—they're calling us to get on the flight. Bye, darling."

The phone clicked in his ear. Will placed it in its cradle and turned to Kim. "You'll be happy to know your favorite mother-in-law is on her way."

As Kim laughed, Will's stomach started to do somersaults. He was sure they wouldn't stop until the lei was out of his life forever, one way or the other.

Saturday, January 15

55

Dorinda's cousin Gus slept like a log in her sublet apartment. It was as if he didn't have a care in the world. When he first lay down on the bed, he pressed on the mattress a few times with his hand and found it a little too firm for his liking. But Gus being Gus, he closed his eyes and went out like a light.

On Saturday morning he woke early. Confused for a moment about where he was, he did what he always did when he woke up in a strange bed and couldn't figure it out. He counted to ten, got his bearings, and his whereabouts finally penetrated his skull. "Cousin Dorinda!" he cried out. "What a pity."

The clock radio next to the bed read 6:12 A.M. "The old time change," he said as he threw his legs over the side of the bed and stood. In the little kitchen he brewed a pot of Dorinda's Kona coffee. As the joe slowly dripped into the glass container, Gus bent down and tried to touch his toes. He never succeeded, but it made him feel good to make the effort. He reached back up, then down again. Up and down, up and down until he felt dizzy.

The coffee was finally ready—dark and rich with a wonderful aroma. He poured himself a cup and promptly went back to bed. He rested the cup of coffee on the end table and grabbed the second pillow to prop up behind him. His eyes rested on a spiral notebook.

"What have we here?" he said to himself. He pulled it closer and opened it. On the top line, printed in large letters in Dorinda's scribbly handwriting, was the title: THE ROMANCE OF THE PRINCESS BALL. IS IT A NIGHT TO FALL IN LOVE OR TO FALL IN LOVE ALL OVER AGAIN? Gus couldn't make out the smaller print below. He grabbed his glasses off the dresser, took his coffee in hand, and sank back into the pillows with the notebook on his lap. He read with interest about how Hawaii was the perfect place for romance. Honeymooners abound as well as people who have been together for years. People meet and fall in love on the beautiful islands. Natives and tourists alike wear leis in a spirit of love and friendship and celebration.

The next paragraph in Dorinda's notebook was

about the planning for the Princess Ball at the romantic Waikiki Waters Playground and Resort—the excitement about auctioning off one of the royal leis that had been in the Seashell Museum for years; the food; the decor; the clothing with the shell lei design in the gift bags; and the charity that would benefit young artists in Hawaii.

Gus dabbed at his eyes when he came to the end of the unfinished article. Dorinda had written, "Finally the night of the ball arrived."

"She never got to write the outcome," Gus whispered sadly. Didn't Beethoven have an unfinished symphony? he wondered. It sounded familiar.

Gus put down the notebook and sipped the coffee. I've always had a knack for reporting, he thought. In high school I wrote a few articles for the paper. He glanced over at some of Dorinda's clothes that were thrown on the armchair in the corner. Poor little D, he thought sadly. She could be a brat, but she didn't deserve to die like that.

"I'll finish the story for you, Dorie," Gus said into the air. "I'll make it a tribute to you from your beloved cousin Gus. Or Guth, as you called me when you were a baby." The more Gus thought about it, the more excited he got. I'll bring the notebook over to the hotel today and show it to Will, he thought. I'll tell him my plans. Then I'll spend the day on the beach and come back to get ready for the ball.

Cousin Dorie, I won't let them forget you.

56

At a little after eight Regan snuck out of the room as quietly as she could. Kit had gotten in at about three. Regan had heard her, glanced at the clock, and fell right back to sleep. On the way home last night she had called Mike Darnell. He told her to drop off the beer bottle at the police station and he'd take care of it in the morning. Regan tossed and turned when she went to bed, wondering again if she had gone overboard.

Down on the beach, Regan began to walk. It was still early, and there weren't many people around. A few morning strollers were out, but only a couple of diehards had already staked their claim of land with their towels, beach chairs, and umbrellas. Regan walked out to the end of the jetty and sat. The water was splashing up against the rocks.

Everything felt so peaceful and calm. It was going to be another beautiful day in paradise.

She sat for about ten minutes and then got up. It was easy to imagine how someone could slip on these rocks, she thought. They're wet and a little slimy. Carefully Regan walked back to the sand and, carrying her shoes, headed toward the hotel. She passed a group of six people in Hawaiian print shorts who were obviously out for an early-morning constitutional.

Regan spotted Jazzy sitting at a small secluded table by the pool with a man who looked like a sourpuss. Regan wondered if he was her boss. She took the path that would bring her closest to the table on her way to the breakfast buffet and made sure to catch Jazzy's eye.

"Oh, hello, Regan," Jazzy said when Regan waved.

"Hi, Jazzy." Regan couldn't believe she was calling her Jazzy. "All set for the ball tonight?"

"Oh, yes."

She'd better introduce me to this guy, Regan thought. He's buried in the breakfast menu, but he'll have to lift his head sometime soon. "I'm so glad the leis are back, aren't you?"

"You better believe it," Jazzy answered. "Regan, have you met my employer, Claude Mott?"

"I don't believe I have." Regan approached with a big smile and extended her hand to Grumpy. "Regan Reilly. Nice to meet you."

He looked up and smiled wanly. "I'm sorry. I am no good before I have my coffee."

"I can understand that. I always feel more human after my first cup of the day. I'm looking forward to seeing your clothing tonight."

"You won't be disappointed," Claude muttered. "After tonight we'll go back to my house on the Big Island, and I will design, design, design."

"Jazzy told me you have a wonderful home over there," Regan said, doing her best to be endearing. She wanted to get some inkling as to why they ended up in Dorinda's dirt file, and she figured graciousness was the best approach. "Where is your house?"

"It's up in the hills a few miles from the Kona airport." Claude kissed his fingers. "It's magnificent. The only problem is that there are people building a house on the next piece of property. I haven't met them, but believe me, they have no taste."

"The problem will be solved when you sell that house and build one here near Waikiki," Jazzy noted coyly.

Regan got the impression that was something Jazzy was pushing. She wants to be where the action is. The Big Island is beautiful but much quieter. "Well, fences make for good neighbors," Regan commented, wanting to prolong the conversation even though it was clear they weren't going to ask her to join them.

"The problem is the fence!" Claude exclaimed. "They just put up a barbed wire fence lining my property. What are they building up in the woods there? A prison?"

"You can't see the house because it's a very wooded area," Jazzy explained. "Very rural and very wonderful. But Claude can't understand the need for the barbed wire."

"When are they moving in?" Regan asked.

"Word is, in the spring sometime. I can't wait to get a look at who these people are. Two women, I'm told." Claude's focus went back to the breakfast menu. Regan took that as a sign that he didn't want any more small talk.

"Enjoy your breakfast," she said. "See you later."

Will was already in his office, looking a little more relaxed. "Today's the big day, Regan."

"I know. Did you have a good night last night?"

"I'm so glad my family is back. Kim is terrific. I told her everything. She didn't even get too upset about my mother being on her way."

"That's great. I just saw Jazzy and Mr. Personality outside."

"Claude?"

"Yes. What a charmer."

Will laughed. "Tell me about it."

"Will, did you get the number for that couple I met on the beach the other night?"

"Yes, I did." He handed her a piece of paper with

their room number and extension. "Regan, you'll be interested to know I just got a report that the girl's mother called this morning. She's worried because she hasn't heard from her daughter since early yesterday morning. She called several times, and no one answered the phone in the room or their cell phone. She was sure Carla would be calling nonstop with ideas for her wedding."

Regan looked concerned. "Have you gone into the room?"

Will shook his head. "No. They could be sleeping. They could have unplugged the phone. We can knock on the door in an hour or so, but I don't want to disturb them yet. It's still early."

"But if they're not there . . ." Regan began.

"Sometimes people take a room for a week but go off for a day or two to one of the other islands. They've already paid for the room, and they don't want to pack up everything. Our guests have that right. If they just got engaged, they could have gone anywhere to celebrate."

"I suppose," Regan said. "But please let me know when you go into their room. I do want to talk to Carla. You know, Will, if this young woman did indeed see something suspicious the night Dorinda died, she might be a target—"

"For whoever might have killed Dorinda," Will finished. "Let's hope that they just had a lot of champagne yesterday and are sleeping it off."

"Believe me, I'll be happy if the worst thing

they're suffering from this morning is a hangover," Regan commented. "Now, about that tour group that escapes the rain to be here thanks to the guy who left them ten million dollars—where would I find them?"

Will looked at his watch. "It's buffet time. The two ladies in charge always manage to corral a large table in the main dining room near the open doors overlooking the beach." He briefly described the members of the group whom Regan hadn't met. "I don't suppose you want to be introduced to the rest of them."

"No. Not yet. I'll try to sit near them. I want to check out the twins. They may be swindling money. It sounds as if Dorinda was definitely on to something there. I just wonder what raised her suspicions about them."

"I don't know. All I know is that they only pay their bills after they've wrung every discount possible out of me."

Regan stood. "I'll go to see what they eat for breakfast."

Outside Will's office, Janet was at her desk.

"You're in early today," Regan noted, "and on a Saturday."

Janet smiled up at her. "After this ball I'm taking a vacation."

"Something tells me we'll all need one," Regan said and headed to the breakfast buffet.

Carla and Jason had spent an agonizing night in the cold cellar. Temperatures dropped to forty degrees up in the mountains, and the heat in the house wasn't working yet. Their bones ached, the ropes cut into their hands and feet, and their mouths were raw and dry with the gags. But those aches and pains were nothing compared to the fear they felt. They were terrified for their lives.

Bound in chairs that were tied to separate cement poles, both Jason and Carla had tried to wiggle around, but it didn't help. It only made the rope burns worse.

Although they couldn't talk, they were both thinking the same thought: They'd never get the chance to marry each other.

"Gert and I have no interest in going to the ball," Regan heard one of the twins saying. "You people go and have fun. Gert and I will find other things to do."

"You're not mad we charged the tickets?" Francie asked. "Because Joy here thinks that—"

"Francie!" Joy snapped.

"All I'm saying is that Joy thought you might be upset we did it without asking."

"Joy is a very smart young lady," Ev replied. "Normally we wouldn't be happy, but we'll let it go this time."

"Why don't we get two tickets for you?" Artie suggested. "It might be fun. We'll go as a group."

Ev was firm. "Those tickets are overpriced. We've already wasted enough of Sal Hawkins's

money on them. Gert and I will go into town and
have some twin time. I don't see that dynamic duo
Bob and Betsy. Are they planning to go to the
ball?"

"I think they had a fight," Joy declared as she
stirred some wheat germ into her yogurt. She was
doing everything she could to keep her figure as
trim as possible, but she knew her discipline would
evaporate when she got back to Hudville. She had
lost most of her zeal for it anyway. Last night Zeke
had revealed that he planned to travel the world
for five years—with his surfboard.

"What did they have a fight about?" Artie asked.

"I don't know. But last night when I came back
from a party they were sitting on the beach. I
heard Betsy complain that Bob was too much of a
square."

"Bob's not a square!" Francie blurted.

"How do you know? He looks like a square to
me," Artie countered.

"Bob's nice. He gave me spending money," Joy
said pointedly as she glanced over at the twins.

"Well, if that makes him feel special, then good
for Bob," Ev said sternly. "The world is full of men
who need to show off to young girls. It's sad."

"Why don't we leave Bob alone?" Joy asked.

"You're the one spreading the gossip," Artie
reminded her.

What a group, Regan thought as she ate a fork-
ful of scrambled eggs. It seemed likely to her that

the twins were pocketing some of Sal Hawkins's money. They were on a tight budget when the group was left with $10 million. That's a lot of money to go through even if you vacation in Hawaii every three months. But how are they going to get away with it? If they did take several million for themselves, it doesn't sound as though they'll have a lot of opportunity to spend all that dough in Hudville.

"You're back in your muumuus," Joy remarked to the twins. "I couldn't believe you were wearing those hot clothes yesterday."

"We explained that to you yesterday, Joy. We were in and out of air conditioning all day looking at hotels all over Oahu. We're doing our best to keep costs down. Otherwise there won't be many trips left for the lucky Praise the Rain members."

Regan watched the twins closely. If they absconded with Sal Hawkins's money, that would have been a big scoop for Dorinda. Could they have known that Dorinda suspected them of stealing? That would certainly be a motive for them to want to murder her. They looked like two sweet old ladies. Are they capable of killing? The blonde caught Regan staring at her. Regan turned away quickly, but in the instant their eyes met she decided that babe could be scary. Her look at Regan had been withering.

Guilty, Regan thought, of at least theft. She took a sip of coffee and pretended to be entranced by the fruit plate in front of her. It's clear that the twins don't want to go to the ball tonight. Why not? They're up to something. If they have all that money squirreled away, another few hundred bucks shouldn't matter. What are they up to?

A woman trying to juggle a full tray and hold her toddler's hand passed behind Gert's chair and knocked into it. Gert's purse slid off the back of her seat and onto the floor. I wouldn't want to be that poor young mother, Regan thought with a slight smile as she watched the annoyed expression that immediately came over Gert's face.

"Well, excuse me," the twin said sarcastically as she reached down to grab her purse. Too quickly she picked the pocketbook up from its bottom. The flap of the purse hadn't been hooked properly, and the contents spilled all over the floor.

"I'm so sorry," the young mother apologized as her toddler, being only about two feet from the floor, attempted to help out by picking up Gert's wallet. Gert grabbed it out of his hands, and he started to cry.

Several coins had rolled beneath Regan's chair. She leaned down and quickly gathered them up, then crouched on the floor where Gert had practically thrown her body, insisting to her group that she could collect everything herself. Regan was the closest to the mess. She noticed Gert hastily put her large hands around a postcard with the word *Kona* sprawled across the picture of a beautiful beach. Regan picked up a makeup bag. Under it was the stub of a Hawaiian Airlines boarding pass; destination: Kona, January 14.

"Here," Regan said, dropping the coins, makeup bag, and ticket stub into the purse that Gert was stuffing with her Tic Tacs, comb, eyeglass case, hanky, and room key.

Gert looked into her eyes. They were both on the floor. "Thank you," she said quickly.

Regan felt as if Gert were searching her eyes for something. Regan deliberately remained impassive. No, she thought, I didn't notice that you had a boarding pass for a flight yesterday to Kona. Not at all. And I would never mention it to your tour group—the tour group you just lied to about looking at hotels in Oahu all day yesterday.

But what, Regan wondered, do you have going on in Kona?

59

Ned had barely slept. He woke as the sun rose and went for an early morning run. All he could think about was the fact that someone, probably Glenn, had taken the leis out of his gift-wrapped box and replaced them with cheap imitations. That's a premeditated crime, he thought angrily. But whoever did it knows I'm a criminal, too.

Ned ran hard for ten miles, something he hadn't done in a long time. When he reached a deserted stretch of beach, he took off his shoes and shirt and dove into the water. It felt good to move, to kick his feet and let loose. When he saw a big wave approaching, he decided to ride it in. The undertow was strong. It pulled him under, threw him around, and then finally retreated. Ned struggled to his feet. A mass of broken shells blanketed the ocean floor.

"Ow!" Ned cried. He had stepped on something sharp. He limped to the sand, sat down, and pulled a shard of glass out of the bottom of his second toe. Blood was pouring out, and it looked to Ned as if it needed stitches. But there was no way he was going to risk that when Will's mother was coming to town, the woman who had been obsessed by that very toe thirty years ago. If he was going to let any doctor look at his feet, it would be after Almetta Brown was long gone from the Hawaiian Islands and all talk of royal leis had ended.

Ned sat in the sand and applied pressure to the cut with one of his gym socks. He was rewarded with the sight of a white sock turning bright red. With the piece of glass he had just pulled out of his foot, he cut a piece off his sock and tied it around his toe. He squeezed back into his shoes and limped back to the hotel. By the time he got back to the room, his foot was incredibly sore and still bleeding.

As he showered, watching the blood trickling out of his toe wash down the drain, all he could think about was that the ball would be over and the leis would be gone tomorrow. That was fine with him. But what to do about that bellman Glenn? He's definitely up to no good. A thought occurred to Ned: Could Glenn be behind the trouble at the hotel? He seems to be everywhere. And Will has him running around all over taking care of things. But if he is up to no good, I can't do anything about it, Ned realized. And who knows? He could already have set me up with the cops.

Now I'm really getting paranoid, Ned thought. He stepped out of the shower, dried off, and tied wads of toilet paper around his toe. He didn't have any Band-Aids and wasn't about to start poking through Artie's shaving kit. Thankfully, Artie wasn't around. He must be downstairs with the Hudville group, chowing down at the buffet.

Ned got dressed, then reached into his closet and tried on the shoes he had worn surfing yesterday. They felt very tight. He took them off and put on his sneakers. When I get the word from Will that his parents are here, I'll change back into the beach shoes. I can't exactly go in the ocean with my sneakers on—Will's mother would certainly notice that. From the sounds of it she hasn't changed much in thirty years. She probably still notices everything.

Ned went back outside to join the world with one goal for the day: to not get arrested.

60

"I'm so worried." Carla's mother was on the speaker phone talking to Regan and Will. "It's so unlike her. She finally gets engaged after all these years and then drops off the face of the earth. It doesn't make sense. My Carla would have been calling me every five minutes to discuss the wedding. No one has heard from her since yesterday. And now you say it looks as if they hadn't slept in their room!" Her voice cracked, and she started to cry.

"Mrs. Trombetti, we're going to do everything we can to track them down. Don't forget, she did just get engaged. Carla and Jason may just have decided to go off and have a few days to themselves, shutting out the world. This is Hawaii, and there are lots of romantic places where couples go to be alone."

"Not Carla. If she's away from a phone for a few hours, she gets withdrawal symptoms."

Regan could hear her sniffling.

"And how much more time alone does she need with Jason? They've been together for ten years. I'm surprised the bloom isn't off the rose. I was so happy they got engaged before they got sick of each other."

Regan raised her eyebrows. "You know the police don't even count them as missing persons yet because they are adults and are free to do as they choose. They've been gone only twenty-four hours. But we're going to do everything we can to find them."

"Wasn't there just a drowning at the hotel there? My husband was looking up the news from Hawaii on the Internet."

"Unfortunately, there was," Regan answered. "An employee from the hotel. But she was alone. It's unlikely that your daughter and her fiancé—"

"I know, I know," the woman interrupted. "But, believe me, I know my daughter. As much as we might spat with each other, she doesn't ignore my phone calls or go this long without talking to any of her friends."

"I understand," Regan said softly. She spent the next few minutes trying to reassure Carla's mother. But she knew how her own mother would feel if she suddenly disappeared. And she knew how excited her mother was about finally planning a wedding. When Regan hung up, she looked at Will and asked, "How many of these kinds of calls do you get?"

"Enough," he answered. "People come to Waikiki on vacation and want to be free. The batteries on their cell phones die. Or they travel around to areas where there's no service. Relatives get worried. These days people are used to being in constant touch. But this couple just got engaged. Maybe they decided to do something wild."

"Maybe," Regan answered cautiously, "but I wish Carla hadn't been on the beach the other night."

"I know," Will said quietly.

"Can I take a look in their room?" Regan asked.

Will stood quickly. "Let's go. I'm sure we have her mother's permission."

Inside the neat room with the king-sized bed, everything looked in order. In the bathroom Carla's toiletries were lined up. Two toothbrushes were standing side by side in a glass.

"Wherever they are, they didn't plan to stay overnight," Regan observed.

"You can buy a toothbrush anywhere," Will answered.

"You can, but—" Regan pointed at the lotions and creams and sprays that covered the marble countertop—"I don't think Carla is the type to wing it. I'd lay a bet she's never gone camping in her life. Certainly not without her face creams."

Regan walked over to the desk and glanced at the notepad with the Waikiki Waters Resort logo that was next to the phone. Regan picked it up and walked to the terrace door where the light was bright. Whoever wrote the last message had written with force and left an impression on the next sheet of paper. When she saw what had been written, she inhaled sharply.

"What?" Will asked.

"It says Kona. There's a flight number and a time."

"You see!" Will said with relief. "They took off for a little fun on the Big Island."

"But, Will, those twins were in Kona yesterday. I accidentally saw one of their boarding passes."

Will's face blanched. "It still doesn't mean . . ."

Regan looked at her watch. "It's noon. Let's go look for the twins."

"Then what?"

"I'll figure it out," Regan answered.

They hurried downstairs and looked around the pools, scoured the beach, and went in and out of all the restaurants but couldn't find anyone from the Mixed Bag Tour group. They went back to Will's office and called all their rooms. No answer. Regan went back outside and spotted the young girl from the group coming out of the women's clothing store. She looked bored.

"Excuse me," Regan greeted her.

"Yeah."

"I was next to your table this morning when the tour leader's purse fell onto the floor."

"Oh, right," Joy said. "She handled that really well, didn't she?"

Regan smiled. "I need to talk to her. Do you know where she is?"

Joy shook her head. "They were going to sit by the pool today and do their dunking, as they like to say, but then all of a sudden they decided to check out more hotels. They don't want to go to the ball and said they'd see us tomorrow." She shrugged. "I don't know what's going on with them."

"What do you mean?" Regan asked.

Joy rolled her eyes. "They usually make us stick together for every meal so they can count every penny we spend. For the twins to be gone for lunch and dinner is highly unusual, believe me. And they said they were going to a sunrise service tomorrow morning so they won't be here for breakfast, either. Praise the Lord."

"Thanks for your help," Regan said.

"No problem. Anything wrong?"

"No."

Regan hurried back to Will's office. "They're gone for the day and night. Will, I'm worried. I'll bet you anything they're on their way back to Kona, and I'll also bet that's where Carla and Jason are."

Quickly Regan sat down and called Mike Darnell. "Mike, I need a passenger list for a flight yesterday to Kona." She explained the situation.

Within minutes he called back. "All the parties you mentioned were on that flight yesterday. The two women returned in the evening, but the couple didn't show up for their flight. They didn't return their rental car, either, and they said they'd bring it back yesterday afternoon. It's a white sedan with traces of yellow paint on the side. The two women just got off a flight that landed in Kona ten minutes ago."

"Oh, my God. We've got to find them."

"That's a big island. It's why they call it that."

"Can you put out a bulletin for the rental car? I'm going to get a flight over there now."

"And then what?"

"I'm not sure."

"Regan, I just talked to a buddy of mine who has a private plane. He said he was heading out to the airport. Let me give him a call and see if he can take us over to the Big Island. Hold on a second." Regan waited tensely until Mike came back on. "I'll pick you up in fifteen minutes outside the hotel. This is probably crazy."

"It's not," Regan said firmly. She hung up the phone and looked at Will. "I need to get into the twins' room."

"Regan, I don't know if I can—"

"Will, I absolutely need to—"

"Let's go," he said for the second time that morning. They dashed out of his office.

In the twins' room there seemed to be two of

everything: two pairs of matching fuzzy slippers, two identical bathrobes, two pink suitcases. Regan went over to the desk and pulled the drawer open. Inside she found a thick file. She pulled out its contents. "Architectural drawings for a house," she breathed. Regan read the words written across the top of the first sketch—"Gert and Ev's Kona dream house." "They're using Sal Hawkins's money to build a house." She stuffed the file in her bag.

"I don't know whether you should take those," Will warned.

"I'm taking them. The twins won't be back until tomorrow." She looked through the rest of the desk, closet, and bureau drawers but found nothing.

They raced back downstairs where Mike Darnell was already waiting.

Gert and Ev had rented a car at the airport. To their distress, the line had been long and the car hadn't been gassed up. By the time they filled the tank and pulled out of the gas station, they were both feeling impatient and edgy. They were now speeding up to their dream house.

"Boy, is this a change of plans," Gert commented.

"Things are getting too tense," Ev answered. "There was something about the way that girl was poking around on the floor today, helping you pick up all your junk."

"I gave her my scary look," Gert answered. "But she did see that Kona postcard."

"I saw her take note of that. I just want to get that couple out of our house before anyone finds them there. And their stupid car. The sooner we get rid of them, the better." She stepped on the gas.

"So we're not going to throw them in the water tonight?"

"We'll see. We'll strangle them now, stuff their bodies in the trunk, and then see if we can abandon the car somewhere."

"I'd rather let it go over a cliff."

"Me, too. But it's several more hours until dark. I don't want to wait that long." She turned off the main highway onto a two-lane road that wound up a mountain. They were only a few miles from the house.

"We're almost there, sister."

"We certainly are."

"When we land, they'll have a list of all the real estate agents for us," Mike told Regan. "Although who knows when the twins bought the land. They may not have had any dealings with anyone for a while."

"And I'm sure the house is being built privately and they're using false names," Regan added. "But those two are easily identifiable. How many female identical twins in their sixties are on the

Big Island building their dream house?" She
looked down at the sketches for the exterior of
the house, the expansive kitchen with a view of
the ocean in the distance, the matching master
bedroom suites. She tried to slip the drawings
back in the folder, but something was in the way.
Another piece of paper. Regan pulled it out and
unfolded it. It was a sketch for a barbed wire
fence.

"Will, Regan needs to speak to you now!" Janet
called to him. He was out by the front desk talking
to Jazzy and Claude. "It's urgent!"

Jazzy and Claude hurried off. Will got on the
phone, listened, dropped it, and ran after Claude.
"What's your address on the Big Island?"

A police car was waiting for Regan and Mike at the
Kona airport. They hopped in, Officer Lance Curtis turned on the siren, and they took off. Let them
be there, Regan prayed. Please. She knew with cer-
tainty that Jason and Carla were in grave danger.
Just let them be alive.

Jason and Carla heard the upstairs door open.
Carla's eyes were wide with terror. They're
back, she thought. It's over. She bent her head
and started to pray again. Jason had already
done so.

The basement door opened. "Here we are," Ev

called. "Back to take care of the bad girl and bad boy." The sisters lumbered down the steps.

The police car sped up the long, curving private road to Claude's house. It was heavily wooded, unpaved, and bumpy. At the top Regan, Mike, and Lance jumped out of the car. They ran around the back of Claude's house and immediately spotted the barbed wire fence along the left side of the property.

"The twins' house must be in that direction," Regan shouted.

"It'll take a few minutes to go back down the hill and around. The entrance to their driveway must be from the other side of these woods." Officer Curtis ran to the trunk and pulled a wire cutter out of the police car. A few minutes later Regan, Mike, and the officer were racing up a hill and through the woods.

When they reached the top of the mountain, they could see the house. It was in the middle of a large piece of land. In the driveway there was a white car with traces of yellow paint on the side.

"That's Carla and Jason's car. They must be in there!" Regan cried.

"Do you have anything to say to Gert and Ev before you die?" Ev asked, sounding half crazed. She was standing behind Jason, and Gert was behind Carla. They were ready to close their hands around their necks and squeeze the life out of them.

Carla and Jason had been silently crying. As soon as the twins pulled the gags out of their mouths, sobs permeated the room.

"Please!" Carla begged.

"Sorry," Ev answered. "You did a very bad thing. We don't want you to spoil our fun. Because we deserve to have some fun."

"We sure do," Gert agreed, her voice agitated. "We put up with a lot our whole lives. Always taking care of other people in that rainy town. Never thinking of what was good for the twins. Well, we finally woke up. Our lives had been wasting away. When we got the opportunity to take care of ourselves, we grabbed it! And we're not going to let people like you ruin it for us!"

"No we're not!" Ev echoed forcefully. "We should have taken control of our lives years ago!" Flexing her hands, she turned and looked at Gert. "Are you ready, sister?"

"More than ready!"

They started to close their hands around the couple's necks when they heard glass breaking upstairs. A moment later the basement door flew open. But it didn't stop the twins. It only made them more crazed. All the rage that had built up inside them was directed at destroying these two young lives.

"Hurry, sister!" Ev commanded as she squeezed hard around Jason's neck.

"I'm doing it!" Gert answered. Her thick callused hands had easily surrounded Carla's slender, silky neck.

Choking and gagging, Carla and Jason could feel themselves blacking out.

Regan, Mike, and Lance galloped down the steps.

"Let go!" Regan screamed as she tackled Gert whose body felt like a brick wall. Mike helped pry her fingers from Carla's neck as Officer Curtis slugged a resolute Ev and knocked her over. The sisters tumbled onto the floor as Jason and Carla gasped for breath. Lance Curtis pulled out his gun and pointed it at the twins' heads while Mike and Regan untied the ropes that bound Carla and Jason.

Carla wrapped her arms around Regan and wouldn't let go as racking sobs filled the room. "Thank you," she whispered, her voice quivering. Jason moved toward them, and Regan started to get out of the way.

"No." He pulled Regan close to him and his fiancée. The three of them huddled together for several moments as Carla struggled to stop crying.

61

W ill's parents arrived shortly after Regan and Mike left for the airport. He escorted his parents to their room and told them to come down to his office after they'd freshened up. He didn't say a word about what was going on with Regan Reilly.

The minute Ned laid eyes on Will's parents, he knew that they were the ones. How thirty years can just melt away, he thought wryly. They were seated in Will's office when he walked in.

Ned looked from Bingsley and Almetta to Will, and a thought that had never occurred to him, because he'd been so worried about himself, surfaced in his brain. If Will's parents bought the lei thirty years ago and it ended up in Hawaii around Dorinda Dawes's neck, could Will be the middle man? He certainly hasn't made it public knowledge that his parents once owned the royal lei that Dorinda was wearing when she died. Do they know? Did they sell the lei without realizing what they had?

Ned's head was spinning. Does Will have something to worry about? Did he give the lei to Dorinda? No one saw her wearing it the night she died. She often checked in with Will before she left the hotel. Did he have anything to do with her death? That's a lot more serious than stealing, he realized. Was Will as freaked out as he was? He does seem on edge, Ned observed. Somehow, as delicately as possible, I will have to bring up the topic of the antique leis with his parents. Everyone at the hotel was talking about the auction. In all likelihood Almetta Brown would have a hard time keeping any information she had about the lei under her hat.

"It's so lovely that you'll be our tour guide this afternoon, Ned," Almetta said, batting her eyes. She had on a floral top with matching shorts and a pair of little white sneakers. Bingsley had on khaki shorts and a Hawaiian shirt. Ned was relieved that no bathing suits were in sight.

"It's my pleasure," Ned replied. "How about going out in one of the sailboats we have out there? There's a beautiful breeze. I think you'll enjoy it."

"I'd be enchanted," Almetta chirped. "We both would. Right, dear?" she asked, turning to Bingsley, whose face was impassive to say the least.

"It sounds all right," he answered. "But I want to get in a nap before tonight. I'm beat."

"Dad, you'll have time for that later," Will said. "I just wanted you to get some fresh air. And if you take a swim, you'll perk up."

Ned led them down to the water, and they boarded a small sailboat. The Browns sat and enjoyed the fresh ocean air and sunshine while Ned did the busy work of a sailor. There was a steady breeze that helped propel the boat past the surfers and swimmers and out into the aqua waters. Almetta peppered Ned with nonstop questions.

"Where are you from, Ned?" she asked, leaning forward with a big smile on her face.

"All over," he answered. "I'm an army brat."

"How marvelous. You must have lived in very interesting places. Did you ever live in Hawaii when you were a child?"

She's playing with my head, Ned thought. "No," he lied. Time to change the subject. "Are you excited about the ball tonight?"

"I can't wait," Almetta enthused.

"Those leis—that's some story, huh? They were made for two members of the Hawaiian royal family. One gets stolen. They keep appearing and disappearing and reappearing again."

Almetta coughed slightly. "It certainly is something." She looked out at the water and went silent, which made Ned nervous.

"I have to use the head," Bingsley declared quickly. He got up and stumbled slightly, stepping on Ned's bad foot.

Ned winced. The nerves in his sore toe were screaming. Bingsley wasn't a small guy.

"I'm so sorry," Bingsley apologized as he kept walking toward the loo.

"Are you all right?" Almetta inquired with great concern, staring down at Ned's foot, just as she had thirty years before. "That must hurt. Oh, look! Do I see a little bit of blood staining the top of your shoe? Why don't you take it off and dip your feet in the salt water?"

"It's nothing. I'm fine," Ned insisted.

Almetta looked up at him and didn't say a word. But she had a funny look on her face.

62

In the festively decorated ballroom, reporters were swarming all over Regan. Reports of the kidnapping and attempted murder of the lovely, young, recently engaged couple had headlined all the evening newscasts.

"The twins haven't confessed to killing Dorinda Dawes, have they, Regan?" asked a reporter from a local TV station.

"No. But that's not surprising. They're waiting for their lawyer from Hudville to arrive. We know that they are capable of murder, so why wouldn't they lie?"

The five remaining members of the Lucky Seven were in shock and had spent the afternoon on and off the phone with the folks back home.

"Can you believe it?"

"I knew they were being cheap, but this is beyond belief."

"Sal Hawkins must be rolling in his grave."

Betsy and Bob had abandoned their exciting relationship chapter and had started to write a book about their travels with the evil twins.

Francie, Artie, and Joy were determined to live it up and spend money for the remainder of their trip. Joy had decided to come to the ball and leave Zeke and his wanderlust in the dust. In the last several hours the Hudville group had turned into a bunch of mini celebrities. It was suddenly more fun to hang around with them. "And I'm the one," Joy kept repeating, "who knew that Gert and Ev were cheating us!"

Carla and Jason were up in their room recovering, their arms wrapped around each other as they lay on the bed. Carla had already talked to her mother about six times and all of her bridesmaids at least once.

"Regan Reilly said she'd be a bridesmaid," she told them joyfully.

If Carla and Jason felt up to it, they said they'd come down and make an appearance later on. But they had barely touched the food and drinks Will had sent to their room.

Jimmy was in attendance, wearing both leis around his neck. "Jimmy is going to donate both leis for the auction," he announced proudly.

Jazzy was modeling Claude's sexy muumuu and

clearly enjoying the attention. She and Claude hosted two tables filled with socialites. Regan was seated with Kit, Steve, Will, Kim, Will's parents, and Dorinda's cousin Gus. He was quite the social butterfly, getting up and down every two minutes to do interviews and take pictures for the article Will promised to publish in the next newsletter. "We mustn't forget Dorinda," he said. "But most of all, justice must be served."

An air of conviviality prevailed. Everyone was relieved that the twins were behind bars.

"You're some investigator," Steve said to Regan. "Kit is so proud of you."

Regan shrugged and smiled at both of them. "Thanks. Sometimes you just get a gut instinct that you have to follow."

Someone tapped her on the shoulder. As she turned away, Steve remarked to Kit, "She's something, isn't she?"

Kit giggled. She'd had a few glasses of wine and was feeling light-headed. She put her arm around his back. "Knowing her, she's probably having you checked out."

He looked at her and laughed. "Little old me?"

"She's very protective. And I'm her best friend."

The band started to play "The Way You Look Tonight." Steve extended his hand. "Shall we dance?"

Kit floated out of her chair, and they were off.

Regan couldn't wait to get back home. She

missed Jack more than ever as she watched all the couples on the dance floor. She had to admit that Kit and Steve did look great together. She also felt that she had done enough for the Waikiki Waters Resort. With the twins in captivity, the place was certainly safer.

"I can't thank you enough, Regan," Will said to her quietly. "I wish I could hire you on a permanent basis."

"Well, I promise to come back and visit."

"They're going to auction the leis in a little while. For my taste they can't be out of here soon enough."

"I can well imagine."

Regan's cell phone began to ring. She had it out on the table. When she looked at the number, she saw it was Jack. They had talked several hours ago after the twins were arrested. Smiling, she turned to Will. "Excuse me. I'll go outside with this." She got up and started to walk toward the door. "Hello there!" she answered.

"Regan, where's Kit?" he asked briskly.

"She's here at the ball. Why?"

"Is Steve Yardley with her?"

"Yes. What is it, Jack?"

"I just got word about the prints from the beer bottle. This guy has a criminal record and goes by a number of aliases. Yes, he worked on Wall Street, but he was fired for embezzling funds. He's run a number of scams since then. He rents a house in an expensive neighborhood with lots of part-time residents and gets people he meets to invest in his schemes. Then he moves on. He had a girlfriend who disappeared about ten years ago and has never been found. He has a bad temper and is considered dangerous if you make him angry."

"Oh, my God." Regan walked back into the room, the phone at her ear. The band had taken a break, and no one was on the dance floor. She looked over at her table. Kit and Steve's seats were empty. The main course was being served. "Jack, I don't know where she is."

"I thought you said she was there."

"She was a few minutes ago, but then she and Steve got up to dance. Now they're gone. Maybe they just went for a walk," Regan said, worry filling her soul. "I'm going to look for her. I'll call you back."

"Regan, be careful! This guy is dangerous."

Regan closed her cell phone and for a brief moment had the surreal feeling that she was leaving her body. Kit. Oh, Kit. She turned around and bumped into Gus. "Have you seen Kit?"

"I just interviewed her outside. She and Steve look as if they're so much in love. I think they're going for a moonlight stroll."

Regan ran out the door toward the beach.

"This is so romantic!" Kit said giddily as they strolled along the beach.

"I just want to be with you," Steve told her quietly. "Not with all those other people. Some of them are so annoying. Let's go sit on the jetty."

They took off their shoes and gingerly stepped onto the rocky surface. Steve tightened his grip on Kit's hand as, in the darkness, they carefully made their way out to the end of the jetty. A breeze was blowing, and the wide open sea lay endlessly before them. When they couldn't walk any farther, Kit laid her head on Steve's shoulder.

"Come on," Steve urged. He crouched, moved down among the rocks that faced the ocean, and turned to reach for Kit. "It's our own little place here. No one will bother us."

Kit smiled as he carefully guided her down beside him. They sat, wrapped their arms around one another, and nestled in their private cove. The water lapped at their feet.

"This is so wonderful." Kit sighed.

Steve turned his head and started to kiss her. Hard. Too hard.

Kit pulled back. "Steve," she protested, trying to laugh it off. "Ow!"

"What's the matter?" he asked gruffly. "You don't want me to kiss you now?"

"Of course I want you to kiss me." She leaned back in toward him. "I want you to kiss me the way you did last night."

He kissed her again, biting her bottom lip as his right hand yanked the back of her hair. Kit pulled away for the second time, fear rising in her. "Steve, you're hurting me."

He grabbed her arm. "Do you think I would hurt you? Do you think that just because you're best friends with Regan Reilly all your boyfriends should be checked out? Is that what you think?" he demanded as his grip around her arm tightened.

"No, I was just kidding," Kit protested. "Regan looks out for me, that's all. She's my best friend. She likes you . . ."

"No she doesn't. I saw the way she was looking at me."

"She does like you. We want you to meet her fiancé Jack. He's great . . ."

Steve squeezed her arm and shook it. "He's a cop. I don't need the two of them asking me a lot of questions. That's what Dorinda Dawes did. She started poking around my house and asking me everything about my life. She thought she was so smart. I had to shut her up!"

Kit's brain, which had been slightly clouded by the wine she'd been drinking, suddenly snapped into focus. The realization that Steve was Dorinda's killer hit her with sickening force. I've got to get out of here, she thought. "Let go of my arm," she said as calmly as she could. "You're hurting me."

"You're hurting me," he repeated in a baby voice, mocking her.

"I've got to go." Kit started to stand but didn't get far. She screamed as he pulled her back down.

"You're not going anywhere."

"Yes, I am!" Kit insisted fiercely as she turned away and hurriedly began to climb up from the rocks. But Steve pulled her back again. She stumbled backward and screamed out for help. He quickly pressed his hand over her mouth, held her struggling body close to him, and dipped her head into the swirling dark ocean.

Out on the beach, Regan frantically looked around. There was no one there. "Kit!" she called. "Kit!" She kicked off her shoes and ran down to the water's edge. "Kit!"

All was silent.

"Kit!"

Then Regan heard Kit's scream. It sounded as if it were coming from the jetty where Dorinda Dawes often sat. Oh, God, Regan thought, thinking of Dorinda's fate. Don't let the same thing happen to Kit! Regan started to run toward the jetty. Then she heard two more short screams. It's her, I know it. Regan was frantic. My best friend. Please, please let me get there in time, she prayed.

Regan stepped onto the jetty and ran across the slick rocks as fast as she could. She slipped and fell, her knee scraped by a jagged rock. Barely feeling the pain, she got back up and raced to the end. The sight of Steve struggling to hold Kit's head under water sent a jolt through Regan's system like she had never felt before. In an instant, she jumped down onto Steve's back and hit him in the back of the neck with a strength she couldn't believe she had. He grunted, released his grip on Kit, and threw Regan off his back. They both fell into the ocean. As Kit lifted her head out of the water, Regan yelled to her, "Get back on the jetty!"

Kit was coughing, but fury had overcome her. "No way, Regan." She jumped on Steve and scratched at his face. He threw her off and then pushed Regan below the surface. Regan swallowed a huge gulp of the salty ocean but managed to knee him in the groin. She resurfaced just as Kit clawed his left eye with her nails. He screamed in pain, turned away, and began to swim out to sea. But his escape was short-lived. A police boat located him twenty minutes later. His stint in paradise had come to an end.

After all the excitement died down and the police had Steve in custody, Kit and Regan, now wearing dry clothes, returned to the ballroom in time to see the delayed auction of the royal leis. A benefactor purchased both of them for a lot of money and donated the pair back to the Seashell Museum. He didn't have too much competition. "Trouble surrounds those leis," he noted. "They shouldn't be separated ever again. They belong together on display. People should know their history and that they once belonged to members of the Hawaiian royal family. I don't suppose we'll ever know how that poor woman Dorinda Dawes got her hands on Queen Liliuokalani's lei. That's a secret she took to her grave." Jimmy beamed while the curator of the prestigious Bishop Museum looked crestfallen. He had hoped the leis would go to his museum.

Will's mother glanced over at Ned, who had just gotten up from the next table, and caught his eye. They both stared at each other. She stood and went over to him.

"I know that you know who we are," Almetta said evenly. "And I know who you are."

Ned didn't reply.

"I won't tell anyone that you sold the lei to us if you won't let it be known that we had it for all those years. That's the last thing Will needs right now. He had nothing to do with Dorinda Dawes's death. Thank God her killer has been caught."

Ned nodded.

Almetta smiled. "You know, your toes aren't that bad. Buy yourself a pair of sandals."

Ned smiled back. "I already did." He turned and walked off. The next day he applied for a job with the Peace Corps. I'm only going to do good from now on, he promised himself.

Everyone loved Claude's muumuus. They were a huge hit. Scores of women had changed into them in the bathrooms and were now out on the dance floor in force. Brimming with satisfaction,

Claude whispered to Jazzy, "I don't think we should do any more harm to this hotel. You don't need Will's job. They'll sell our clothing anyway. I'll make you my partner. And if you'll have me, I'll make you my wife."

Jazzy kissed him. "Oh, Claude. It's what I always wanted."

He kissed her back. "Me, too. Now tell Glenn to cut out the pranks. We'll give him a good job with the company."

"I love you, Claude."

"I love you, too, Jazzy. From now on, we always do the right thing. Life's too short. Especially around here."

The next morning Regan and Kit were at the Honolulu airport together.

"Another adventure, huh?" Kit said sheepishly. "We've been through a lot together in the last ten years, but this outing really takes the cake."

"The next guy will be the right one for you. I just know it."

"Promise me one thing."

"What?"

"You'll be sure to check him out. No matter how gaga I am."

Regan laughed. "That's a guarantee. Especially if you're gaga." Her cell phone began to ring. She quickly answered it. "Aloha, Jack. Nothing's changed since we spoke ten minutes ago. I've had two more calls from my mother. She's still freaked out, but Kit and I are fine."

"I need to see you, Regan. They just reopened the airports here. I'll get a flight to Los Angeles. I can't wait until next weekend . . ."

"I can't either. Kit and I are about to board a flight to New York."

"You are?" Jack's voice was exuberant.

"Yes. I wanted to surprise you, but I guess we've had enough surprises lately. Kit will get a connecting flight to Connecticut, and I'll take a taxi to your apartment. After everything that happened, we didn't want to make the long trip back alone. My bachelorette weekend is finally over."

"And not soon enough, your life as a bachelorette. I'm thinking we should move up the date of the wedding. We can talk about it when you get here. And you're not taking any taxi—I'll be at the airport waiting for you with open arms."

Regan smiled broadly as the announcement that the flight to New York was now boarding came over the loudspeaker. "I'm on my way, Jack. I'm finally on my way."

SCRIBNER

Invites you to read a chapter from

Hitched

by Carol Higgins Clark

Hardcover available April 2006

Turn the page for a preview of *Hitched*, and enjoy!

Saturday, April 2nd

Regan Reilly descended the staircase from the second floor of her parents' home in Summit, New Jersey, as she had on countless Saturday mornings in the thirty-one years of her life. As usual, she was headed for the kitchen, where her mother would be putting out breakfast. But this Saturday was different.

It was her last Saturday as a single.

Regan's hand lightly brushed the banister as she reached the bottom step and turned toward the living room. The presents from her bridal shower, held the night before, were neatly stacked in the corner—everything from the latest and greatest cappuccino machine that Regan was sure she'd never be able to figure out to a clock radio that blared "Today is the first day of the rest of your life" when the alarm went off. The set of gleaming kitchen knives had intrigued Regan the most. A private investigator, she had examined them closely. The only other present that could have been considered a deadly weapon was the cookbook, her father, Luke, had remarked.

Luke and Regan's fiancé, Jack "no relation" Reilly, had escaped to a restaurant in town and then returned to join the women for an after-dinner drink. All the obligatory oohing and aahing over the household goods and lingerie was merci-fully over. Jack's mother, sisters, and aunts were there as well as many of Regan's old family friends. It had been a lively party.

Regan had flown in two days before from Los Angeles where she had her own P.I. agency. There was now one week left to finalize all the arrange-ments before she went from Ms. Reilly to Mrs. Reilly. Today she was heading into New York City with her mother, Nora, and her best friend, Kit, to pick up her wedding gown.

Getting married is a lot of work, Regan had thought more than once since she'd gotten en-gaged six months ago. It was easy to see why women turned into Bridezillas. But all the hassle was worth it. Jack was what she had waited for all her life, and they both wanted to celebrate with their friends and family by having a great wedding.

After years of enduring dates with losers,

weirdos, and worst of all, cheapskates, Regan often felt that she would never meet her soul mate. It took her father getting kidnapped for her to find Jack. He was the head of the Major Case Squad in New York City and had worked day and night to get Luke back. In the process, he and Regan had fallen in love.

At the large butcher-block table in the kitchen, Nora and Kit were sipping coffee and munching on blueberry muffins.

"Good morning," Regan said cheerily. "Kit, I can't believe you're up. We don't have to head into the city for another fifteen minutes."

"I was sleepless, thinking about seeing you in your wedding gown today," Kit said wryly. "I never thought the day would arrive. I never thought my day would arrive. Yours did. Mine, I'm sure, never will."

Regan laughed as Nora cooed sympathetically, "Of course it will."

"Mom, don't worry about Kit," Regan said as she poured herself a cup of coffee. "Kit, we'll get through everything that this next week entails, get me married off, and then I'm sure we'll be planning your wedding before . . . before uh . . ."

"Before what?" Kit asked as she spread butter on her muffin. "Before the cows come home?"

"Way before that," Regan answered with a wave of her hand. "Life can change in an instant, Kit. I still have a week before I walk down the aisle. Who knows what could happen before then?"

Nora jumped up, an alarmed expression on her face. "Don't even think like that, Regan. Everything is going to be wonderful. Now let's finish our coffee, get in the car, and drive into the city to pick up the gorgeous dress you will wear one week from today. I must say I'm glad it'll be the last time we have to deal with those crazy designers and that drafty loft they have the nerve to call a bridal salon."

Regan and Kit looked at each other and laughed.

"Mom, Charisse and Alfred are a very talented couple, and they are starting to make their mark in the fashion world. They're booked a year in advance. I'm glad they were willing to squeeze me in. Pretty soon they're going to be household names."

None of them could have predicted that Charisse and Alfred's quest for fame would be sped up by their appearance on the front page of the following day's New York *Post*.

With Regan at the wheel, Nora's Mercedes-Benz glided into the Holland Tunnel.

"It's a lovely day," Nora sighed as the sunlight disappeared behind them. "I hope it's like this next Saturday."

"I do too. But it's April. You never know . . ." Regan's voice trailed off.

"A girl in my office scheduled her wedding for late October on Martha's Vineyard. Wouldn't you know a northeaster hit that very day? When they got to the reception, the restaurant was without power," Kit remarked. "And the generator had gone kaput."

"Thanks, Kit." Regan smiled. "I'll be sure to pray for good weather."

Fifteen minutes later they parked the car in a lot not too far from the heart of Little Italy. "Alfred and Charisse's Couture" was located in a loft on the entire third floor of a building that, in Nora's opinion, was in need of a makeover.

"I don't know what the draw of places like these is," Nora muttered as they walked down a side street that looked like the Broadway set for *Cats*.

"People love it down here," Regan explained. "And if you're in fashion, it makes you seem hip to have an address like this. It's where old New York meets the new. The pushcarts of yesteryear have been replaced by trendy boutiques."

"What's wrong with Madison Avenue?" Nora asked as she stepped over a piece of broken glass.

They stopped in front of an old building and caught the door as a young couple were coming out. Regan held it open as she pushed the buzzer for Alfred and Charisse's loft. There was no answer. She pushed it again, and they waited.

Kit looked at her watch. "It's eleven o'clock."

"I can't imagine where they'd be. They live here, and they're expecting us," Regan said.

"We've already made it through their security..." Nora remarked wryly, glancing around at the empty lobby.

"That we have," Regan answered. "Let's head upstairs."

The three of them got on a large groaning elevator that took its time about everything. The car slowly ascended to the third floor, where it stopped with a jerk. A loud click and a mournful moan followed. After an agonizing six seconds, the door opened.

Right away, Regan could tell something was wrong. The door to the loft was ajar. Whenever she'd been to the salon, Alfred always made a point to keep it closed. He was paranoid about people somehow stealing the ideas for his designs. Regan hurried across the hall and pushed the door fully open. There was no one in sight. The dress racks were empty. But one lone gown was in shreds on the floor.

"Charisse?" Regan called again, her voice rising. "Alfred?"

There was no answer.

Nora grabbed Regan's arm. "Regan, be careful."

"Charisse?" Regan called. "Alfred?" She slowly moved farther into the loft and saw that the shredded dress had drops of blood on it. Regan inhaled sharply and hurried to the back of the loft and around the corner to where she knew their bedroom was. Gingerly, Regan opened the door.

"Oh my God!" Regan cried.

Charisse and Alfred were stretched out on their bed, bound and gagged. Regan hurried over and removed Alfred's gag first.

"Regan!" he cried, struggling for breath. "A couple of thieves broke in here in the middle of the night. They tied us up. I thought they were going to kill us. They smashed our safe here in the bedroom and grabbed our cash and jewelry."

"They did more than that," Regan said quickly as she ran around the bed and untied the cloth covering Charisse's mouth. "It looks like all your dresses are gone. Except one that could use a lot of help."

Two screams pierced the air: One belonged to Alfred. The other emanated from the owner of that sorry bridal gown who had just arrived in the next room.

Regan couldn't decide whose scream was worse.